MORE THAN TWO

a novel

MORE THAN TWO

a novel

JAMES ESPOSITO

The New Atlantian Library

THE NEW ATLANTIAN LIBRARY
is an imprint of
ABSOLUTELY AMAZING eBOOKS

Published by Whiz Bang LLC, 926 Truman Avenue, Key West, Florida 33040, USA.

For information contact:
Publisher@AbsolutelyAmazingEbooks.com

978-0692718278 (New Atlantian Library, The)
0692718273

For Pavla

much more than one

*"Everything is plausible here, because nothing
is real"*

Thomas Middleton, The Black Book, *1604*

MORE THAN TWO

a novel

Contents

Introduction

The two stories in this book are factual, in the sense that all fiction is factual. I have been in the privileged position of knowing, and befriending, both Andrew Dalton, whose diaries are published here under the title "N," and George Manners, whose *The Thief of Reason* was found in his library after his death. Even though they were implacably opposed to, and antagonistic towards, each other, I was able to maintain the friendship of each of them, provided I kept each out my conversations with the other. I am the shadow, the slender link, the *corpus callosum* between two minds that are so alike as to be unlike. For these two hemispheres of the mind, to meet is as unlikely as a union of the north and south poles. We have only this narrow stretch of membrane – me – to permit the traffic between the poles, between these two ideas with which I have been familiar for so long. Almost as long as I have known myself. I am the tympanum of their worlds.

Through me they speak both to each other and to themselves. Their stories are their own; the way I tell them is mine.

A curious position for me to find myself in? Between two such different and distinct writers, whose rivalry on the narrow ground of academic literary criticism was well known among their long-suffering colleagues. Both George and Andrew were friends, or at least acquaintances, of John Fowles, and the competition between them as to who would get to write the definitive study of his work was unspeakably bitter. George won, Andrew lost. That is reflected in their memoirs. All I need say at this point is that it was our mutual background in academe that brought to me this unlikely pair of friendships.

I was a contemporary of George Manners at Trinity College, Dublin. My great-grandfather, Michele Esposito, a highly regarded composer, had been professor of piano at the Royal Irish Academy of Music for several decades, having settled there from his native Naples. His children had been involved in aspects of the republican movement towards Irish freedom. After great-grandfather retired to Italy, some of the family remained in Dublin; Michele's son Mario, my grandfather, had bequeathed me a love of Ireland and an appreciation of Irish literature, on which he had written authoritatively. One of my great-aunts (Mario's sister) had had a brief affair with James Joyce, which the family had frowned upon at the time, but which, in later years, had been glorified into the romance that it certainly wasn't. Another had married – and then separated from – one of the leaders of the 1916 rebellion, by whom she had a child, so there were still cousins living in Dublin, even if not under the Esposito name. So when the time came for me to seek a university place, Dublin seemed an obvious choice.

George, who was Irish on his mother's side, was a lively and pleasant colleague, but with an unhappy home background. We became very close friends, with more in common than we perhaps realized at the time, and remained so until his death.

George had spent all his professional life at Lincoln (and, as we shall see, for an unfortunate period, in Scunthorpe) but he left his university position somewhat abruptly, for a life-changing experience, and we lost touch until nearer the end of his life, when a different kind of life-changing episode – his near-fatal alcoholism – made me aware of a responsibility towards him which I was only too glad to perform.

Andrew Dalton was my colleague whom I met when we both did post-grad at Oxford. I will say little about his background, chiefly because he wanted little said about it, and what there was to disclose is contained in the following memoir. After he took a sabbatical from his university job at Leeds to take up the – as it seemed – temporary work as a screenwriter in Hollywood on a film about Leós Janáček (on whom he was a recognized expert) we actually became closer than we had been in our previous professional life. He was lecturing in popular literature, on which he had published a couple of books, including the well-received *Minor Mythologies*, and I was teaching film studies, both of us at Leeds. As he hints in *"N,"* it was partly at my suggestion that he pursued the position of screenwriter, so that the entire story of *"N"* might be laid at my door – to praise or blame as you see fit.

And lay it at my door Andrew did, in the sense that he left instructions that after his death the memoirs, known to him and me as *"N,"* would be edited by me for publication.

Thus for many years I was the confidant of both of them. Their passions, or the lack of them, their hopes and fears, their unique perspectives, become one parliament of reason in my own mind.

In Andrew's case, as you will see, I was intimately involved with him in the saga of *"N"* when his partner was diagnosed with twins. In George's case, after his withdrawal to Greece the relationship was more postal, more restricted to professional matters, but with a continuing undercurrent of mutual attraction.

Naturally, as I've already intimated, I had to keep my

two friends well separated. Neither could tolerate my friendship with the other – so much so that I sometimes thought that Andrew felt a sort of sexual jealousy when I was with George, as if I were cheating on him, and George would accuse me, likewise, of betraying him by even speaking *of*, let alone talking *to*, Andrew. But each had to accept that my friendships were equal and honorable, and they both respected that. What Andrew would think if he knew that I was publishing George's memoir, or what George would think *vice versa, and* between the same covers, doesn't bear thinking about. As the Irish saying goes, if they were alive today, they would be turning in their graves.

They died, so close in time, so far apart in spirit – Andrew in 2013, George the following year. In editing their work I have observed their wishes: I have made no attempt to rectify their obvious errors regarding time and place; nor to draw attention to the many inconsistencies in their imaginations, which, it could be argued, are part of the fabric of narrative. The imagination, which I think is something different from the mind, is a place where the facts of one's life are transmuted into fiction, fantasy, the *merveilleux* – the dreamland on which we all depend for our access to an "other" world. But they remain rooted in the facts that gave rise to them.

Neither Andrew nor George would have struck the average person, meeting them for the first time, as imaginative. Both had achieved academic distinction on the basis of *not* being imaginative. Both had passed through a phase – Andrew with "N," George with Jessica – where imagination had taken hold and swept them up into the stratosphere of dreams that they both describe so well. And then had dumped them down again into a reality quite different from the one they had left, in which the only imagination was this hankering after something that *was*, and yet remained elusively a might-have-been. In the aftermath of their whirlwind romances, both Andrew and George "reverted to type": tweedy, nondescript scholars chasing after a future which was in fact behind them.

Quite separately, Andrew and George had said to me that the essential ingredients in any story – novel, drama, thriller, even a work of literary criticism – were *quests*, *confessions* and *puzzles*. I'm not sure where they got that expression, but they both used it, and the fact that it provided the elements in their own lives suggests, to me, that there were two actions taking place simultaneously: Andrew and George were creating "quests, confessions and puzzles" in their writing but, more significantly, each was already possessed by the "quests, confessions and puzzles" within himself that had made those lives possible. In fact, two Andrews and two Georges: the one who lived as a storyteller, and the other who was lived by the story.

In editing their memoirs, I've realized more and more that it was my responsibility to hear their confessions: to show you, the reader, how far each had progressed in his quest, but always to acknowledge that the puzzle, the enigma, the contradictions and misleading clues, the dilemmas of their lives, remain.

Samuel Beckett is supposed to have said "the key word in my work is 'perhaps.'" The key word in the works, and indeed the lives, of Andrew and George is "maybe" – the acceptance of the unpredictable, the presence at all times of the unknown, a consciousness which *might* be explained but perhaps was best not. Andrew's perplexity about "N" and George's incomprehension as to why he was engaged – and by whom – in his "dispatches," as he called them, for a supposed secret service, are of the same order of "maybe." Psychologically, especially since, in their own ways, even with an academic bias, they were storytellers, "maybe" was very close to "As if ..."

It can be argued that in *"N"* and *The Thief of Reason* the characters are never fully developed – they are in danger of becoming cardboard cutouts. Even George's "Uncle David," for all his humour, strikes one as a caricature. I think that is intentional, rather than a stylistic flaw. Andrew and George saw themselves as cardboard figures, striving to be rounded through experiences with, on the one hand, "N," on the other, Jessica. But never quite succeeding. That may be a disappointment to the reader, but, as their editor, I think it was much more a disappointment to themselves. I wouldn't go so far as to call either of their stories a "tragedy," although Andrew's break-up with "N" and George's loss of Jessica (and his refusal of Aleksandra) may have seemed like that to them. But it isn't fully expressed in their memoirs.

To say that their 'adventures' with 'N' and Jessica were unsuccessful might be seen as a slur on the women in question. That's not the case. When I say they 'never quite succeeded' I mean that the fantasy, the romance, in each case came to an end, and they returned to life still involved in a quest. While they lived that 'other' life, each was utterly fulfilled, became a rounded person for the first time. Is it a coincidence that both were drawn to women at the very top of their professional class? And in what was, broadly speaking, the entertainment industry, which had previously been a *terra incognita* for both Andrew and George? Each gives plentiful evidence of fulfilment previously unknown in his life. Andrew was thrown together, by an inevitable but inexplicable fate, with the woman with whom he had been infatuated for many years. George, through his whirlwind affair with Jessica. In each case, a charismatic, stunningly beautiful woman who, for reasons neither of them could understand, had chosen to initiate these somewhat dowdy academics into an 'other' life, to transform those dowdy, academic lives into something unspeakably different.

Andrew was absorbed into the kingdom of make-believe in which 'N' was a queen, and through her, and his experience of observing her amazing creations of her screen rôles, he entered a world which gave him a sense of home. George was immersed, in a similar way, with Jessica's music-making – intense, passionate, totally demanding, but a life that invited him to partake and sit at the table of her music-making. His book on Brahms is, subliminally at least, the child of that relationship.

Both had a secret that kept them from the 'real' world. Andrew, because his relationship with 'N' was never made public, George because his work for what he thought *might* be MI6 was never spoken, never acknowledged. Andrew went to his grave holding his secret close to his heart. George had expected to do the same, but events turned out differently. Of course they did. They always do.

Whether 'Margaret' – to whom they both seem to have been married – or 'Jessica' or 'N' ever existed outside the minds of their author-lovers, we shall never discover. I did know both Margarets, or at least I *thought* that I did; I was, as Andrew makes clear, a participant in his life with 'N'; I had personal knowledge that each man had become the father of twins, one giving them the absurd names of "Oscar and Lucinda," the other 'Victoria and Albert'; and I was well aware of Jessica's international status as a concert artist, even though I knew little of her place in George's life until after their separation. But *who were they*? Just as both men respected my friendship, so I in turn have respected their real fictions, their fictional realities. What went on inside their heads is reflected, somewhat, in what they wrote. Their fears, hopes, memories, belong ultimately to them and are only partly articulated in their memoirs. If memory is fickle, selective, misleading, then both Andrew and George made imaginative leaps not into the future but into the past, in order to confront these memories, to be misled, to be fickled. I am merely the recording angel.

The sharp-eyed literary analyst will notice parallels between the two memoirs. Andrew's lunch with Solly Hofberg and Mart Sullivan is not unlike George's lunch with two anonymous mandarins of British Intelligence. In each case, it's possible that the conversations at those two lunches, however different they may have seemed on the surface, had helped each to recognise that he was an outsider, an exile. Andrew may not have recognized it explicitly, but George makes it very clear in his diary that he – and I think the same goes for Andrew – were perpetual exiles.

And this despite the fact that they were both long-term owners of houses – or maybe the same house – in Greece, on the tiny island of Karponisi: a bolt-hole, a rat-run where they might, but only might, feel more secure, more enfolded in the protection of the Englishman's castle. But can an exile ever know 'home'?

They both explore the porous borders between fact and fiction, the nature of faith and betrayal. An Irish writer once said that in his memory, events that *did* happen merged with events that *didn't* happen – couldn't have happened – but that fact and fiction became indistinguishable. He wrote: "*The fact is a fiction.* For some reason the mind has shuffled the pieces of verifiable truth and *composed a truth of its own.* And because I acknowledge its particular veracity, it becomes a layer of my subsoil; it becomes part of me. An autobiographical fact can be pure fiction and no less true or reliable for that." For both Andrew and George, memory has, it seems, played a similar trick – or is it in fact a 'trick'? Isn't it just possible that these borders between fact and fiction, between real and imaginary, are perfectly valid lines on a metaphorical piece of paper, *not* rigid frontiers with a stern notice: 'No Man's Land! No Woman's Land! Thou shalt not cross!' Quite the opposite. Andrew and George believed what they wrote in their respective memoirs, and therefore they represent their truths.

Keats said – and I'm not sure anyone really understands him – that 'beauty is truth, truth beauty – that is all you need to know.' These 'truths' that are spoken by Andrew and George respectively are their 'beauty.' There is no doubt of that. They prove Keats's idiosyncrasy by means of their own. And they go one step further, because they seem to tell us 'that is all you need to know.' To be economical with the truth, even if "composed," is one thing; to be economical with beauty is their way of saying that there are higher truths, and higher beauties, than those on the page.

Nor should we overlook the parallel facts that 'N' disappears for a mysterious eighteen months, during which she gives birth to the twins, Oscar and Lucinda – and I can vouch for that, because I was there – while, some time after George's and Jessica's separation, Jessica 'disappears' for two years during which she seems to have had a breakdown, whether mental or musical we do not know.

One was a disappearance celebrating the joy of togetherness and fruitfulness; the other was an absence signalling despair and emptiness. But in terms of Andrew's and George's lives, both were significant silences. The fact that one was a presence, the other an absence, is of little account when we consider that the women were prepared to 'take time out' in order to examine the nature of relationships, their potential and their dangers. Both Andrew and George reflected very deeply on what this meant for them.

Both men had become alcoholics or, to be more

precise, in each of them the genetic predisposition to drink had gradually asserted itself, with the predictable effect. Some drinkers go through their alcoholic life untouched. Others live as though in addition to two lungs, two kidneys, two eyes, two testicles, two hemispheres of the brain, they also have two livers. They don't. In Andrew's case, he simply continued drinking until it, in partnership with his liver, killed him. In George's case, the doctors read the riot act before he could go the full distance, and he was rescued and restored to sobriety.

The fact that they both, in their minds, came to live on the island of Karponisi, where they are both buried – two adversaries who came nearest to each other in their final resting-place – is entirely fortuitous.

Karponisi itself, of course, does not exist. A fiction. And yet, it is a fact...

- James Esposito
Villa Ipothesi
Karponisi
August 2015

"N"

by

Andrew Dalton

as told to James Esposito

CONTENTS

1
Editor's Introduction by James Esposito

When Andrew Dalton died in 2013, his executors, knowing that I had been his friend and long-time colleague, approached me with the proposal that I would edit, for publication, his memoir of his career: first, as a rising academic in the UK university world, and then in his fairy-tale, whirlwind involvement as literary advisor on *Intimate Letters*, a film about Leoš Janáček, starring Nicole Zoffany as the student Kamila Stösslová with whom Janáček became infatuated. I say 'fairy-tale' because the story is so unbelievable that you could reasonably be forgiven for thinking that he had made the whole thing up. In the course of working as a scriptwriter on the film, Andrew fell in love with the leading lady – or, it might be fairer to say that *she* fell in love with *him* – and his meteoric rise to Hollywood fame – and an Oscar – became a romance. Up to the time of his death, the only account of Andrew's romance with 'N' (as he habitually referred to her) was to be found in his diaries, which I have now edited for publication.

After their separation, he and 'N' remained on amicable terms, and Andrew was scrupulously protective of her identity and the identity of their twin children. Only towards the end of his life, when he retreated to his hideaway on the Greek island of Karponisi, did Andrew become indiscreet about his "Life with Nicole," as he entitled the memoir, and that indiscretion was due to the heavy drinking which eventually foreshortened his life. Throughout the years of their relationship, Andrew and 'N' were so guarded about the affair that it was Hollywood's best-kept secret, better than some of the CIA's or Pentagon's most precious mysteries. They had both been married before, and, after their separation (the cause of which is painfully described by Andrew in the memoir), 'N' married again. Andrew did not; he carried within him during his remaining years what he called 'the icon of beauty' – by which he meant not only N's stunning physical appearance and her warm, embracing personality, but also the entire aura of magic and fulfilment which transformed his life and surrounded him with happiness and a sense of completeness.

I can't say that this is "the greatest story ever told," but, as Andrew's friend and as godfather to his children, I can say with all sincerity that the tale you are about to read is greater than make-believe, more powerful than fable, truer than fiction. Andrew was a painfully honest character, and what he has written here never slips sideways from the truth, *his* truth; never tries to hoodwink you, the reader; and above all, never betrays "N," the love of his life.

I should add one crucial fact about Andrew's story that doesn't invalidate it in the slightest. The course of his relationship with "N" was exactly as he describes it. But the chronology he presents is all wrong. He presented it in order to put a smokescreen between "N" and him on one side, and the Hollywood gogglers – the *paparazzi* and society gossips – on the other. He says, for example, that he first saw her in the television series *Hotel Shanghai*, which was screened in 1989. "*I could hardly believe what I saw*," he writes. "*A young, confident, actress of such beauty that her dazzling appearance became in my eyes the subject of the film. The actual storyline receded into history as N stepped out of her childhood and into the spotlight with which beauty is rewarded in the public gaze. But for me, the private gaze of my adoration was a million times greater and nobler than anything Hollywood might subsequently offer her.*"

Beautiful words indeed, and leaving us in no doubt that his adoration of 'N' certainly began with this, or some similar, epiphany. But when he refers to this as her screen début he is all astray. He says that he instantly fell in love with her, and that it was therefore a massive surprise in 1995 when he discovered that she would be starring in *Intimate Letters*, that they were fated to sit in the same room, working on the same script. But *Intimate Letters* came several years *before Hotel Shanghai*.

Deliberately, it seems, Andrew gave no specific dates for the years with 'N' – neither the beginning of their relationship and the birth of the twins, nor the bust-up that ended it. Any sleuth trying to work out the sequence of her films, and how her life with Andrew fitted into that sequence, would be baffled – or so Andrew hoped. In fact, he really failed to throw anyone off the scent who had the slightest knowledge of her career – as all film buffs and fans invariably do.

I have no doubt that it was indeed with *Hotel Shanghai* that Andrew 'discovered' N. After all, he was hardly an avid cinemagoer. DVDs hadn't been invented, and if he hadn't had a television at home, and if *Hotel Shanghai* hadn't been a made-for-television series, it's doubtful if he would ever have come to know about her at all. And so, a beautiful story would never have been conceived.

He implies that there was a gap of eighteen months in N's schedule which was when 'N' became pregnant with the twins, and they retreated to the beach house on Long Island to start their family and their truly private life. But the only such gap in her schedule was in 1984-86, when Andrew and she hadn't even met. It's another of Andrew's smokescreens, the truth of which is known only to a tiny number of people, none of whom, myself included, will ever speak of the more private and intimate details.

Unless, of course, it was a different 'N' of whom he speaks, an even more secret 'N' whom none of us will ever know...

- James Esposito

2

Andrew Dalton's Diary

Nicole. At first, she called me 'the thinking woman's crumpet.' Later, she revised her opinion. I was 'like something out of a Graham Greene B-movie' – this on account of the shabby cream linen suits I habitually wore. But I suppose I was flattered. A none-too-young, rather shy academic from a distinctly non-celebrity background, thrown into a world in which I had no footing, no sense of direction. The princess and the pauper wasn't in it. This was class with a difference. A "literary advisor" on the film – sorry, the movie – on Leoš Janáček, in which she was starring as the student with whom the composer becomes infatuated.

Maybe she felt sorry for me – so obviously out of my depth, not exactly star-struck but looking around me with eyes of wonder at the scene into which I had been somewhat precipitately – even cruelly – pitched.

One of my remaining treasures is the portrait of Nicole by Annigoni which hung in our home and which she agreed I would keep after our separation. (We couldn't have a formal 'separation agreement' because we did not, officially speaking, have any reason to separate, since as far as the world was concerned we had never been together in the first place.) Considering the aesthetic value of the work – to say nothing of the monetary value of a work by an artist who had painted, among others, Queen Elizabeth – it was amazingly generous: it was one of the many signs that, despite our acrimonious and sudden split, she cared very much for me. Or was she just making sure that, every time I looked at it, I would feel *deep despair at having lost her, over what now seems to have been a stupid tantrum on my part?*

Someone as ignorant of the film world, as I was, even after eleven years with Nicole, had no grounds whatever for making the kind of criticism of Windmill *that I did. In fact, she was totally right and I was totally wrong. Or was she partly, almost entirely, right, and I was almost entirely, or partly, wrong? The truth of the matter, if there can ever be truth with hindsight, when there was never a shred of truth at the time, is that I was in no position at all to make judgements about the quality of her rôles, or indeed how she played them. She'd done dodgy films before* Windmill *and she did brilliant ones after it. So it seems, with this famous hindsight, that it was merely a hiccup in her superb, meteoric rise to stardom. She, to be fair to her, was willing to acknowledge this, but only after the storm that pulled us apart – not, of course, at the time. And I was ill-equipped to criticise because, although she gave me her scripts to read before she accepted a part, I had fuckall idea of how the script got translated onto the big screen, how Hollywood actually 'worked' – and this after I had worked on* Intimate Letters, *the film that brought us together.*

At that stage, I was too screen-struck to understand what it was all about, even though it was my script that was being daily mauled about by ignorant wankers who wouldn't have known one end of Leoš Janáček if he had walked into the script room and bid them gooday. Not in English, not in Czech, not in the odd language they speak in Hollywood. And then, before I could catch my breath, I was star-struck, or, more to the point, N-struck, instantly immersed in a passionate collision that, to this day, sustains me, especially when I look at Annigoni's masterpiece and see N soulfully but playfully eyeing me

James Esposito

*like some poor mutt that has strayed into her caravan –
sorry, trailer.*

*That portrait, and the album of photos of us with the
children, sustain me in my loneliness. It's not all lonely, of
course. N and I speak on the phone as often as possible, or
necessary, and the children visit me here at least once a
year, usually twice. Until they reach the age when the
excitement of seeing their otherwise distant father wears
off, and teenage excitements are found in other
directions. They were ten when I left Long Island – and
they are seventeen now. Almost time to go. There are
signs of that already. But my visits to them in the States –
almost always on Long Island, in the home where they
were born and grew up, where N and I grew our love and
understanding – are more regular and will continue,
come what may. There, we have the guards to discourage
the paparazzi; here, we have just ourselves.*

*Only once has N been here, a calculated risk, with no
escort, modestly, completely unrecognized, just like that
first day in the Snow White Café. You couldn't call it a
reunion, certainly nothing approaching a reconciliation.
Artists' vanity, when it is hurt (or thinks it's been hurt)
always prevents that. But although she never ceases to
remind me that I know nothing about the business, and
that my views on movies in general are of no value
whatever, she can't deny the love that bonded us and
which we stupidly threw away. We didn't allow it to fade
or wither: we simply abandoned it in one mad, frantic,
senseless night of insult and counter-insult, tears,
recriminations, truths and lies, until in the morning I
knew I had lost her. I had found paradise, and I had
thrown it away. L'enfant abdique son extase.*

*The idyll of those few years is now a part of movie
history. I was a side-show – as indeed I always had been
– who should never have been allowed through the gates*

7

of any film studio, let alone those of the sainted and revered N. So when she came to stay here, so briefly, and even though we did not have sex, or even contemplate it, a sense of a passion-that-once-was haunted our few days together. We knew she would not be recognized because the tavern-keepers were elderly folk who had hardly any interest in the cinema. Only once, when we sat near some American tourists, was the mask nearly snatched away. We heard one of them say, "Gee, I think that's Barbra Streisand at that table." I laughed. N was furious.

It wasn't N who drew me to Intimate Letters, *because when I had been approached, her name had yet to be mentioned as a potential star. The rôle of Janáček, it had been agreed, would be played by the Romanian actor Ion Caramitru, but that of his passion, the student Kamila Stösslová, was still on offer – Keira Knightley, Cate Blanchett and Jennifer Lopez were all under consideration, but for various reasons of prejudice, who-slept-with-whom, and budget, they all went up in smoke. Thankfully, in the case of Keira Knightley: the same inane grin that made Princess Di an icon for those even more stupid than herself. Good for* fellatio *and little else. Vanessa Redgrave does it so much better – I mean the vacant, open-mouthed expression, not the other thing.*

But when I knew that N was to play the part, all my previous admiration for her and, I must be truthful, my voyeur's lust for her graceful womanhood impelled me towards my glorious fate.

I'd better explain a little more clearly, and in more detail, how my infatuation with N began. I was never a 'film buff' and seldom went to the cinema, so it wasn't until 1989 that I first saw N on television in Hotel Shanghai. *It came on after the 9pm news and something in the storyline caught my fancy. A young girl, on the cusp of womanhood, is on a quest for her lost father – it* had all the ingredients of the literary mystery genre that had taken up so much of my professional life (I lectured at *Leeds* on *Popular Literature*). The ins and outs of the story are neither here nor there. Of course the girl gets the man (or, rather, daughter and father have a tearful and tragic reconciliation), and all ends happily or unhappily ever after, depending on your preferred outcome. But it was N's absolute beauty – and I say 'absolute' knowing so well what I am saying – that called to me. An innocent on such a steep learning curve that N the girl-starlet became, in the course of four hours, the woman-star. But in my mind and memory she remained a girl-woman, on the cusp not only of movie greatness but of her own femininity. With all her experience today, she is still the wide-eyed little girl, wondering at the way the 'other' world can become her reality, the way she can make it her reality. Getting lost ... and needing to be found.

If it's true that "the boy who leaves home has to meet the man who returns," then it is even more true, and more challenging, for the girl who leaves and becomes a woman. N, with me, was the woman who nourished the girl who had left her simple background to encounter complexity and danger.

I became one of her off-screen lovers. Like millions of other, unfulfilled, middle-aged men. A young, confident, actress of such beauty that her dazzling appearance became in my eyes the subject of the film. The actual storyline receded into history as N stepped out of her childhood and into the spotlight with which beauty is rewarded in the public gaze. But for me, the private gaze of my adoration was a million times greater and nobler than anything Hollywood might subsequently offer her.

Her juvenile innocence wasn't the part she was playing, it was N herself. And I fell in love with that *innocence, that playful innocence that, I later found, could be cruel in the very same moment that it was loving; teasing and delivering all in one instant of revelation. My wife would find me secretly rewinding the episodes I had recorded on VHS, just to use the pause button – a technical challenge for me – and savour N's beauty: the small breasts, the long slim legs that I always coveted. One day they would be wrapped around me... 'Stop the fantasy, Andrew, and get on with the story' I hear myself saying.*

It was her mouth and smile. In fact, the way her entire face exuded a character that developed as one observed it, revelled in it, adored it. It was mesmeric. It drew you to her, as the sphinx lured you with her secret – the secret of her identity, not hidden in her depths, but readable on the surface of her pure, untrammelled skin. Even when her lips were closed, she was smiling. It was always a smile. It would light up the world even if there were no sun or moon or stars. Radiant doesn't describe the dynamo that came from her heart and showed itself through her eyes and her smile. The mouth was innocent, insouciant, ingénue, capable of the most disarming openness, but at the same time, a mouth not to be touched with anything other than the profoundest respect. It was the meeting-point of strength and innocence that mesmerized me, the perfect confluence of the eyes that smiled in total harmony with the mouth. Saying all things at every moment of time, or, with the minutest, split-second flicker, change from youthful bewilderment to steely understanding. Steel and softness, timid and assertive, it frightened me.

All the time, this duality. In her eyes, in her mouth, in her profile, in her full face. Two women in one. Many women in one. In one glorious body. One inexpressible expression. I'm biased, of course, but most film buffs would agree.

Her look could be petulant, truculent, wilful, and as she matured – as she did, minute-by-minute over the four hours of Hotel Shanghai *– it would change to panic, anger, determination. She did not shed her innocence: she used it to find herself, and to bewilder a world which, it seemed, only a moment before had bewildered* her. *From little-girl-lost to woman-in-command. A face that was total character. And enigma. She enslaved me, and millions of other speechless voyeurs of her beauty.*

Yes, I became her lover, so of course I am prejudiced, but that face, that character, becomes the whole world – a poem that becomes an epic, a testament of beauty, with everything within it: all human knowledge, all longing, all persuasion, all joy, all fear. How she can exude innocence and longing and strong temperament all at the same time still confounds my intelligence, but not my love.

When she came to make Love, Fear, Hate *and* An Other World, *N had stolen the screen in so many movies with that unbelievable face, that she could become her character simply by being herself. If you look at her films, one after another, you could be forgiven for thinking that she was just herself, unchanging, in every rôle. But as her career developed, providing her with increasingly challenging rôles, so too did her persona, both onscreen and in real life. But that did not diminish her beauty. It enhanced it. It was the mastery of nuance, the knowing exactly how to make a fractional alteration that brought her from girlhood to womanhood, from innocence to experience, that was her most prized quality. All her speech, her movements, gestures, hints, came after this encyclopaedia of nuance. Look at those films and realise just how much the directors depended on the close-up to convey the whole range of emotions, almost without a word being spoken or a step taken.*

In An Other World, for example, we saw apprehension in the face of the unknown, and eagerness to confront it. In Love, Fear, Hate, where she was so cruelly treated by Joanna Hampton and John Danolič, she was, in her own words, "working at a pitch" that brought her close to madness, so intense were the emotional changes demanded of that impeccable face. Capable of being submissive in her desperation, yet resistant at the same moment. When I had first seen her, I had seen a girl unhappy and desperate to regain the state before unhappiness, to be loved again, to belong, to be held. That, as I would discover, was what she sought from me. That sense of longing without lust, of seeking something, someone, with perhaps no chance of finding it. And that is what she thought she had found in me. Did find in me, until I behaved like the world's stupidest cretin and let her go, all for the sake of a stale, aesthetic, pointless and worthless argument.

I realized early, and many years before I knew N, before I found that my screen-reading of her was a true one, that this was a face of piercing yet mellifluous eyes and tender mouth, all combining in smiles that were, let's face it, dangerous and bewitching. She was searching for an unknown quality, asking questions of the unknown, and at the same time tearing into your soul and planting there seeds of passion and alarm.

My marriage was already one only in name. Margaret and I had been the victims of kid-love, a childhood "pash" that we mistakenly thought would sustain us through adulthood, whatever that was. When she found me drooling over N's screen image, neither of us thought it was serious: just a fantasy on my part and jealousy on hers. N didn't break us up, it was coming anyway.

From that point on, my enslavement to my screen goddess marched side-by-side with my increasing realisation that Margaret and I were finished, that it was only a matter of time before we went our separate ways. How could N have had anything to do with that? I might have fallen in love with a hundred screen nymphets – the aforesaid Blanchett or Lopez, the androgynous Gwyneth Paltrow, the sulky gamine of Scarlett Johansson; even gawdelpus, the mindless grinning Knightley.

In career terms, even with my very limited knowledge of the celebrity world, I realized that this was a junior talent that would take N to the very top of her profession. And she would bring me with her, to the very top of my life as a lover, a father, a man from whom middle age fell away and left simply me, the man and she, the icon. I write this in the aftermath – some might say the ruins – of that life.

3

My Journey to Hollywood

How did I come to be in a script office with a roomful of film nerds, working on the Janáček project? I had been, as they say, 'plucked from obscurity' – not in academic terms – but as far as the film nerds were concerned, anyone from a university was a non-entity, not worth crossing the road to piss on.

Perhaps I should go back to the beginning, even though it was a worthless beginning, hardly meriting an explanation. I was born in 1949 in Croydon, south London. My father was a schoolteacher and my mother kept house. I was an only child. My parents were determined that I should have a good education that might open the way for me to a successful career. I suppose that my father's profession already pointed me towards some kind of teaching. In due course I attended Whitgift Grammar School in the town and won a scholarship to Oxford. They were thrilled at first, less so when it appeared that I wanted to continue in academe, pursuing a PhD on Walter Pater and then successfully applying for a junior lectureship at Leeds, where my mentor was the late Derry Jeffares. Until *Intimate Letters* came along, that was where I stayed. The thesis on Pater was unpublishable, not least because it vied with a similar work by my contemporary, the aristocratic George Manners, whom I came to despise.[1] In the course of all this academic work I had married a childhood sweetheart, Margaret Holmes;

---

[1] Editor's note: George Manners was distantly related to the family of the Dukes of Rutland – hence Dalton's use of the term 'aristocratic.'

we were childless.

My attention moved to twentieth-century authors like William Golding, John Fowles and L.P. Hartley. My main concern as a teacher was that generations of students had been conditioned to think that there were 'great' works and 'lesser' works – and it wasn't only 'airport fiction' (the doorstep-sized stuff by Danielle Steele and others) that was looked down on, but in fact most popular fiction, including the detective genre, thrillers, 'quest' literature like Tolkien; these, we had been taught to believe, were 'lowbrow' books which couldn't compare with Austen, George Eliot, Dickens and others of that ilk. You *either* liked Proust and Kafka, and said so, loudly, *or* you liked P.G. Wodehouse, but probably didn't admit it. I thought I had a responsibility to deflate this pomposity, and had therefore persuaded my department head to let me teach a course in Popular Literature, which I supported by writing two books on the subject.

But the reason for my coming to the attention of the *Intimate Letters* producers was due to entirely different circumstances: the fact that at Oxford I had also written a minor thesis on the Czech composer Leoš Janáček. Which leads us to my arrival in Hollywood.

I suppose I was equipped to do a scriptwriting job because I had always studied music (I had taken literature and music as my twin subjects for my BA) and wrote a regular critical column for *The Yorkshire Post* after Gerald Larner's retirement. Somehow my Janáček article had found its way to whoever was researching the movie. I only later discovered that two other 'experts' – one at Oxford, the other at Cambridge – had been approached before they came to me; both had turned it down, presumably because writing for the screen was somehow *infra dig*. A fat tome on Janáček's operas in the one case (Oxford) and, in the other, entirely devoted to the *Glagolitic Mass*

(Cambridge), which sat on library shelves and which nobody read; fine achievements in themselves, no doubt. Jasper Pilkinghorn, who wrote the book on the operas, saw them simply as expressions of the working class stirring in their sleep. And until the *Letters* were published, no one, but no one, had had the slightest idea that the Glagolitic Mass might have been Janáček's way of 'marrying' his fantasy-love, Kamila. But their books got them invited to international conferences in obscure parts of the world where they could play away games with little fear of discovery – Rio de Janeiro was a favorite for this kind of thing, the Brazilian women were noted for their willingness and enthusiasm.

So the producers were left with me. And it wasn't even Hollywood, but in its own way a sub-let of the moguldom. An independent company which had excavated for itself a niche in literary and musical films, several of them aping Ken Russell's success with the genius-plus-sex formula, and had already produced films on Virginia Woolf, D.H. Lawrence and Henry James in the literary sphere and Sibelius, Mahler and Benjamin Britten in music. And now Janáček: the story of his separation from his wife and infatuation with Kamila Stösslova, not a million miles away from my own circumstances, since I had recently separated from Margaret and, unbeknownst to me, was heading for N. In polite meaningless banter during our preliminary skirmishes, I had gathered that there was also a bio-doc (I was learning fast!) on John Fowles in the pipeline, and, since John was a personal friend, I argued that they would much, much rather have a script from me on Fowles. But no, that was already done and dusted: George bloody Manners had got the job. I never really disliked him, although I think he believed he had a grudge against me – why, I can't imagine. He had got to the winning post on Pater *and* Fowles before me. I didn't envy him at all, especially considering he made a complete mess of the Fowles books. And anyway, if I had taken that job, I would never have ... well, you know. There were two of us in it. More than two, I suppose, really.

I allowed my genuine devotion to Janáček, with the flattery which, even as number 3 choice, they poured over me in several well-watered lunches in some exclusive London eatery, to overcome any worries I might have about what I was embarking on. It would be fun. I had no idea of just how much 'fun' would be involved, but I was keen with anticipation. My meteoric rise to a status somewhere between a minor actor and the studio night-watchman gave me an entrée to an undreamed-of world; a hotel suite (not quite the best, but a luxury as far as I was concerned, with my limited experience of international travel and the annual excursion with Margaret to our cottage in Greece for what are laughingly called holidays). *And* a chauffeured car – not a stretch limo, no question of bulletproofing, but a car nonetheless that I personally didn't have to drive.

That, until that incredible day in the script room, was all the fun I knew, more or less compensating for the excruciating frustration of working with people for whom Janáček might as well have been a Neapolitan organ-grinder or a peddler of *bratwurst*. I wanted to bring him, and Kamila Stösslova, alive with the passion of his music and the "intimate letters" that inspired him. *They* wanted something they could sell at the box-office. Having Caramitru, a brilliant but unknown Romanian actor who had also been Minister of Culture in his own country, thrust on them through diplomatic pressure – something to do with east-west entente – meant that they needed a superb player as Stösslova. It's called entertainment. It's called bums-on-seats. It certainly ain't called art. Art Garfunkel, maybe.

My first step towards the Oscar I would eventually win for best screenplay was the background memorandum I'd written on foot of their original enquiry. Sometimes I doubted if they had ever read it, but the way the whole thing developed, and in doing so subverted all the subtlety, the nuances, the whispers, of the Janáček-Stösslova relationship, its innate *beauty*, convinced me that they had indeed taken a cynical but, to them, realistic decision on how that relationship was to be screened. My agent had insisted on a clause in my contract that stipulated they couldn't change my script without my say-so, and they couldn't take my name off the screen credits unless they paid me a star's ransom. Up to that fateful day in the script office, I could have engineered it so that I became such a pain in their collective posterior that the star's ransom would be mine, and they could do what they liked with the "intimate letters" – use them to staunch the pain in their you-know-where for all I cared. And then... the star arrived, and I was ransomed in a quite different way.

So, to jump the storyline, anticipation became 'N': joy, trauma, passion, heartache, the sheer exuberance of N – how any one word can describe such a phenomenon, such a goddess *ex machina*, is beyond the comprehension of a professional writer like me. One would have to be a poet on methadone, or worse, to find that word. I had to settle for two words: *incandescent ecstasy*, and it lives with me even now, looking back on the fantasy into which I so easily and willingly fell. It was a never-never land that would become a land of always.

But to get back to the story. This memorandum I supplied, on which all the misconceptions of the film would eventually be based, was lifted, shamelessly, from the thesis I had written years before:

In 1917 the Czech composer Leoš Janáček had begun

a trial separation from his wife, Zdenka, whom he had married in 1881 when she was almost sixteen and he was twenty-seven. Due to the acclaim accorded to his recent opera Jenůfa *he was emerging at this time from relative obscurity, and was now on holiday in Luhačovice with his mistress Gabriela Horvátová when he met Kamila Stösslová, who had been happily married for two years. She was twenty-seven, Janáček sixty-two. Janáček was immediately struck by Kamila (his feelings for Gabriela were already waning) and began to write her passionate letters – over seven hundred during the next eleven years. (Hers to Janáček were almost all destroyed by him, at her request.)*

(Gabriela was eventually played by Greta Scacchi.)

These letters are considered by most musicologists to represent the clearest and most revealing statements by Janáček about his compositions, his career, his marriage to Zdenka (which had settled into a form of companionship) and his love for Kamila. Those of hers which survive indicate that she was unquestionably devoted to her husband and children, was by no means convinced that she could fulfil the rôle of muse into which Janáček had projected her, and was hesitant about meetings and correspondence itself. It is almost certain that, as far as their emotional relationship was concerned, it was exclusively platonic with the possible exception of a "kiss" in 1927 to which Janáček attributed enormous significance. In "fact," they seldom met, and were hardly ever alone together, yet for him, Kamila became his "soul," and he frequently addressed her as such in the letters, constantly and increasingly affirming that she and he were as one, and that the burning passion that this engendered was the source of his artistic inspiration.

Whether or not he was a self-deluding old man,

Janáček's work became increasingly and intensely passionate. He produced a stream of music that, he said, had Kamila as its sole begetter, and represented their offspring. The song-cycle "The Diary of One who Disappeared," the operas The Cunning Little Vixen, The Makropoulos Affair, From the House of the Dead *and, above all,* Katya Kabanova, *were, he said, directly inspired by Kamila's physical beauty and her temperament. Even the* "Glagolitic Mass," *formerly regarded as a straightforward pan-Slavonic, pantheistic work, was revealed to be a nuptial mass for the composer and Kamila when his letters (in one of which he even referred to himself as "your husband") were published in Czech in 1990 and in English last year [1994].*

The letters begin in a stilted, but nonetheless passionate, fashion: 16 July 1917, "Dear Madam, accept these few roses as a token of my unbounded esteem for you. You are so lovely in character and appearance that in your company one's spirits are lifted; you breathe warm-heartedness, you look on the world with such kindness that one wants to do only good and pleasant things for you in return." Whenever Kamila delayed in replying, Janáček became petulantly impatient. Five years later, "I need your twittering and your scrawling as the dry weather needs the rain, the dawn needs the sun, the sky needs the stars. Yes, that last comparison is the best. What's the sky without that little star? You're the star that I look for in the evening. Out of love? Out of sincere friendship." Sexual longing was never absent from this passion, and was frequently expressed: "How can one not want you, when one loves you? But I know, don't I, that I'll never have you... We dream about paradise, about heaven, and we never get to it. So I dream about you and I know that you're the unattainable sky. But not to want you – that's an impossibility."

And yet this precious passion must be closely guarded: "Do you know, my soul, why it's necessary meticulously to conceal things? If we really had belonged to one another, would anyone believe that after eleven years there was only that longing, that yearning? No-one would believe it."

In 1927 – whether or not provoked by the "kiss" – the relationship deepened considerably. "Perhaps something was fated to give us both unutterable pleasure? Never in my life have I experienced such an intermingling of myself with you ... In the thought that I have you, that you're mine, lies all my joy of life ... The seed from Luhačovice has grown tall; a tree has grown from it on which hangs the red of your lips."

In January 1928 Janáček told Kamila that he had begun a string quartet (his second), entitled "Love Letter"': "our life will be in it ... In that work I'll be always only with you! No third person beside us. You know, don't you, that I know no world other than you!" The quartet would, "in fact," be their love-child, and the elimination of the 'third person' meant the exclusion of both his wife and her husband – they could only be totally together in music. The frustration was enormous: "I'd like to dedicate it to 'Mrs Kamila Janáček.' We want to love one another, we want to belong to one another, we want to experience with total passion the fact that we'll declare we belong to each other and for ever, inseparably."

The title of the work evolved into the more subtle, more guarded and yet more suggestive "Intimate Letters," and Janáček began to wonder whether the enforced secrecy of the relationship would become too obvious: he wrote to Max Brod "would it be taken amiss if the spiritual relationship, this artistic relationship, were to be openly admitted?"

To Kamila, he described the composition of each

movement: the first was "the impression when I saw you for the first time"; the second, "my sweetest desire – you are giving birth"; the third, "the earth begins to tremble"; and the finale "reflects the anguish I feel about you ... not fear but the fulfilment of longing." The entire work was an intense outpouring which was committed to paper within three weeks. He died in August 1928, while on a rare holiday with Kamila and one of her children. He was seventy-four, she was thirty-eight.

Janáček's letters to Kamila were themselves a "performance," a massive soliloquy on the nature of longing and passion. Kamila's silences were a withdrawal, a series of empty bars or rests in which the listener – Janáček – strained to hear her absent meaning. For the composer, the only medium he could trust, or at least understand, was music; he came to think that music and silence may be "the real thing."

I can't say that all of this should have been the entire film, or that other aspects of Janáček's life shouldn't have been included, but it provided the researchers with enough background to understand what the central theme of the film should be: love, love, love. Unfortunately, their conception of what love is, or was, and what to do with it, was radically different from mine.

4

Frustration

Well, you can imagine how outraged my Britishness and my sense of justice were by the way in which the producers molested this beautiful story. When I had written the original thesis, a colleague at Leeds, James Esposito, had gasped: he knew nothing of the facts behind it, but he did know his way in the art-cinema: "Andrew, this has the makings of a truly wonderful art film! Let me pass it to some contacts I have in that world." And so began the disintegration of my storyline into the romantic, Ken Russell-ish travesty of the "real thing." I'll come later to the way the producers took every part of this memo to pieces, as if they were excisemen with sniffer-dogs, intent on exposing the slightest grain of sincerity or, god forgive me, "truth" and confiscating it. (I later discovered that some of what they secretly regarded as the "good bits" found their way into another film, on Béla Bartók, but that, as they say, is another story. One I didn't get paid for.)

As I tried to sketch out the finer points of my idea – how Janáček and the relationship with Kamila were to be portrayed, the musical themes which were to be brought to the screen – I saw their eyes glaze over. This was my first realisation that there *were* in fact no "finer points." I had the upper hand, in the sense that, as their no. 3 choice, they had damn all chance of getting another scriptwriter with my recognized expertise as an "authority" on Janáček, but a further realisation was that they could just as easily decide to scrap Janáček altogether and find a Mozart expert (if fashion dictated an eighteenth-century treatment) or a Strauss expert (if they were told that Strauss was "in"). I doubted whether they would have known, or cared, whether it was "Johann Strauss the Waltz King" or Richard Strauss, the stormy associate of Hitler. That choice would have been made by whoever felt like nineteenth-century romance at breakfast time, and just as quickly changed his mind by lunchtime if fascism became the flavour of the day (that wouldn't be Solly Hofberg, of course). Or they could move away from music and decide on a bio-doc on William Golding, with Malcolm Bradbury in the hot seat.

Even though this was a low-budget, non-Hollywood movie, and certainly not conceived as a blockbuster, the Hollywood mania for re-scripting had taken hold. The producers, the director, N herself, the representatives of the Janáček estate (his work and, more importantly, the "intimate letters," were still in copyright), all had a contractual right to make observations on the script and, in the last resort, to exercise their veto and insist on a rewrite. This happened several times.

My original screenplay had been diverted three times into what I regarded as unnecessary and untenable variations on the basic theme, before the rôle was even offered to N. I had been consulted on the process only because of my "star's ransom" clause. I was stuck with them and they were stuck with me. I never felt like that with N.

So often during the script meetings I had found myself exclaiming: "but what you're asking for is pure slush – no style, no finesse, no class – what you want is romantic gobbledegook." I was tempted to say "pap for the dispossessed" but I knew there wasn't a snowball's chance in hell they would recognise the literary reference. "What you are asking for has nothing to do with real life – with what really happened" I fulminated. "The estate will insist on a return to the truth of the matter." "Andrew," they would explain, at first with patience, almost kindliness, as if talking to a small child intent on entering an adults" world, but with increasing annoyance at my Britishness, my insistence on "the truth": "This isn't real life." "Well I can't see Nicole swallowing this make-believe. She has a higher intelligence than that."

At this point one of the executives guffawed. "Intelligence? Nicole? Oh boy, what planet are you on Andrew? She's an actress. She says the lines we give her. No intelligence required. How many clothes-horses have brains?" What he didn't know was that N was just outside the door. When she came in, the icy silence that fell could hardly be called embarrassed. It was mortification multiplied a million times. After a few moments of this professional limbo N, with the sweetest possible expression, said two things. To me: "Andrew, dear" – as if she already knew me, and knew me well – "Could we step outside?." To Mr Guffaw, very quietly, almost in a whisper that masked her controlled rage, "Goodbye." If he ever worked in the film industry again, it would be as a tea-boy. N saw to that.

Emerging from the script office, Andrew and "N," little did they know it, were on the threshold of one of the most exciting, passionate and secret affairs that Hollywood has ever known.

5

The Snow White Café

When we left the script room, N took my arm and pointed in the direction of her trailer. "I'd like to get out of this space, and these clothes, if you don't mind, Andrew, and then we could go somewhere quiet where we can talk. If we stay in the trailer, there will be a string of PAs, make-up people, maybe that creep from in there" – she nodded back at the script room – "come to apologise." With a smile I would come to know so well later, one that combined innocence with conspiracy, she said: "And Sol or Mart have a habit of just dropping in, and I think you can do without that for one day." At that stage I had only met the producers, Solly Hofberg and Mart Sullivan, at one brief assembly of the writing staff. The worst was yet to come, and I think N knew that.

I waited in the lobby of her trailer while she did mysterious things within. And she was right. A non-stop stream of visitors, all no doubt on legitimate business, and an equally non-stop ringing of her phones. I was still waiting, wondering how even a superstar could take so long to fetch a pair of dark glasses, when someone I can only describe as a broad stepped up to me. Denim jacket, short – *very* short – denim skirt, ordinary blouse, and raybans. "Are you going to stand there all day?" I started, trying to be invisible. "Andrew, let's go." The broad was N. Totally *gamine*, street-urchin, she was completely unrecognisable.

The disguise was just as well, since she steered me out of the film lot and past the Chinese Theatre where, a year later, we would collect our Oscars. A little further along, we came to the Snow White Café, plastic banquettes and a 1950s jukebox. "One of Hollywood's national treasures" N whispered. "Only for tourists."

We sat opposite one another; N ordered a coffee for herself and, without consulting me, told the waitress "And he'll have a Grumpyburger." I stared at her in astonishment. "A What?" "Think where you are, Andrew dear. After what you've been through this morning, a Grumpyburger is what you need." "And you," I blurted out, "After that slimy bastard's insult, don't you need a Revengeburger?" She gave a little laugh from behind the Raybans: "Something good, something bad, happens every day on the lot. That freak was just a bit worse than the normal. But when I put the word around, he'll wish he had never been born. We won't see him again." She paused, lifted her glasses, smiled with mouth and eyes: "And today, something good happened, Andrew. I met you."

"Look, Miss Zoffany" I tried to stammer in reply.

"Andrew, my name is Nicole. On the set, it's a rule, I'm Miss Zoffany, to everyone, including you. But when we are together, I want to be Nicole. Trust me, Andrew."

Trust her! I'd have given my life for that one smile, from the woman who had been my dream – oh, let's be crude, my pin-up – for so long. Even to sit with her, with or without a Grumpyburger, was heaven.

I tried stammering again, to see if I could do it a bit better this time. "Miss – sorry, Nicole, if this is just a thank you for what happened in there, I do appreciate it very" –

"No, Andrew," she took over. "It isn't because you value my intelligence." A smile close to a smirk; thereafter, any mention of the word "intelligence" would bring smiles to both our faces. "It's because I've been watching you. I like you. I would like to be with you. I value your – your" and here she herself started to stammer. "Your honesty. The way you've put the script together. The way you've had the sense to accept Sol and Mart's driving force." The smirk returned. "*And* the way you spoke of me. That's why I've sought you out. If it hadn't been today, it would have come some time soon." She saw my look of alarm. "Don't worry, Andrew, this isn't a man-hunt, I'm not a man-eater. In fact, I don't mind saying this to you – since my divorce from Jim, I've been living alone. I haven't wanted to be with anyone, and with you it's a cry for friendship, not an invitation to my bed." (Jim Bates was a second-rate actor whom N had decided to marry when she was a mere nineteen - "Master Bates" as his detractors, and Hollywood gossip in particular, called him.)

I would soon discover that "living alone" was a Hollywood term for a house with a butler (English), two cooks (French), what we in England would call three parlour-maids (Filipino), a chauffeur (Spanish), a private secretary (English) and two gardeners (Mexican). No Americans in sight. But she had not been with a man since that messy breakup and divorce from Jim.

The re-writes were nerve-wracking, exhausting, frustrating and they always wanted them by yesterday. It's the same on every film, sorry movie. N was very gentle in explaining it to me. She did so in humorous terms, and yet she spared no punches because she knew I would have to fight every inch of the way to save my script from a sex-change, a personality disorder, a bipolar condition and reincarnation as *Gone With the Wind*.

"Look, Andrew, it's like this: one producer wants to change the central character, the other wants to change the period in which it is set. Some characters are deleted, mostly when the plot gets too complicated for the Hollywood mind; yes, believe me, some of them *do* have minds, warped and shrunken though they may be. Others, who often have nothing to do with the original story, get added, usually when the producers decide the thing isn't sexy enough (i.e., add a bimbo) or lacking in suspense ("We need an extra villain here"). A film that starts off as *The Man in the Iron Mask* could move from the eighteenth century to the twentieth, the central character is no longer a member of the French royal family but a Serbian politician, he's rescued by the CIA until the CIA tell the producers to back off, and then he's rescued by a gang of lesbian mountaineers who'd put Pussy Galore to shame. And it's set in Dublin. Or Canberra. Or Antarctica."

She sat back and laughed. I didn't care at that stage what they did to my script as long as they left that laugh, and its caring, patient author, frozen in aspic for all time.

Intimate Letters would go through most of these metamorphoses. At one point the boss producer, Solly Hofberg, even wanted to delete Janáček completely and replace him with Ernest Hemingway, mainly because they had a lot of plot left over from a film set in Key West in which Hemingway was a minor character. Just the same way that they took my leftover Janáček material and stuck it onto Bartók. I call it theft of intellectual property. They call it business. And after all, what is the cinema except a great illusion, so enthralling that you don't realise they are picking your pockets as you sit there ogling Britt Ekland's tits? Entertainment? It's theft, by another name.

And fashion changes meant that the 1920s weren't as "sexy" as they had been when the film was conceived and they wanted the whole thing moved forwards into the 1960s or even the 1990s. "Andrew, you've got to accept that, whatever the critics may say about the movie, it's the box-office that counts – it's the man at the box-office who counts the pennies that add up to dollars that add up to millions. So the buzzword right now is "People have had enough of this costume drama stuff. They want *now.*' So we have to go with that."

But she went on: "Sol and Mart will be calling you in,

and if you survive that, you can certainly tell that roomful of creeps back there where to stick their re-writes." She waited for her determination and professional expertise to make themselves totally clear to me. "I'll always be there, not only because it's *my* movie, and *my* career, but because I recognise a soulmate, someone out of their depth, and I want to protect him." Him. ME! I slobbered; I wallowed; I genuflected; I stood on my head and sang *Ave Maria* – all, of course, metaphorically, which was appropriate because most of this project, and in fact the rest of my life, would be indentured to metaphor.

The fact that N's presence would begin with protection, proceed through a series of encounters that you could calibrate with a calendar in one hand and a loveometer in the other, towards the greatest love imaginable, and then out the other side, was beyond me at this stage, but something told me that that "not an invitation to my bed" was not the closed gate it seemed, and hadn't been intended as such.

"Dear Andrew."

6
Solly and Mart

My most painful experience of being re-written was when Solly and his sidekick (co-producer) Mart Sullivan, ganged up on me to – well, to tear up my ideas and make a new film out of the confetti. Solly's family had come to the States as the remnants of once prosperous Vienna merchants, the rest of whom had perished in Dachau. He basically wanted every film he made to be about the holocaust. Mart's people had come much earlier, as refugees from the Irish famine. So insistent was he on his Irish heritage that he listed his name officially in Gaelic, as "Mairtín Ó Suilleabháin," which no one, not even the Irish, and certainly not Solly, understood. He wasn't quite as hung up as Solly on the deep subliminal hurt to his family which he carried on his shoulder (if that isn't an anatomical contradiction). But it was a close-run thing.

Between them, they had amassed a small-to-medium fortune from movies that explored deprivation, cruelty, pain and extermination, and as a result become national heroes in a country that (apart from the aborigines) had hardly known any of those essential human experiences. So much so that they were known as "Solly Sullivan," whom many people thought was an Irish-Jewish hero of some war of liberation. The only war Solly and Mart had been involved in was the liberation of cinema audiences from their cash and, in that, they were the victors. Some day someone should make a movie about the losers in that war – the Joe Soaps (sorry, John Doe) who'd been hooked on the drugs that Solly and Mart peddled on every high street (sorry, shopping mall) in the US of A. I thought "SolMart" was a better trade-name – since what they did was just like a discount chain store.

Well, crunch day was when they sent the car to take me down the coast to a swanky restaurant at Santa Monica. After three very pleasant, if pointless, martinis administered, no doubt, to render me more pliant, Solly produced my memorandum from his briefcase and proceeded to read it. Actually *read* it! "OK Drew" he began.

"Actually, my name's Andrew," I stuttered.

"Drew, Andrew, what the hell. This stuff stinks." Mart looked uncomfortable. "Yeah" Solly continued, unaware of any discomfiture on anyone"s part. "Take this first part: *In 1917 the Czech composer Leoš Jack* – he stumbled over the composer's name – I could see trouble looming and decided his name was "Jack" – *had begun a trial separation from his wife, Zdenka, whom he had married in 1881 when she was almost sixteen and he was twenty-seven.* That all has to go."

"But it's essential background information," I protested. "We've got to get that across to the viewer."

"Look Drew, *you* write the crap – *we* get it across. See?" I dried up before he could tell me to. Mart gave me a sorrowing look, as if to say "There's worse to come."

"*Due to the acclaim accorded to his recent opera* Jenůfa *he was emerging at this time from relative obscurity, and was now on holiday in Luhačovice with his mistress Gabriela Horvátová when he met Kamila Stösslová, who had been happily married for two years. She was twenty-seven, Janáček sixty-two. Janáček was immediately struck by Kamila (his feelings for Gabriela were already waning) and began to write her passionate letters – over seven hundred during the next eleven years. (Hers to Janáček were almost all destroyed by him, at her request.)*

"OK Drew, you may have something there. This music guy meets this dame, while he already has two on the go, and he starts writing her. Drew, writing letters does NOT make a movie."

"But the film's called *Intimate Letters* and that's what it's all about" – but even as I said it I had lost faith in myself to defend it, and as I was on a losing streak it seemed best just to shut the fuck up.

"Letters, intimate, mistress, music – that can all be changed if necessary. If we say" – and here Mart looked even more uncomfortable as he was drawn into his co-producer rôle – "If we say it's going to be called *Undying Lust* and if we say it's about a gay playwright in 1960s Paris, that's what the public will see."

"Well in that case, you won't need me any longer" I said, gathering my notes and preparing to leave with as much dignity as I could muster. "But you'll have to meet the penalty clause if you dismiss me."

"Hell, Drew, don't take it like that," Mart intervened. And I realized that I was in a good cop/bad cop situation. Solly would beat me up, and then send in Mart to soften me, smooth my bruises, and extract the confession that had been coming all the time.

"We can reach a compromise," Mart offered.

"Yes," I said, regaining some of my composure. "Call it *Postcards from Heaven* and set it in the French Revolution when they didn't even *have* postcards, and star Dirk Bogarde and Raquel Welch." They looked at each other, a conspiratorial smile spreading on both their faces.

"Drew," Solly said, "You're on our side. You're beginning to make sense." My heart sank even further than I had thought possible. It reached my feet, passed on through, and was burrowing its way into the restaurant floor. This was good cop/bad cop working to perfection.

Take the pernickety bastard with his belief in the truth, kick him hard enough in the shitbag that he uses for brains, and soon he'll agree with us that it never was truth in the first place. Certainly not as truthful a truth as we can put on the screen.

"Gentlemen," I said, using the most inappropriate term at my command, still on my feet, still ready to walk out, "If you want me to continue on this project, we will indeed have to reach a compromise, as Mr Sullivan suggested" –

"Mart, Mart," Mart exclaimed. "We're all buddies here!"

"As Mart suggested. But you'll have no use for me unless you stick to the identity of the central character and the exploration of his emotions. After all," I added cheekily (but I had nothing to lose), "Your first two choices turned this project down because their heads were so far up their rectums that they couldn't write a script to save their lives. Here" I tapped my forehead "You have not only an expert on Janáček but a professional writer – and one with a veto."

I stood back while this idea did its best to find an entrée into Solly's cranium. Mart got it first. "Sure, Drew, this Jack guy, he's the star, and sure, you're just the man for the job, and – well, no hard feelings, but there *are* a few points we need to touch on before we go to the next stage." He nudged Solly, who gave up his futile attempt to absorb what I had said, and smiled disconcertingly. "Drew, let's talk some more after the lobster."

After the Lobster would, I thought, be a good working title for a sad story about a scriptwriter whose ideas are served up to two unscrupulous highwaymen as an *amuse bouche*.

So the main part of my destruction came with the sweet trolley. "*These letters are considered by most musicologists,"* Solly read *"to represent the clearest and most revealing statements by Janáček about his compositions, his career, his marriage to Zdenka (which had settled into a form of companionship) and his love for Kamila.* OK Drew, let me be honest – what the hell are musicologists? Where do they come in the script?"

"No Solly," I made quick steps to reassure him – "that's just by way of background. They don't actually appear in the movie. It's what people in the music business consider that the letters are about."

"The *intimate letters* from Jack to Kamila" Mart interjected, fearing that his colleague might once again have got lost in my explanation. And with a look that implored me "Keep it fucking simple!"

"OK, got it. I don't want to hurt your feelings, Drew my friend" – I shrivelled – "but could we just possibly lose the wife, kind of thing? Stick with the dame."

"Sure, Solly" I replied at my most expansive (the Pouilly Fuissé had been superb and copious) "Let's keep it to a composer who adores Kamila from afar." I was digging my own, if not Janáček's, grave.

"Does this Jack guy really *have* to be a composer? And if it's not for changing, does it *have* to be this opera shit?"

Here I was on surer ground. "Yes, Solly, because if it isn't Janáček, then I'm out of here, and if it *is* Janáček then, no, he didn't write 'White Christmas' or 'Singing in the Rain.'" Mart actually had an admiring look as I said this. "Apart from the operas, which are essential because he wrote them with Kamila in mind, there's the work which the letters are leading up to – his second string quartet." You could barely hear the end of that sentence, as the Solly warhorse leapt out and looked as if to trample me.

"String what!?! Never let me hear those words ever again. Opera is good. Opera we can shoot – if we have to.

39

The other thing – kill it."

So the afternoon went on. The upshot was that the letters, at my insistence, remained in the script *and* the title, but I had to concede that writing letters isn't exactly the stuff that epics are made of. Then Solly came up with a twist about Janáček's *"I need your twittering"* that he thought was earth-shatteringly brilliant: "That's it, Drew – Jack sends Twitters. Or better still, a blog, Drew. He keeps a blog. And we can do better than that – we got wuh-wuh-wuh." This, I confidently thought, we could later bury somewhere where Solly wouldn't find it. "He loves this dame, he fantasises about her" – here I swallowed hard and nodded meekly – "and he never gets what he's after."

I must have looked blank, for Mart followed up his partner's statement: "Drew, according to your story, he never gets laid."

"Well," I began, but realized immediately, from the look of denial I got from both of them, that Janáček was going to have to get laid.

"So all that stuff about platonic – that's out, right?" (I'd written: *It is almost certain that, as far as their emotional relationship was concerned, it was exclusively platonic with the possible exception of a 'kiss' in 1927 to which Janáček attributed enormous significance.*) "I want that kiss BIG, and early, and leading up to the full job, geddit? And these letters – sorry Drew, but it's been done before. That Ken guy, with that Russian guy – musician too – they did letters and stuff and *his* fantasies were HUGE." He made "huge" sound like it filled the whole universe – a world in which there was nothing but lust and, one would hopelessly hope, redemption.

"That's Ken Russell's *The Music Lovers* – about Tchaikovsky" I said.

"Yeah, lousy."

"OK Solly, you're the boss."

40

"Attaboy Drew."

I was dead in the water. Beyond this point, they could make Janáček the greatest whoremonger since Casanova and I'd go along with it.

"Now Drew baby, I've just one or two final points, and then the car will take you back to the studio for the next re-write."

"Please tell me what you have in mind" I said submissively, meekly, realising as I said it that Solly was incapable of having anything in the part of his body that passed for a mind except the sound of dollars cascading into the box-office. But I would have cast my own grandmother as a madame-brothel-keeper with feral lesbian tendencies, *and* signed the contract in my own blood, so punchdrunk had I become at the hands of two of Hollywood's most ruthless manipulators.

"Let's move on from the kiss. You say *He produced a stream of music that, he said, had Kamila as its sole begetter, and represented their offspring.* Then you give a list of these offspring. I want, and Mart wants, that you make these part of the script."

"How? I'll do anything within reason" – realising, again, that reason was at this stage the last thing on anyone's "mind."

"He calls them 'love-children, right? So I want to see love-children on screen. First they have this Gigantic Mass or what, and they get spliced. Then along come the love-children." I couldn't argue, because it was in fact the string quartet that Janáček had called a "love-child," but I dared not utter the word "quartet" for fear of causing Solly an apoplexy.

Mart could see my dilemma and diplomatically interposed: "Sol, they ain't love-children if they come *after* the marriage. A love-child is a bastard, Sol. I think we should drop that." Solly seemed to see some sense in his partner's opinion. I wondered how rare that was.

"So there's this Gigantic Mass, or something. That's church, right? That makes good camera. Especially if you play up what you say here *revealed to be a nuptial mass for the composer and Kamila*. I want that on camera. He marries her with this religious music in the background."

"I think I can work that into the script Solly," I said with, for me, a surprising show of confidence.

Solly persisted about the operas being the offspring. "She – the broad, that is, gets to sing. And change the names of the songs. Cunning Little Vixen is stoopid – make it... 'The Clever Fox.' And this Mak-something Case, either cut it or give it a sexy name like 'Franchise Affair.' There's no Greek vote in this kinda movie. And this 'From the House of the Dead' – is it vampires?" Solly looked like a small child who really, really wants Father Christmas to bring him vampires. It seemed uncouth and churlish to dash the hopes of childhood.

Mart caught my eye. "Not quite, Solly, but I'll look at it again," I managed.

"And this Katya dame. OK you say she was *directly inspired by Kamila's physical beauty and her temperament*. Can we do a scene with her? We can get it sung and synched to the actress. Nicole can pretend to sing. *You* can make her *zing*, Drew. Make her *zing!*" I'm glad to say that in the privacy of our bedroom, I was able to do just that. But not on screen!

"And all that 'unattainable' stuff. Make it attainable! You got this bit right" – he looks at his sheaf of papers: *Never in my life have I experienced such an intermingling of myself with you... In the thought that I have you, that you're mine, lies all my joy of life... The seed from Luhačovice has grown tall.* Do the intermingling. Dammit, he says 'I have you' – get that on screen. Let's see him having her. And plenty of seed. Spunk everywhere.

You can do it, Drew."

That was the end of the lunch, and, if it hadn't been for the epiphany of "N," the end of me too. As it was, it was certainly the end of Andrew Dalton the reserved, dull academic out of his depth, who got transformed, one might say by a single kiss, into the lover of N. How ironic it now seems that I had quoted Janáček's letters to Kamila, *And yet this precious passion must be closely guarded: Do you know, my soul, why it's necessary meticulously to conceal things? If we really had belonged to one another, would anyone believe that after eleven years there was only that longing, that yearning? No-one would believe it.* And of course they didn't. The eleven years in which I loved and lived with N. Eleven 'closely guarded' years, 'meticulously concealed.'

Janáček began to wonder whether the enforced secrecy of the relationship would become too obvious: he wrote to Max Brod 'would it be taken amiss if the spiritual relationship, this artistic relationship, were to be openly admitted? If James Esposito had been my Max Brod (who's this Brod guy, I hear Solly complaining) I might have had some guidance; as it was, I didn't really draw James into the frame until we were looking for a godfather for the twins. But it was uncanny how Janáček had predicted my life with N: a secret passion that was deeply sexual, deeply spiritual and utterly unbelievable.

7
Opera

When I got back to my apartment from my 'lunch' (aka slaughtering) with Solly and Mart (more like feeding-time at the zoo, when I was the ragged bits of raw meat being thrown to the hyenas), I took my courage in my hands and phoned N. She guessed immediately what was going on. "How did it go? You're still talking, so they obviously didn't eat you alive, or cook you *al dente*, or cut out your tongue, and you haven't thrown yourself over a cliff." "Can we meet? I'd like to tell you before you hear it from them." "Come over now."

So I found my driver, and was taken out to N's house in Beverly Hills: a modest twenty-room split-level palace with an infinity pool cantilevered out from a cliff. One parlour-maid showed me in; another took my hat; and the butler smoothly brought me a drink while I waited in the conversation pit.

She walked in demurely, but on edge. I was afraid that she might already have had a call from either Solly or Mart, but that wasn't the case. She read my look correctly. "Yes, I'm on edge Andrew, because I was afraid that you'd thrown it up and I wouldn't see you any more. I know that sounds like a silly little girl and her "crush," but I think you already know what you mean to me. I'd hate to lose it. You."

She sat beside me and I began to describe the lunch – the conversation, if you can call it that, not the food. A bit of Solly-Mart showed itself in N. "Andrew, dear, let's get to the point. It obviously involves me, us, so I'd like to know what it is."

I explained that the producers had played with the basic facts so far that the part of Kamila would involve opera singing, or at least acting the part of an opera singer. And synchronising a professional singer. She looked pensive, sat quietly for a few minutes. At last: "Andrew, tell me please about Jenůfa and Katya and Makropoulos and the Little Vixen. I'll learn them, if you will help me."

I began by warning her that I couldn't get it all across in a few sentences – that, in addition to what she'd read in the script to date, she needed to know the background. A typical academic's long-windedness, but I apparently made the point well enough to be granted a hearing.

"I don't want a few sentences, Andrew, I want the full story. I have all the time in the world."

"But you're already waiting for the next re-write, which Solly and Mart think I'm working on right now!"

"Andrew, if I tell them to wait, they wait. This is *my* movie – sorry, film." She smiled (of course) to underline her diplomatic use of a Brit term for what she did every day in another language. "If they don't like it, they can get Streep or Winslet. But I don't want that, because I want us to work on this together, to work on the script and to work on friendship." Oh my god. I quivered.

She rang a bell; a parlour-maid came in. "Please ask Janet (her secretary) to cancel my evening appointments and tell Alphonse (chef) I'll be here for dinner with one guest, Mr Dalton – simple, but special. Two courses and salad."

"So we have all evening, Andrew. Don't look alarmed just because I've cancelled a drinks party and a boring dinner with (she named one of the top flavours of the month). And you are *not* staying the night. You will tell me, as a teacher would tell a student who's eager to learn, all you can in one evening, about ..." she giggled as she said it, "Jack – isn't that what Solly calls him? Let's start with the name. How should I say it?"

So, like a speech coach, I explained how to say "Janáček," with the accent on the second syllable rather than the first, where most people put it. She got it at once. I realized that, like all great actresses, she was devout in her attention to the way she was taught, since the rôle depended not only on her inner magnetism, and her interpretation of the character, but on the way that her speech would project that character. I had heard how patient and dedicated a student Meryl Streep would be when learning an accent, and had seen the proof of it in *The French Lieutenant's Woman* (which became quite a talking-point for N and me). Now I saw N, at first hand, absorbing my teaching, and in doing so she drew me into the process whereby she would transform herself from "N" to "Jenůfa" or "Katya," and yet at the same time remain the indefinable N.

"But when you are his lover, you'll be calling him by his first name. Unless of course they don't like that idea."

"Well then, lesson number two. It isn't Leos is it?" She pronounced it as if it were a pride of lions. Within a couple of minutes she was saying "Leoš" perfectly.

That afternoon and evening went in a few seconds. Yes, I am incurably romantic – I wish it had lasted for ever. What I didn't realise at the time was that it *would* lead to a partnership that seemed as if it would last for ever. I suppose we have 'Jack' Janáček to thank for that.

"The operas I mentioned in my script are *Jenůfa, Katya Kabanova, The Cunning Little Vixen* and *The Makropoulos Case*. In that order of composition. There were several other operas, but I think" – I was gaining confidence now in my capacity as a scriptwriter – "that we can limit the next treatment to just *Jenůfa* and *Katya*. There's more than enough material to support the storyline. Then" – I hesitated, and she read me correctly –

"then there's the Glagolitic Mass, when Solly wants you to..." I trailed off.

"I think I can guess. But we may have to go along with a mock-wedding, even if it moves the movie from bio-pic to fantasy." I hadn't mentioned the vampires, and thought better of it.

But I did say, as if N and I were now locked into a world which neither of us had envisaged, "I have to admit that I've had to give in to them so much that it's no longer the film I thought it would be, but I think we can steer it sufficiently, with both our vetos, so that it doesn't get too ridiculous."

"But you aren't quitting?" She sounded a little afraid. My answer must have contained all of her afraid and all of mine.

"No, I'm not quitting. I'm staying with it because of..." I couldn't complete the sentence, because I wasn't sure how to.

Totally professional, and totally aware that I had just avoided making a love-lorn fool of myself: "Andrew, let's just get on with the job. It's no longer *your* film but it is *our* film, and that makes it stronger and easier to handle. Let me play student to your teacher. I'm sure you'll be good." Business-like! Abruptly, decisively.

"OK, then let's start with *Jenůfa*. Do you know *The Bartered Bride* – Smetana?"

"Andrew, let's just assume for the moment that I am completely ignorant of opera. I've just about heard of Verdi, but otherwise, please treat me as an absolute ignoramus. Tell me the story of *Jenůfa*."

I couldn't resist it: "Are you sitting comfortably? Then I'll begin. In the beginning..."

"Andrew, I'm not a child, this isn't a bedtime story. Please proceed."

"No, but it's a love story."

"Good so far."

"Jenůfa has a stepmother – not exactly a *wicked* stepmother, but one with difficulties, shall we say. She's a big noise in the village, and rules Jenůfa's life. She – Jenůfa, that is – has two lovers who are half-brothers" –

"That sounds promising" –

"and she's pregnant by one of them."

"Sol is going to *love* this!"

"I thought we'd agreed to leave Sol out of this?"

"Sorry. Really sorry. Go on, respected teacher."

"Lover number two (not the father of the child) is jealous of Lover number one (who is), and slashes Jenůfa's face with a knife."

"You would have expected him to knife Lover number one, wouldn't you?"

"Yes, but operas aren't so easy. Otherwise it would all be over at the end of Act One."

"Ok, go on. I like it so far." And I think she meant not just the storyline, but the way I told it. At least, I kidded myself that was what she meant.

"Jenůfa gives birth. Then it all gets very complicated. There's no point in trying to explain all the complications of the plot unless we are going to put it into your script. I think it's best if we concentrate on the main themes." I realized as soon as I said '*we*' that I was presuming too much. N saw it too – she had an unfailing ability to read my feelings through my face, just as surely as she made it difficult if not impossible to read *her* feelings through *her* face.

"Yes, Andrew, 'we.' If we do it, it will be you and me putting together *our* script." I can't say how deeply this touched me. It was the warmth of her sincerity, the fact that I hardly knew the 'real' N, could only recognise the N to whom I was speaking, with whom I was sitting for only the second time, in whose house I was working. All my life thereafter I would struggle with the two 'N's – the woman I loved on the screen, and the woman I loved in my arms. The fact that she had drawn me into her company – me, the lowly scriptwriter – into her working life as a partner, someone she not only respected but, I dared to hope, actually *liked*: this was a heaven I had only dreamed of, a dream in which I would continue to live.

Back to business. "So the stepmother takes the baby and drowns it. Meanwhile, the first lover – the baby's father – has got engaged to someone else, and the slasher, Lover number two, eventually marries Jenůfa, while the stepmother is taken off for trial. That's it."

N was utterly beautiful, wrapped in consideration of the bare lines I had given her. I began to see how deftly she could imagine herself into the situation required in the yet-to-be-written script, how she could empathise with Jenůfa, a tragic heroine. I could see 'N' *becoming* 'Jenůfa' before my eyes.

"Before we get too deep into Jenůfa, could we move on briefly to Katya? I don't want to sound superficial or hasty, but Jenůfa is going to be just one part of the chain between Janáček and Kamila, if it gets into the script at all, that is, so I'd like to get an overview of all the works, if you don't mind."

Did I mind!? I could have spent whole days and nights, weeks and months, slobbering over *all* Janáček's women, real and imaginary, if it meant having N all to myself, the attentive N who, over that wonderfully long evening, visibly entered into a world which, only a couple of hours before, had been almost unknown to her – and to me.

When dinner was announced by parlour-maid number three, we sat down to what N had ordered, a 'simple' two-course feast: the most succulent langoustines, in a cream and champagne sauce, I had ever – in my short culinary experience – tasted. She smiled at me: "I knew you'd probably throw up if I had served you lobster." The langoustines were followed by an old-English beef, which her cook had found in Eliza Acton, ornamented with traditional potatoes, both roast and boiled (the latter smothered in buttered parsley). The green salad of rocket, wild spinach and *kos* leaves, which N dressed and mixed herself, was served as an after-course, with a cheese-plate that obviously didn't count as a 'course' in its own right: a melting *Chaource*, a dry, salty *pecorino* and a blue goats' cheese from Ireland which she had discovered in Kerry when filming *Here and There*. Needless to say, it was imported to LA especially for her.

The langoustines were accompanied by a champagne; the beef by a full-bodied Chambertin. Dinner was almost interrupted by an aborted phone call from Solly – or was it Mart? Probably Mart, considering the tact that would be required when talking script-changes with N.

"Tell him not now," she said, in such an imperious voice that the superior butler, even though he had no doubt heard it a thousand times, retreated immediately with a mumbled "Yes Miss Zoffany, of course Miss Zoffany."

"I hope this is ok, Andrew?" I nearly choked on my cheese. The last – and only – time I had eaten with her had been the Grumpyburger at the Snow White.

"Superb," I managed to mutter. "Superb. Thank you so much."

"It's simple. I like the food to be straightforward. So many cooks want to smother the food with couscous, which I *hate* – or mix together bits and pieces that would be best served separately. So I dislike anything cooked with nuts, for example, or *sole véronique*. If I want grapes, I'll eat grapes. All these messed-up things are *so* pretentious." As I couldn't agree more, I just kept silent.

To have said "I couldn't agree more" would, in itself, have been pretentious.

But I could not keep the doubts from my mind. I wasn't a film buff, but I *was* an opera buff. I knew my stuff, and, after all, that was why I'd been hired and that's why I was here in N's home. But although we could each of us sense that there was an electricity running between us that was quite definitely more than professional, I nevertheless wondered whether she was using me just to learn her part, in the same way that she hired a speech coach and a personal trainer. Was I just part of the entourage? And was this electricity something she could generate in order to attract moths to her flame?

During dinner, she could sense my nervousness, and put me at my ease. She had both power and charm. As far as power was concerned, it felt like dining, unexpectedly, with Vladimir Putin *and* Mao Zedong. And for charm? Princess Grace and Katherine Hepburn. And N outdid them all. She spoke a little of politics, a little of travel, carefully keeping away from Hollywood gossip or the technical side of moviemaking. Her limitations as a conversationalist revealed her strengths as a consummate actress. I don't mean that she played a part with me. Looking back, I still don't think she was ever anyone except her enigmatic self when she was with me – alone with me, I mean – but she *became* an N I had never known, a full, strong, intelligent (are you reading this, Mr. Guffaw?) and committed personality. If I don't mention beauty, it isn't because I'm afraid of over-using the word, or running out of synonyms, but because, although I never, *never*, took it for granted, it did go without saying. Her beauty was in everything she did. The way she mixed the salad, the way she wiped a smidgen of sauce from her lips, the way she poured the wine (she had dismissed the maids), just as much as the way in which she spoke about the work in hand – *our* work – or the obvious love she had of traveling.

Coffee came to us when we returned to work in the conversation pit. Having 'dealt with' Jenůfa and Katya, we moved on to Emilia Marty, the opera-singer in *The Makropoulos Case* who has lived for 300 years. Preposterous? No more so than some of the films N had made – the sci-fi stuff – or the whole genre of 'Space Invaders' or 'ET.' And, besides its origins in European folk-myth – a touch of the vampires here – there was a respectable precedent in Rider Haggard's thriller *She*, and the *King Solomon's Mines* trilogy. I was afraid I was boring N by mentioning these, reverting to type as a bookish don, but no, she was as alert as ever.

"Would it help if I read her... *She*?"

"It wouldn't help directly, but it would give you an angle on the mysterious power of a woman who is ageless, who, in the dénouement, changes from an unspeakable young beauty to a wizened, skeletal hag."

"I'll read it." A pause. "If you'll read it with me, Andrew."

I panicked. This was well out of my depth. "Let's not go too far on that line," I cautioned, little thinking until after I had left the house of the *double entendre*. "Let's stick for the moment with Janáček."

"Yes, I'm sure you're right."

It wasn't late, but I thought it best if I suggested I should leave, and we could resume the 'singing lesson' another day. I suppose I was secretly hoping that she would invite me straight away for another tête-à-tête, but that didn't happen. But neither did she show any sign of wanting me to leave. She wasn't working the following day, so her 'beauty sleep' wasn't as important as it would have been if there had been a 6am make-up session. In fact, we stayed talking till late. And so continued one of the most extraordinary days in my life, one that had begun with mounting despair as I was demolished stone by stone by Solly and Mart, and which was now restored, as N reassembled my confidence and my stability with her own mastery of the situation, her intuitive command of what was needed and her determination to get it.

She was anxious to face the realities of this particular job: "I've got to think Solly here. If I can work out how Solly will want me to do 'this broad,' as he calls her, I'll know better how we can manoeuvre him so that I don't have to be quite as cheap as he would like." That was why she had implicitly asked me to stay longer, to tease out how *we* – how I revelled in the idea of togetherness, of the way she said "we," as if it meant the whole world, a world in which she and I were the only people.

If that evening had, indeed, lasted forever, the next episode in our falling in love might never have happened. We would have been in suspended animation, waiting for the evitable to happen, fearful of the next step. But it did come to an end, and we did move on to falling in love. Again, we have 'Jack' Janáček to thank, because it was the pursuit of his work and, by that means, the pursuit of his love for Kamila, that created the love between N and me. A love that, I think, began that evening with N listening patiently, studiously, alert and concerned, to my brief descriptions of what Janáček's heroines had been like, how their dramatic destinies might be used to illustrate his devotion to Kamila and the deepening love that united them. And as I spoke, I could again see two Ns: the professional, who was eager to learn her part, and the girl who was fascinated by the 'tell me a story' turn of events, her own identification with Jenůfa and Katya deepening into a passion for the part, living their lives, believing their stories and, although neither of us knew it at that moment, deepening into our own love and devotion.

The quickest way to make N familiar with the music was to send for recordings. I asked the studio to find the recordings of *Jenůfa, Katya Kabanova* and *Makropoulos* by Elizabeth Södeström, which were the classic interpretations. But they were no substitute for the thrill of the opera house, the anticipation, the first notes of the overture, the curtain up, the heroine comes on, to what will be her tragic fate. Maquillage, chevelure, choreography, all serving the needs of the *drama*.

And so we decided that we would find any productions of Janáček's operas that were available. N would see what others did with the parts, and then go a million miles better. Professional, amateur, student performances, anything would be grist to my teaching mill. But Janáček doesn't get productions every day of the week. Not like Mozart or Verdi.

One day N said, quite suddenly, "A surprise for you Andrew. We're flying to Santa Fé for *Tosca*."

"Flying? Are there any flights?"

"This one is mine. I hired a Lear jet for just us. And where did I get the idea? From *Pretty Woman*, of course! If Gere and Roberts can do it, so can we! But not a word to anyone – the staff here don't know, the studio mustn't know, no one. I've told them here that the limo to fetch us at six is to take us to a very special dinner in a very special place about a hundred miles from here, and I don't want my regular driver involved."

They behaved like giggly schoolkids mitching from school. The flight; the limo from the private airport to the opera house; a (in Andrew's opinion) not brilliant but very passable *Tosca* which thrilled N the neophyte; a private supper with Tosca, Cavaradossi, Scarpia, and the conductor.

That night we flew back to LA very late, but it was essential for N to be on the lot the next morning for production meetings that she couldn't avoid. So it was around 1am when we were in the limo taking N to Beverly Hills. I assumed she would drop me at my apartment *en route*. I was wrong.

"Andrew, tonight wasn't just fun. It was magical. I don't want the evening to end. Please stay with me." It was magical for *her*? What was it like for *me*? Not only had we taken our first step towards her immersion in opera, to a point where a new dimension to her portrayal of Kamila was manifest; we had moved from writer-actress to teacher-student and now, to pre-empt the remainder of that night's togetherness, man and woman, lover-lover.

Having, thanks to Puccini, fallen in love with opera (and me?), N had no difficulty when I made the case for Janáček. She responded immediately and intuitively – as she did in all her rôles – to both the idea of the man and his meaning. Was his music strange to her? No. Coming from a background in which music was not even that, she plunged straight into it as part-and-parcel of the whole scenario – as opera is supposed to be, of course. It was a case of "Andrew, this is a part. I'm Kamila and I'm also the singer who brings Jack's imagination into life. That's all I need to know. That's my brief. Now we have to make it happen."

And while Janáček's weren't exactly the most performed operas in America, or even in Britain, we found productions that inducted N into the mindset of Kamila/Jenůfa/Katya. We met and became friends with Charles Mackerras, N making an easy bond with him because of their origins in the southern hemisphere, and we listened over and over again to his landmark recording of *Katya Kabanova* from the 1950s.

We saw *Jenůfa* at Edinburgh, conducted by Haitink; and at Covent Garden with Anja Silja and Karita Mattila, who became a very dear friend and went on to a triumph in *Katya*. We saw *Katya* again at the Met, with Charles conducting the Jonathan Miller production; we saw *Jenůfa* again almost on our doorstep in San Francisco and we even made it to Glyndebourne for another director who became a great friend, Nikolaus Lehnhoff, for *Katya* and *Jenůfa*, again with Silja and Andrew Davis conducting.

We never managed to see a production of *Cunning Little Vixen* and that wasn't such a problem as we hadn't written it into the script, but I sensed that N hankered after it simply because of its title – she saw herself as just that...

N admired the way Janáček had achieved such clarity and economy in his writing; she understood the scores as filmscripts, a factor that went a long way to winning her the Oscar. And my tutorial rôle remained vibrant right through the preparations and the filming, because I was her point of reference: a route-map back to the first inspirations whenever she queried a scene or even a note. To say that it deepened our love would be a gross understatement: we became professionally envious of each other, and at the same time profoundly intimate: N loved Janáček, I loved Janáček, therefore N loved me: the equations don't make sense mathematically, but it's the best I can do to explain how our work on *Intimate Letters* liberated our love by bringing the professional demands of the cinema to the natural longing of two essentially lonely people. That's what the cinema does for its audience, perhaps: putting a spectacle in front of them that brings them together into a shared emotion. Well, in our case, Janáček was almost the priest who married me with N.

Quite apart from Janáček and the music that would be central to *Intimate Letters*, N wanted to immerse herself in the whole business of what opera actually meant. She approached it as she would any acting job: she wanted to understand the nuts and bolts of composing for the stage, just as she knew intimately the techniques of writing for the cinema.

So it wasn't only Janáček's operas: Verdi, Donizetti, Mozart and of course Puccini because of that one first night of love. Even Britten's *Turn of the Screw* fascinated her and lit the emotional bonfire, which was her hallmark as an actress. During that performance I thought I would have to take her out of her seat, so much was she wracked with tears and sobs as she witnessed the damned love between Miles and his governess.

Only at Wagner did she draw the line. "Fucking fascist" she declared, and nothing I could do (and I was never really a Wagner fan myself) could reconcile her to the greatness of the Ring quest; so unthinking was I that I had not taken into account that N's grandparents had, like Solly's, suffered under the jackboot. And quite apart from that, "No passion; no love; no humour; no human spirit."

"What about *Tristan* – the greatest love story ever told?," only to be met again with "Fucking fascist!"

We often had to make a last minute dash to see a show: the Lear jet had been a once-off treat; but Concorde gave us the chance to get to London and back almost before SolMart had noticed we were gone. If N turned up on set any time looking a little red-eye, her gamine and wily smile would explain it away. On those mornings we still felt like kids who had slipped out of school for an all-night party in someone's garage and got back only just in time for morning assembly. Kids. But kids who were living make-believe lives in every direction: growing up emotionally, growing into each other physically and spiritually, growing into the rôles that N wanted to play, within the overall rôle of Kamila. A whole world opened, for me as a complete neophyte to Hollywood, for her as a lover and a professional stepping tentatively, but with complete assurance, into the latest make-believe that her life would offer.

Introducing N to opera was like bringing a child into storyland. And, when I think of how her whole life *was* storyland, I'm amazed that she was so innocent and naïve in her wondrous entry into this kind of make-believe. The world of opera was Aladdin's cave: "Did that statue *really* come to life?" (*Don Giovanni*); "Does she *really* have to die?" (Violetta) and even "They couldn't do that, *could* they?" (*Così*). I will never know whether she was pulling my leg when she turned to me, like a six-year-old, towards the end of *Otello*, and asked "Has he *really* killed her?" and then, minutes later, a little excited gasp as Desdemona revives, if only for a brilliant moment. If only also our love, after we had killed it, had recovered for even one brilliant moment... But that is to anticipate a murder that should never have happened and for which no Iago was to blame, except the Iago lurking within the blackness of my own Moor.

It was N's naïve excitement that intensified my love for her. If *Hotel Shanghai* had been my introduction to her innocence, from the distance between voyeur and beloved, *Intinate Letters* was my re-introduction to her soul, because every opera we saw was N rediscovering what she herself did for a living, but seeing it in a new dimension. She re-learned herself through her admiration for, and intense study of, her peers such as Silja and her close friend Karita Mattila. In order to become Kamila, N explored every dimension of Janáček's work, every cavity and every nuance, until she could step onto SolMart's stage as if it were the Met or Covent Garden, and sing her heart out. It was all a part within a part within a part within the greatest part of all – or so we thought – our own intimate letters.

8
Pillow Talk

If the prurient reader expects an account of a torrid bed-scene observed by an unseen camera, I must disappoint. I'm not fuck-and-tell. Not only do I absolutely refuse to be tempted into that kind of revelation, but I owe it to N to protect our intimacy from anything outside its total embrace – if, indeed, there was anything outside the walls of the world we made for ourselves over the next few months. And those walls were not made of glass, they were made of steel, to hold us in as much as to hold others out. This was the essence of our privacy, and the strategy we used successfully to keep the relationship so secret from that world of prying, gossip-mongering, dirty minds who contribute nothing at all to the real world, the world of love and passion and commitment.

Here was one of the most eligible women in the whole world, for whom I would have crossed the Atlantic in a pair of concrete boots – or the Pacific, whichever was the wider – inviting me to her bed! It would have been churlish to refuse.

If you want to know how 'N' performs in bed, look at *Anniversary*, look at *Romping*, look at any number of movies where 'N' takes off her clothes and gives herself to *coitus* or rape. Suffice it for me to simply record that our love-making was so complete, so exciting, so *different* for both of us, so joyous and celebratory of our secret freedom, that it makes any other sex-life look like Enid Blyton's "Toytown" – which maybe it was.

It was amazing that we succeeded in hiding our love from everyone – even N's household staff, those who are

usually the first to detect their mistress's *amours.*
Absolutely no one knew. We managed this because, firstly,
I kept on my own hotel suite – after all, Solly and Mart
were paying for it – and, secondly, N's palace contained a
guest suite, so that whenever I stayed with her, which was
so frequent that I in fact became a resident, I occupied, as
far as anyone was concerned, the guest rooms, which I
took the trouble to make sufficiently lived- and slept-in to
convince all but a super-sleuth. And luckily, there was no
super-sleuth. Our anxiety that the relationship should
remain secret started from the simple danger to N's career
if she was known to be co-habiting with a mere
scriptwriter.

Whatever she and I might be to each other, she was
the star and I was the minion, serving up delicious
dialogue and scenes where she could look misty-eyed into
the camera or exert the power of that charismatic smile.
The fact that we were lovers and, in our loving, didn't seem
to give a damn whether we were dust-farmers in
Oklahoma auditioning for parts in a remake of *The Grapes
of Wrath,* or downandouts in Irish Boston (as she had
played them with George Clooney in *Here and There*); it
was just "us," with no tags attached.

But Hollywood wouldn't see it that way. Solly and
Mart would try everything to get me either reduced to
wood pulp or even pay my ransom to sack me and change
the storyline completely (as Solly, anyway, would dearly
wish); the *paparazzi* would have helicopters hovering over
the house before you could say "whirlybird"; the world's
press would have blown the story out of all proportion,
either casting N as someone who would stoop so low for a
lover, when she had (and maybe they would say she *had*
'had') the choice of her fellow stars, or me as an
unprincipled climber who would do anything to get his
script on screen and had just picked the plum from the

cake, when all he deserved was a cherry-stone that someone else had already chewed over. And N's publicist would have torn her hair out, trying to make a convincing story out of the most improbable material, which is what she was paid for in any case.

No, if we could be at all secret, it would protect our privacy, N's reputation (mine was hardly worth talking about) and *Intimate Letters*, which we were both, at this stage, determined to see through to completion, on our terms.

But I was a shadow, whose existence was denied and whose non-existence could be proved at any moment. I was in her closet. I didn't exist. I could have written "Oh my god, I'm one of her fictions." But she is the *actress*, not the scriptwriter! Oh no. Oh yes. Oh N...

Daytime, from breakfast till dinner, was for work and work-talk. Especially when N was considering a script and asking my advice. By common consent, bedtime was for pillow talk and loving. Hollywood never got a look-in to our nights together. Of course it was sex, too, but it was also joke-time, when I revelled in the laughter I coaxed from her – girlish, raunchy, raucous by turns. It was *fun*. Lovemaking opened my eyes to the little girl who still lived in N: "Tell me a story."

The 'teacher' in me was brought into the bed, too. "I want to be able to say 'whore' just as well as Meryl Streep does it in *The French Lieutenant's Woman*. It's such a dirty word, and yet she manages to dignify it. Could I do that?"

"I'm not a voice coach. Streep has a different voice coach for every film she does. Besides, 'whore' is difficult, whether it's dirty or dignified or what, because it's a single syllable spelling volumes."

"Andrew, I have voice coaches too. Did you think I did

it all myself?"

"Well yes, I did, actually."

"Actually" – she mocked my Englishness.

"You're mocking my Englishness."

"Actually, yes I am. But I still want to be able to say 'whore' in your English way." Only years later would I be telling her that that was what she made herself in *Windmill*. Not the whore's part that she acted, but that she whored in the part, prostituted herself.

I took sadistic pleasure in telling her tall stories masquerading as jokes. "Only kidding" was my way of escaping a bash over the head if N was sufficiently outraged by what she called my "droll sense of humour – so British." One story was about the Polish conductor, Jerzy Maksimiuk. "Is there such a person?" she asked, suspicious that a bad one was coming up.

"Yes, of course, he's giving a concert next week in Symphony Hall with the Polish Chamber Orchestra."

"Well, what's the story?"

"His father chose 'Jerzy' as a first name; his mother didn't like it and calls him 'gansey' (N knew that this was an Irish woollen because she'd bought one when filming *Here and There*); he perspires a lot in rehearsal, so the orchestra call him 'the sweater.' And, because he's not circumcized, his girlfriend calls him 'the pullover.'" A pause.

"Andrew, are you... Oh! Oh! You rotten bastard! That's disgusting!"

Not as disgusting as some of my 'drollery.' But I usually kept it clean-but-naughty. "How do you put a giraffe into a refrigerator?"

"You open the refrigerator, put in the giraffe, and close the door."

"Brilliant, you've passed the first part of the test."

"How many more parts are there Andrew, I'm sleepy?"

"Three more, all quite simple unless" –

"Unless *what*?"

"Unless you're under four or over seventy."

"Four and seventy IQ, or age?"

"Wait and see. How do you put an elephant into a refrigerator?"

Sleepily: "Andrew I don't know how you put an elephant in a refrigerator, and I don't really care, but I can see I won't get any sleep until you tell me. So please fucking tell me!"

"If you were thinking" –

"I wasn't thinking, Andrew! I was dozing!"

"Yes, well, if you'd said 'Open the refrigerator, put in the elephant, and close the refrigerator' you'd have been wrong, because the refrigerator is already full of giraffe. So..."

"Andrew, how much longer does this *thing*, this so-called *joke*..."

"I never said it was a joke, it's a kind of intelligence test."

"Well, in that case it's a test of *your* intelligence, not mine. I suppose I'll have to hear it to the end."

"And so you shall, my sweet. You take the giraffe out of the refrigerator and put in the elephant in its place. The idea is to test your ability to be responsible for your previous actions. It would *not* be a good idea to put the elephant in with the giraffe, even if there *were* room for them both." I actually had to wake N to administer the final part of the test: "The Lion King is hosting an Animal Conference. All the animals attend except one. Which animal does not attend?"

"Dunno and don't care."

"The elephant. The elephant is in the refrigerator. You just put him in there. This tests your memory. Last part: There is a river you must cross but it is used by crocodiles, and you don't have a boat. How do you manage it?"

"You jump into the river and swim across."

"Haven't you been listening, Nicole? All the crocodiles are attending the Animal Conference. This tests whether you learn quickly from your mistakes. And all of this comes courtesy of Anderson Consulting Worldwide, who say that around 90% of the old folks they tested got all the questions wrong, but many pre-schoolers got several correct answers – which conclusively proves the theory that most oldies do not have the brains of a four-year-old." I looked down in triumph, only to find a recumbent N, thumb in mouth, cheated out of her bedtime story by a questionnaire of Einteinian profundity. A little snore, which made me both love and forgive her, broke from her gently parted lips.

Another bedtime was rather more successful. Was it because it was full of sex, not a refrigerator full of Noah's ark? *A woman meets a man in a bar. They talk; they connect; they end up leaving together. They get back to his place, and as he shows her around his apartment she notices that one wall of his bedroom is completely filled with soft, sweet, cuddly teddy bears. There are three shelves in the bedroom, with hundreds and hundreds of cute, cuddly teddy bears carefully placed in rows, covering the entire wall. There were small bears all along the bottom shelf, medium-sized bears covering the length of the middle shelf, and huge, enormous bears running all the way along the top shelf. She found it strange for an obviously masculine guy to have such a large collection of Teddy Bears. She is quite impressed by his sensitive side, but doesn't mention this to him. She turns to him and kisses him lightly on the lips. He responds warmly. They continue to kiss, the passion builds, and he romantically lifts her in his arms and carries her into his bedroom where they rip off each other's clothes and make hot, steamy love. She is so overwhelmed that she responds with more passion, more creativity, more heat than she has ever known. After an intense, explosive night of raw passion with this sensitive guy, they are lying there together in the afterglow. The woman rolls over, gently strokes his chest and asks coyly, 'Well, how was it?' The guy gently smiles at her, strokes her cheek, looks deeply into her eyes, and says: 'Help yourself to any prize from the middle shelf.'*

A shriek of laughter (just as well, I thought with relief). If you know N only from her screen laugh, you'll know that she has an enchanting laugh. But if you knew her as I knew her, shrieking with unrestrained enjoyment, you would have seen a return to girlhood, to the 'is it really true?' of the bedtime story. And then she turns the tables on me: "If you wrote scripts as well as you write jokes, we'd all be millionaires."

"But you *are* a millionaire, Nicole."

"Ah, just testing you, you four-year-old!" "Well Andrew" – this with the rather sinister look I had come to respect – "Do I get the big teddy, the medium teddy or the small teddy? Choose your words carefully." I had no choice but to show her how much she deserved the big teddy.

It wasn't all jokes. Sometimes we talked about operas, as we were still absorbed in the whole world of opera make-believe, the reality of pretence. I happened to mention that Verdi, whose music we had particularly come to love, had been a national hero, at the time when Italy was in the throes of making a nation out of a disparate collection of independent states. "They used his name as an acronym for" – I was stopped in my knowledgeable, professorial, tracks.

"I know, Andrew. Vittorio Emmanuele, Re d'Italia – V.E.R.D.I. See! I may not have done opera at school, but we did do history." That put me in my place. So I tried to get my own back by suggesting that "Gounod" stood for "gigantic orgasm under Nicole, or die," and "Mozart" for "must offer Zolly a right thrashing" (I cheated a bit there). She retorted "Bizet: 'Bloody idiot Zolly easily thrashed'." Not bad, N, not bad. "Berlioz" was "big elephant runs loose in Oslo zoo," and "Bartók" was "Bach's anus rogered thoroughly ok." That last one was mine, not N's.

Lying beside N, I also made jokes about the rewrites. It was the only way of coping with them. We had competitions, as a variation on the theme of "Consequences," to see who could think up the most stupid change of scenario. From the starting point of the Janáček-Kamila-letters, we ended up, shrieking with laughter, at Attila the Hun, besotted with Queen Victoria, building the Taj Mahal to celebrate her beauty and, in a moment of absentmindedness, jumping off the roof instead of having the architect do so. Attila would be played by (who else?) Charlton Heston, Victoria by Vanessa Redgrave. The whole thing would be set in Paris in the next century.

I thought about the fact that, at his death, Bruckner's effects were found to include the photographs of nine café waitresses from establishments he frequented in Vienna. Bruckner had died as he had been born – a virgin. I thought that if Ken Russell, or, now, Solly and Mart, had got hold of this fact, and coupled it with the fact that he wrote nine symphonies, their creative genius would know no bounds. One of the greatest, most extreme sexual fantasies of the age. Bruckner, a profoundly devout Christian, had dedicated most of his compositions "to God." Solly and Mart would have turned that into "goddess," with one saucy waitress standing for each of the nine symphonies.

"I reckon Janáček and Kamila get off lightly," N said thoughtfully. And less thoughtfully: "And when you die, and they find all my photos in your album, what will they make of that?"

Then quite seriously, she turned to me: "Andrew, this may seem like blasphemy, but I actually *like* Sol and Mart." I couldn't answer that for a few minutes. Then, trying very hard not to burst out laughing, and even harder not to look sorry for her, I said:

"Well, you have to work with them. I could paint a sad portrait of you, locked into Sol-Mart Productions, with a contract making you unable to gain your freedom other than by jumping off a high building. Or letting your long hair down the wall of the ebony tower in which you are their prisoner, waiting for a passing knight to rescue you."

"Rapunzel. Hmm."

"Well, I *do* understand that, in a certain way, you can respect them. After all, they are only doing what comes naturally – turning Mozart into Margaret Thatcher, played by John Hurt..."

"Yes, but I actually *like* them," N repeated. "They are pure slush, of course, and yes, they *do* belittle us all in the interests of turning a quick buck, but they really do believe that they are making *good* movies, that they are providing their public with valid entertainment. It's a very, very long time since the first leading lady took her clothes off, or jumped into bed with Randolph Scott or whoever. Sol and Mart didn't invented cinema nudity. Nor vampires. Nor historical films that said goodbye to the facts before they left the drawing board. When you get to know them, they can actually be quite *nice* – even *fun* – to be with."

"You see them from a different angle. You're a star. They need you. They would probably much rather have a new star who wouldn't get the obscene fees you can command" – here, a sharp but playful bash in the ribs from N, and a stifled "you mean bastard!" – "but Nicole Zoffany puts bums on seats. In my case, I'm so low down the pecking order that there must be times when they can't even remember my name. And I am still trying to recover from the gruelling lunch they put me through."

"Remember your name? Oh, David, how could they forget?" Peals of laughter as I exploded with indignation, part real, part feigned. Like our whole life together – part real, part imaginary, even illusory, made up by one or other or both of us to account for how we had found our way into this script.

"But seriously, that's how I feel, except when I'm with you. Do you know how that term – 'pecking order' – came into use?"

"No, tell me..." And so our evenings would pass, with banter, jokes, teasing, make-believe, and, of course, loving. The deepest, most satisfying, most unimaginable loving that a devoted couple has ever known – or so it would be in a storybook, 'the greatest story ever told.' Which is where we were. But we could joke about that, too. One night we played the opening of an imaginary film, using the *El Cid* theme as our starting-point. Opening sequence, background music of Rodrigo's *Concierto de Aranjuez*. Me, singing: "Diddle-dee, dee da dee dee diddle dee ..." (she always said she loved me to sing to her). "This is the story of a man (cue Charlton Heston) who fought the infidel and saved Spain. And of the woman (cue Sophia Loren) who loved him... Diddle diddle dee dee dee ..."

"Yes, Andrew, the woman who loved him." I wasn't sure how to speak, or whether speech was necessary. I waited, heart in mouth. "Yes, Andrew," as she drew me closer, "the woman who loved him." Maybe this was a game. Maybe N was just playing with me, with my affections, with my weakness. I was someone so far down the pecking list of possible lovers that I often wondered how I had arrived in this bed.

"I don't know what to say."

70

"Andrew," she smiled that innocent, girlish, beguiling face, "just say 'Nicole I love you.'"

"Nicole, I love you."

"Good boy. I thought we would never reach this part of the script. I don't have to read your mind, my darling, I can read your face. You're thinking 'Is she about to burst out laughing and throw me away like a used condom?' I'm sure you feel like that sometimes, because of all the differences, but, at the heart of it" – she put her hand on my heart – "it's what we just made up – a man, and the woman who loved him. And" – that dangerous smirk was starting to appear – "you *did* your best to defeat the infidel. Poor Sol and Mart, I almost feel sorry for them, with my lover, *my* Andrew, standing up to them. But you didn't have to save Spain, or even Janáček, to find the woman who loves you. *I* love you, my darling, my sweetheart."

Back to our old jokes, the composers' acronyms: she set me a real conundrum, from which I found the easy answer, the lover's answer. "Janáček? It's no acronym. It's the word for love, our love. If it hadn't been for Jack, we wouldn't be here being stupid." And we were still working on the last month of shooting *Intimate Letters*. "I used to think that falling in love was something you did when you had nothing else to do. But when I'm doing that marriage scene with Ion, and – " she paused – "and the bit after, I think I'm marrying you and loving you, Andrew."

We were in bed, and N, as was her custom, had given me the plans for her next project. I hadn't noticed that she had something else on her mind, even though she was less playful, more thoughtful, than usual at our bedtimes. I put it down to the fact that I'd been trying to tell her why I thought this next possible project, *Hamlet*, would not suit her. I'd gone to the bathroom, and when I came out I was still giving my reasons when –

"Andrew, will you please shut up for a moment?"

"Sorry, I'm merely giving you my" –

"Andrew, we're going to be parents."

As I ran forward to embrace her, I thought instantaneously that she might have said, "I'm pregnant." But because she said, "We're going to be parents" she had spoken of an 'us.' The fruit of our love was ours; not hers, not mine, but *ours*, and her immediate inclusiveness of, as it turned out, the four of us, were some of the most beautiful words she ever spoke to me or, I suspect, to anyone.

9
Long Island

And so began the eighteen months when we were not only happy, but happier than I would ever have imagined, for me, for her, for us – and, after the births, for our children. N's natural leadership had enabled her, without consulting me, to make a far-reaching decision: we would move to what she called 'a cottage on Long Island' which, it transpired, was a 17-roomed 'cottage' with several acres of closely guarded grounds.

That was the first part of her decision. The second was her announcement, first to me, then to her agent, and then to the public, that she was resting from work for at least a year, probably longer. In the outcome, we spent seven months together before the births, preparing to be parents, and about a year after, until she was ready to return to the screen.

The third decision was the trickiest: what we were doing and – as far as her own career was concerned – what *she* was doing, would be absolutely confidential. She would tell no one, not even her agent, the reason for this temporary retirement; I was encouraged – and in any case I insisted on it – to tell one person only, James Esposito. I trusted James implicitly. There was nothing wrong with James, except that he was also friendly with that shit George Manners.

The staff in Beverly Hills were kept on the payroll, butlering, tweenying and gardening an empty house, while a completely new household was assembled in the 'cottage.' No one ever mentioned N's identity and, although they must have guessed who was their employer, they would never have dared to disclose it, in view of the colossal pay they received and the confidentiality contracts they had signed.

N's strategy for securing this silence was simple: she had been looking at *Hamlet* with a view to emulating Bernhardt and playing the title rôle. N had many times been on the verge of withdrawal from a movie, even on the eve of first rehearsals, and it had become a Hollywood truism: don't roll the cameras until she walks on set. So when she actually told the producers and director that she wouldn't do the part, they had no difficulty in believing her and, at her behest, made no attempt to change her mind. Her hesitancy over every part was due to the lack of self-confidence which assails every artist at the moment when they are about to walk onstage, but she made it very clear that her withdrawal on this occasion was nothing to do with her ability to play a man's part – she'd done it to acclaim in *Orlando*.

Quite apart from the pregnancy, it was the best career decision she ever made. And *Windmill* was the worst. No doubt she could have *been* Hamlet – she was, as I knew well, supremely capable of thinking herself into Hamlet's mind, and she had the balls to do it – which is probably more than Hamlet had – but the world would not have been able to take it seriously. It would have been a terrific box-office attraction, and that's of course why the producers wanted to pull off this coup, but critically her reputation would have been on a knife-edge, presenting her as a circus-act, and the punters would go merely to gawp at a transsexual, not to appreciate N's artistry.

Two months into the pregnancy – before it began to show – we heard news that shook me but which N took in her stride. We had each won an Oscar for *Intimate Letters* – she as best actress, I for best screenplay. When I say it shook me, of course it was no surprise that N had achieved hers (after all, it was one of the defining rôles of her career), but *mine*? Well, in a way it was a victory against the gobshites who'd been producing their version of *Intimate Letters*, set on a Caribbean island with the intimate letters being French ones, in a bottle and coming back (oops) on the next tide. Come to think of it, as a black "MontyPythonesque" comedy, that wouldn't be too bad. But it vindicated the stand which I – and N of course – had taken over the whole project, the integrity and inherent value of *Intimate Letters* as a love story with a difference. And it – do I have to say it? – endeared me to SolMart. Not endeared, perhaps, so much as made me one of their surrogate family, made Sol kiss me repeatedly (while Mart stood embarrassingly beside him) and utter the magic words "Drew, you're a god!" Followed by "Anything you write for us from now on, we'll take care of it."

"Yeah," I thought, "you would." Back to Mahler cast as a vampire, avalanches and the compulsory Hitler.

As N and I were "hidden" in our cosy little retreat with only seven indoor staff and two Kalashnikovs prowling the grounds (we called them K1 and K2 but they were almost indistinguishable), and had shunned not only tv but also newspapers, *Hello!* magazine – everything, in fact, except a subscription to *Mother-to-be* – we had no means of knowing about the Oscars. We actually got the news indirectly. N had nominated a faux-agent, to whom her real agent would forward mail, offers of the Légion d'Honneur, the Croix de Guerre, the DBE, the throne of Kazakhstan and other junk mail. The faux-agent would delete most of these, or reply to them in gracious terms declining the honors ("Miss Zoffany regrets she's unable to ..."), signed lovingly with a faux-N signature, and he damn nearly deleted the news about the Oscars, suddenly paused above the relevant key of his iPad, and realized that this was *big* time. N's first Oscar. Better by far than becoming Queen of Kazakhstan (the Oscar would probably last longer) or being kissed – and probably groped – by the French President.

So it was N who opened her faux-poste and found the news. It was a conventional setting: the breakfast table. One of the tweenies brought a tray with the letters. N discarded most of them, which to my mind meant that the faux-agent wasn't doing his job. But spam will fly under the radar, it seems, even of a Hollywood superstar in total seclusive purdah. But this one she opened. "Oh Andrew, you've done it!" I worried a bit at this remark, as it could have meant anything good or bad. Could it be anything to do with my getting the Nobel Prize for Literature? For Fatherhood? For Love? The PEN Club of Guatemala had elected me honorary president? Seemed unlikely. Nothing for it but to ask for an explanation from a more radiant-than-ever N, who after my microsecond of alarm was now jumping up and down (dangerously, I thought, in view of her condition) with unsuppressed joy.

"Oscar."

"What?"

"Oscar."

"You mean a name if it's a boy?"

"No, you wally. You've won an Oscar."

"Nicole, please stop making silly jokes at this time of the morning."

"It's not a joke, fuckhead" – this was meant playfully – "for *Intimate Letters* – the script – you're the king of Hollywood – for a year, anyway," she added with a giggle. It seemed like a long time. I couldn't believe it. I had to believe it. This wasn't a joke. Then N opened another letter. Calmly:

"And so have I."

As my Irish grandma used to say, "Oh holy fuck." That

was hardly news. N deserved that Oscar, and yet, out of love for me (as I later discovered), she had suppressed her own letter to take joy in mine. And her career depended so much more on hers than mine did on mine, for mine, as I had already determined it (wrongly of course) would go no further.

There was only one sadness: we could not go to the awards as a couple. We would probably have to sit at separate tables. That was the price of our secrecy, our privacy, our togetherness, our soon-to-be parenthood. Was it time to tell everyone "Hey, we're together!"? 'Hollywood Double for Nick and Drew' would have been vulgar but satisfying. It was not to be. N, needless to say, got all the glitz, while I stumbled into glory as an adjunct. The writer. The drudge. If only those goons that night in the Chinese Theatre had known how hard and viciously we had fought for that script, for the film itself, had threatened walkouts (well, hers anyway), had bled for 'Jack' Janáček. But above all, they would never know how that script had created the love that dared not speak its name (apologies to Wilde).

The awards night was just as you've seen it on TV – a circus. N, stunning in a minimal gold dress, of which there was almost nothing except the color for *Tittle-Tattle* to describe, with her minders forcing the way through the crowds; me arriving in a much smaller limo ten minutes later, requiring no crowd control whatever. Who was I?

N's acceptance speech, gracious, witty, with no giveaway loving look as she acknowledged me, SolMart and everyone else all in one breath, justifying her entitlement to stardom. Me, still incoherent from the shock, mumbling a few words and making the same sycophantic obeisance to SolMart. And our separate exits until, under cover of undercover, we were together in the jet back to Long Island and apprehensive parenthood, the only difference now being the two Oscars on the side-table where my made-in-Taiwan Buddha had previously stood.

The twins loomed into our life, our togetherness, after a scan that, in some couples, will produce alarm, but in our case pure joy, especially when, at a later stage, we knew that they were a boy and a girl (feminists, read "a girl and a boy"). N, I need hardly say, blossomed into motherhood. If there had been huge love between us up to that point, the love now was transferred into a new dimension: the love of N and me redoubled and, in addition, our love for the duo growing inside her.

When the birth came – and, unlike so many of N's films, it was an easy birth – the girl slid out first, much to N's joy, followed thirty minutes later by the boy. We had resolutely refused to think of names until the birth(s) and it was a few days – spent mainly in adjusting ourselves to life with two sentient, clamouring creatures who, to N's delight, had made it safely from inside to outside – before we realized that "the girl" and "the boy" had no names, no identity other than the cliché of babyhood.

N had been so preoccupied with the adjustment from pregnancy to reality that the mechanisms of motherhood – breastfeeding, catching up on sleep – absorbed her whole energy. That, despite the two nurses, the nanny Jessica Conneely, and the other retainers who would live with us for the first few months.

Eventually, however, we put our hearts and heads into the *caerimonia nominationis* - in plain words, giving names to the babies. On the basis of my Englishness we played with "Victoria and Albert," "Elizabeth and Philip" and, even for a *very* short moment, "Charles and Diana." There seemed no reason to look at my parents' or grandparents' names for any sentimental reason as, being dead, they could show no appreciation. N's family was, she insisted, laboured with such awful names that she would not even discuss them.

Then we had a parental version of our bedtime fun-fucks: we thought of her producers, Solly and Mart, and laughed over the idea of calling our kids "Solomon" and "Martina," but we couldn't have lived with it, neither could they. The only people who would have been pleased were Solly and Mart, and we were on a sabbatical from Tinseltown.

One morning, N woke giggling: "Andrew, remember the opera in San Diego? Remember I said I got the idea of the jet from *Pretty Woman*? – Gere and Roberts?"

"Oh NO!" I cried, "NOT 'Richard and Julia'?"

"No, but something along those lines."

"Charlton and Sophia," I murmured, hoping she wouldn't hear. But she did:

"Sean and Audrey?"

"Where did you get that from?"

"*Robin and Marian*, where Connery plays the elderly Robin and meets Marian who is now a nun and at the end he's dying and she gives him hemlock to help him to die more swiftly."

"Bloody hell, what a way to go! For Robin *and* for Sean. I think I would count it as a great honor, as well as a sexual thrill, to be given hemlock by Hepburn."

"Ok, we'll drop that one."

And so it went on – a catalogue of the great names on celluloid, until I came up with an alternative: the *character*, not the *actor*. "Nicholas and Alexandra," "Henry and Sally" –

"I don't think the girl should have an orgasm-related name to live up to."

"Not like her mother, no. Sorry, I was just thinking of Meg Ryan."

"I know – that's the problem."

"Yuri and Lara?"

"No way!"

"Sodom and Gomorrah" –

"Cut it out Andrew."

And then, *un bel di*, we got it. Not Ralph and Kiera, but Oscar and Lucinda. And that is how the children, like the creatures in the *Just So* stories, got their names, identified as two great screen lovers fated to ... well, we won't go into that.

I swear that the 'Oscar' on our metaphorical mantelpiece had nothing to do with it. Really I do.

Was it irresponsible? Many children go through life teased because their parents have lumbered them with unfortunate names or acronyms. I was at school with a boy whose initials were M.A.D. Shere Hite's parents couldn't have been too kind either, and she'd fulfilled their advice by writing a load of, well, S. Hite.

Oscar and Lucinda: calling them by those names – which they love, by the way, even though, at such a young age, they have no idea of the origin – was a naughty joke, just like the day they 'stole' the jet and fantasy-flew to the opera at Santa Fé. A rather more serious joke, when it was two little lives we were playing with, but it was our way of thumbing our noses at the industry and all its pretensions.

So we absolved ourselves from irresponsibility, despite James's disbelief. I should explain James.[2] James Esposito and I had been at Oxford at the same time, during our respective postgrads – I on music (mostly), he on film adaptations, on which his scholarly and critical reputation is based. The only thing we had in common was our detached but subjective admiration of N as a screen goddess. James became my best friend. No, we didn't spend our time together drooling over N's videos. I may

---

[2] Editor's note: I leave Andrew's words about myself as written.

have done that, but James succeeded in sublimating his interest in N in other ways. We developed a second interest in opera, and, as I've already told, it was James who recognized my passion for Janáček and who put me in touch with people who put me in touch with people who put me in touch with ... Solly and Mart, and thus brought N into my life.

So James had a lot to answer for – the misery of my script being constantly rewritten, the degradation of that lunch with "Solly Sullivan," and the ambrosian heights of love and life with N.

Therefore, when Oscar and Lucinda were born, it was only natural, on my part, to contact James and ask him to come over to the "cottage" – could we find a wee room for him? – and share the new dimension of our joy. N offered no resistance, nor did she require anyone for girl-support at that time – no family, no film buddies, no friends.

As O'n'L (as we lovingly called them, while they came to call each other "Oz" and 'Cinders') grew from baby to small person, which of course is all I saw of them in the home life, they were shielded by the bevy of nannies, the Kalashnikovs and advertising executives. Kalashnikovs, because N was fearful of a kidnapping, advertising executives because they pestered us with offers of lucrative contracts for the twins in ads for diapers, kiddyfood, Mothercare and – this surprised me – early reading manuals. We – or rather O'n'L – could have earned telephone numbers if we had permitted them to do so. Had they been identical, same-sex babies, the telephone numbers would have had a zero at the end. And maybe O'n'L, despite their undeniable wealth today, regret the money *and* the early stardom that would have put them into the same league as their mother.

When N *really* wanted to annoy me (have I mentioned this before?) she'd called me 'Drew' and she did it with a superb Solly voicealike. As the babies became sufficiently sentient to merit a bedtime story, N announced one day "Drew, bedtime stories for O'n'L, are *your* baby. You'll be a star, Drew."

"Shut up, N."

"Won't."

"Try 'shan't.'"

"Shan't, won't."

"Why does it have to be me?"

"You're the scriptwriter. You've written the best story in the world, just trade up a little and charm the diapers off O'n'L."

"It won't work, N. It's a different ballgame, a different genre (we both pronounced it 'genner' as a private joke) I'm a parent, not a bloody scribe in SolMart's warehouse."

"Try it Drew."

"And are you, Ms Solly, going to edit? Call in a team of sub-scribes to change the prince and princess into a werewolf and King Kong? Change Snow White into Ivan the Terrible? Tell me my story is 'crap'?"

"Well, this love might not have happened in quite the same way if I hadn't brought you to the Ivan the Terrible Café. A grumpyburger might have had a rather different effect. Like cutting someone's head off, John-the-Baptist style, on a plate."

"Would you stop, Ms Stösslova?"

Anyway, joking aside – but only for a moment – the bedtime story fell to me, and I fell almost immediately in O'n'L's estimation. Fallen Idol? Hitchcock was only trotting after me as far as nursery fables were concerned.

Here's one of my earlier catastrophes.

"Dada" – that's what they called me – "tell us a story." L, as senior twin, was always the spokesman.

"Sure." A pause for instant inspiration. I was in a hurry as I wanted to phone James at a pre-arranged time.

"Once upon a time" – how else does a fable begin? – "Once upon a time there was a very beautiful princess and a very handsome prince." Pause to allow this idyllic possibility to register in the ever-growing and ever-alert brains of two two-year-olds. "And they lived happily ever after. Goodnight my darlings."

I was halfway down the stairs when a shriek came from the nursery. They couldn't get it into words, not words that an adult would understand, but L, and then O taking his big sister's cue, but not entirely sure why he should do so, let out the sort of shriek that you only hear in the best houses. It brought K1 running from the kitchen where he had – predictably as stories go – been screwing a tweeny, assuming that nothing could have penetrated K2's vigilance outdoors; not in the way that he was penetrating the tweeny, anyhow. I must be murdering N, or maybe she was murdering me. Which paid his salary? That would affect his response to the shriek. It brought Nanny Conneely running, assuming that I was murdering O'n'L (not, strangely, that O'n'L were murdering me, although at that moment they had plentiful cause and probably plentiful intent). It brought temporary ruin on my fatherhood, as O'n'L did not require any bedtime stories from me for some days, preferring them from a book, read by Jessie (Nanny Conneely) – 'Jekanan' as they called her in their emergent language.

And it proved me to be correct in one thing: "Andrew, you may be a writer, but you're no good at telling a bedtime story." Told you so.

So, for eight years after the births, while the children were growing up, I lived a quadripartite life: lover, father, returned academic and renewed – Oscar-winning, for god's sake – screenwriter.

I had published one big study of popular literature in 1992, *Minor Mythologies*, and I had been working on a sequel when the *Intimate Letters* project came along and transformed my life. Now, with N's encouragement and goading, I asked James to unearth my research papers from my college rooms, so that work on that sequel, *Myth, Ritual, Story*, could be continued.

But while N exhibited the natural interest in my academic work which one would expect from a lover, it was my continuing involvement in the script world of Hollywood that, predictably, came first.

In those years, in addition to completing *Myth, Ritual, Story*, I wrote three scripts, the first with pleasure and enthusiasm, the second reluctantly and with misgivings. The pleasurable project was a script for N: a black psychological thriller based on an original story by Edgar Allan Poe. The other was done just to keep SolMart off my back: a ghastly remake of *The Prisoner of Zenda*. I didn't even enquire what it turned into eventually – probably something involving Alexander the Great and the Garden of Gethsemane.

As an Oscar winner, my name would – even if slightly – enhance a movie that might otherwise attract little interest. 'Screenplay by Oscar winner Andrew Dalton (*Intimate Letters*)' would embellish the posters. It obviously didn't matter in the case of the N film, because it would have star attraction even if it had been written by Mr Guffaw and revealed N as Mrs Mickey Mouse. But in the case of the third script, *Ephesians*, with a B-movie cast and one of SolMart's less distinguished accomplishments, my name meant *something*, even if the actors couldn't deliver my deathless lines except in deathful tones.

Ephesians was a skit on St Paul's letters which, some clever dick had observed, never got any replies. Ephesians, Corinthians, Philippians, Colossians, all had received epistles advocating love, charity and other inestimable virtues, but none of them had ever written back: "Paul, fuck you and your bloody charity." *Ephesians* remedied that lacuna. Sol, of course, saw it as a Jewish film: "They're not Christians, so why should they reply? They're like me – fucking Jews." Mart as a good Catholic had to object: "But Sol, they *became* Christians. That's the dramatic turning-point of the story – Saul-Paul converted them." Sol: "Dramatic! There's more drama in a dogfight. And there's no drama in fucking letters." Where had I heard that before? It was the only time I ever witnessed a row between Sol and Mart.

I was approached by numerous other studios – Twentieth Century Fox, Miramax, Columbia, you name it – and numerous other stars, including Meryl Streep, Glenn Close and Dustin Hoffman, but I turned them all down. I was tempted by Andie MacDowell, purely (well, impurely) by the enigma of her smile. Andie's smile was so different from N's, that I felt I had to write a different kind of script, but I didn't get the chance. N, sensing my attraction to Andie, vetoed that one out of hand. Meryl did tempt me, for entirely non-sexual reasons: she was interested in an adaptation of a Russian novel in which she would play a Russian *au pair* in San Francisco or LA, and would have to learn the language and the accent. It was the sort of challenge Meryl would rise to, but in fact N got the part – *Anniversary*, it was called, but I wasn't involved.

One night Andrew had a nightmare in which he received a phone call from an unknown caller – a voiceless voice – who, in tones of authority, informed him that his dreamtime was concluded and that he was to report back to his desk in academe forthwith. He was no longer the plaything of the stars, but a pen-pusher whose future life would consist in teaching morons, while always dreaming back to his fantasy life. He was back to being a nobody. And, as he was dragged away by the head of his department, he saw N being held back as she cried out "Andrew, I'll save you!"

He woke, screaming "No! You can't do this to me!" – to find a concerned N trying to soothe him as he wept his despair. "It's ok Andrew, it was a nasty dream." He continued to sob, until he began to make some sense of the episode. She was comforting him, when in the real life of fantasy he was supposed to find her flooding the bed with tears and, holding her in his arms, restore her to tranquillity. "I'm sorry – I'm sorry," he kept saying, as if the upset were his fault.

It's a commonplace that all dreams, all nightmares, are projections of the fears and anxieties – and sometimes, but less frequently – the hopes and joys of our unconscious that dare only to come out under cover of darkness. Andrew hadn't imagined the summons without reason, and when he saw the confusion between reality and fantasy he wasn't importing anything from a book of bad things, but dredging it up from where it had been buried between him and N. They had already decided that he would resign his lectureship at Leeds, although Andrew had yet to notify the university.

So, on reflection, it was his fault. "Andrew, no one is going to take you away from me, unless it be myself." When he explained that the dream had been a reversal of his worst fears, that in fact she would be taken away from him, and incarcerated in a house of corruption for women who thought they were beautiful, world-famous movie stars, while he single-handedly arranged for her release to his arms, his bed, his love, they both burst out laughing. "It's Hotel Shanghai, you fool," she said playfully. "You're reliving the fantasy that brought me to your imaginary life in the first place."

Could that be true? Had he, all these years, carried with him the idea that it would be he who rescued the young, innocent, N and 'they lived happily ever after'? How fantastic could it be? How had it actually happened, their being so much together, and yet he still had that fear of what, in fact, had already been fulfilled? But, as he lay in her comforting arms, the rôle reversal made him ask again, was all of this a sabbatical from reality?

10
Love, Fear, Hate

The principal difficulty in writing about N is the fact that one cannot avoid the clichés: indomitable, incomparable, unforgettable. How can it be, the reader asks who does not know her, or who only knows her superficially from some of her films, that one woman can embody all these qualities? You talk about beauty – ok. But now you add 'indomitable, incomparable....' Is she a superwoman? Is she a goddess? The answer, I make shamelessly, is 'Yes!' N *does* embody an indomitable spirit, she *does* create incomparable screen characters, and once you have looked beneath the *superficies* to the core of the character, you find the core of the woman, and *that* is unforgettable.

All of this was made even clearer to me than previously, when I watched her misery, stress and suffering in *Love, Fear, Hate*, working with director Joanna Hampton and co-star John Danolič. If N were not an indomitable character, she would not have survived the near-fatal bullying that she received from both of them in making that movie.

I had seen – the world had seen – a face that could show apprehension in the face of the unknown (in *An Other World* or *New Worlds* for example). In *An Other World*, N seemed to relish the challenge presented by a character, so much so that, as in almost all her rôles, she *became* that character: "She is slipping into my consciousness," she said. And that meant not merely that N was becoming the character, but that the character was becoming *her*. The film was nothing more or less than *atmosphere* and, as the director said, N *was* the atmosphere. Another director says "She is an actress, first and foremost, not a film star"; and a third: "go beyond good acting and it's something else – life itself." Watching her moving into the mists of uncertainty, a player in and of the darkness, was, I suppose, magical, because N was acting, possessed by the part and thus making real life from pretence: nature imitating art.

But *Love, Fear, Hate* was a torture almost beyond endurance which etched itself into her face in rehearsal, in make-up and onscreen. 'Apprehension' comes easily to the innocent. And N does not court safety: quite the opposite. She once said not only that "I love movies that are psychologically frightening" but also that she was always drawn to "black comedy." She has given many examples of both – of the former in *An Other World*, of the latter in *Anniversary* – but there comes a time when one moves into territory that is more frightening, blacker, than one could ever have anticipated, and for which, however professional one's background and experience, one is ill-fitted.

In *Love, Fear, Hate* N and her character lose that innocence, drawn into a malice the intensity of which she had never before experienced. And all in the name of making a good, a brilliant, movie. *Which it did!* The stress under which N was put by Hampton almost killed her, and it cured me of any misconception I might have been harboring, that all and everything was permissible on the part of a good director in order to get a brilliant performance.

Always, N is on the threshold of life; her career may have led her into a wealth and depth of experience, but – and not only for me – she returns every time from that journey to the girl of *Hotel Shanghai*. Youthful, enjoying life, *méchante*. Only when she is in a soul-searching and potentially soul-destroying situation in rehearsals does she leave behind – and only for a moment – the innocence and insouciance that have followed her all through her career.

Even when she is in the throes of misery, cruelty, despair – all the worst that life can throw at one – she nevertheless exudes a sense of just stepping out into life. Sometimes she seems embarrassed by her own naïveté and the laugh becomes tentative. At other times it is timidly raunchy. Is that a mixed metaphor? I don't care. Is it because she rejects a future which she sees as unsatisfying, too dangerous, even too ordinary? And retreats back into girlhood? Not so, since she seems to embrace danger, and to transform ordinariness into magic. She was fully aware that, as she put it, "there's reality and there's pretend, and those lines get crossed. It's a very exciting thing to happen, and a very dangerous thing to happen, and when it *does* happen, that's when the work becomes so much more than making a film. Film-making is about getting lost, and it's exquisite when it happens."

She was speaking of her work in *Seeing in the Dark* but it was mercilessly true of our lives together. She certainly transformed the ordinary me into something beyond despair. The crossing of Andrew's line with N's line was "very exciting" (that's putting it mildly) and that's when our friendship became so much more even than being in love; it was 'getting lost' in and for each other. Yes of course I'm a sentimental and, today, drunken reminiscer, turning the pages of a storybook, but you could rewrite the history of love and the future of love by looking into that book.

In the first month, I watched N working with Hampton, dutifully taking instruction on how the director wanted the part to be played. I had seen that attention to detail; it was a 'back-to-school' look that I'd first met in our own case, of my coaxing her into the Janáček heroines. But this went much further: deeper, more intensely, cutting through to the heart of misery that takes place in Sophie (N's character) as she realises how her bid for freedom, her crying out to be loved, had turned against her and introduced her to a circle of evil where she was lost, where apprehension turned to utter dismay, where the capacity for resistance was worn away, expunged, and in its place came the contamination that evil spreads in even the purest, most pristine mind.

It was as if Hampton and Danolič were intent on projecting the malice and horrid nature (which Danolič did so perfectly, apparently without acting), onto both Sophie *and* N herself. Sinister was hardly the word. It wasn't the word. The word was evil, evil, evil, through and through and through. Cynicism that you see in the eyes and leering mouth of an insatiable beast moving toward *engorgement* and destruction. Did Henry James envisage this treatment of his novel? He had written somewhere "Evil is insolent and strong; beauty enchanting but rare; goodness very apt to be weak; folly very apt to be deficient; wickedness to carry the day." But could he have lived with it? For an answer, we would have to consult Paola Brunetti, the James expert, whose husband, the Commissario, would have detected Hampton as a criminal. And not directing a *crime passionel* for which one might expect forgiveness. A crime against humanity – N's humanity.

At day's end we would go briefly to N's trailer and, having given her PAs the running order for tomorrow and, usually, "cancel all appointments, and I mean *all!*" we'd repair (how inappropriate a word) to the hotel suite where we could do little, in fact, to 'repair' the psychological damage that had been inflicted that day. And they call it 'work'! Intimidation in the workplace is clearly something

actors sign up for in their contracts, and the fact that N
was on a $10m fee plus a percentage did little to assuage
the damage.

To say she earned her money would be a travesty of
the idea of working for money. However much N was –
and continues to be – paid, it wasn't merely for the money,
and the comfort and security it could buy, that she did it.
She put her talent first, and here she laid it on the ground
like a priceless Shiraz carpet and allowed Hampton and
Danolič to trample on it. The result, of course, was genius.
But at what cost? Later, when *Windmill* exploded in our
faces, I would accuse her not of laying down her talent as a
cheap rug for all to defile, but of prostituting it. Where was
the difference? But I ask myself this too late, from the pits
of Karponisi.

Because of her utter perfectionism, N could be nothing
but tactful in discussing her part with Joanna Hampton.
When, if the truth were to come out, she had found it not
merely professionally challenging but destructive. She was
screaming, but on the inside. It took many months of
retreat in Long Island before she could look at anything
stronger than a comedy that required little or no effort on
her part.

N used to say her trick was "Breathe and relax. You
need to be in a relaxed state." That isn't what I saw. I saw
the opposite. I saw the mother of my children being
reduced to emotional rubble, to a state in which no child
should ever see its mother; and I wondered whether she
would ever be able to come home to us in one piece and
resume her loving self. Or would she carry that hurt with
her, back into our lives, a lesion on our love? If this was a
selfish thought it was not only on my own part, but on
Oscar's and Lucinda's.

At one point she was on the verge of walking away
from the thing and selling her part to Meryl Streep or

Glenn Close; maybe they would be more resilient, or more capable of fighting back. At another point, she was tempted to call in a counsellor for after-work therapy but, as she said, "It's too much like an *après-ski* apéritif – and it's not restoration I need, it's reconstruction. Look, Andrew" – she was the closest I have ever seen to tearful screaming – "I'm IN BITS!" And she held up her arms in helpless surrender, almost seeing Hampton and Danolič bearing down on her in her own suite, adding more poison to the chalice. "I don't know what's happening to me." Little-lost-girl no more. Lost woman. Over the next few weeks, until shooting began (the point at which I, as "consultant," ceased to have a valid reason for being around), it was my responsibility to help N to understand what was happening, to work it out from the inside, to re-find herself, the "real" N, so that she could be the "real" Sophie. She had put herself in the way of danger, little realising that she stood in the path of a relentless, all-devouring irresistible force and that she was no longer an immovable object.

Even now, it's a matter of pride to me that I was able to help her through this ordeal. Pride is another "wrong word." I didn't take pride in my desperate attempts to put her back together again at the end of each day. And I didn't help her entirely on my own. If that steely determination to come through, scathed but still whole, had not reintroduced itself into the old N, I could not alone, or even with a team of therapists, have sustained her. No, it was N and I together, and that togetherness was, in its own horrible way, as precious to me, *is* as precious to me today, as the joyous times, the victorious times, the times of laughter, the times of love shared with Oscar and Lucinda, that were the pillars of our life, and remain the pillars of memory for me, as I write here in Karponisi.

And there was a tiny bit of fun for us in this adjustment: room service became a joke, as I instructed the hotel kitchens in minute detail how to prepare and serve the most basic English dishes – fish and chips, steak and kidney pie, brawn – to give her some plain nourishment rather than the fancy stuff on the menu. "Hmm. Good. Boring but good. Just like you, Andrew." An admonitory whack on her arse from an equally exhausted but still sensitive Andrew. And it worked. No langoustines for Miss Zoffany. By the end of the *Love, Fear, Hate* nightmare N had actually come to like – even love – plain, honest fare. If only everything else had stayed plain and honest ...

N once described the intensity of working on a film – any film – as "working at a pitch": if it didn't happen, if the tensions and reservations weren't released into nervous, creative energy, the film would lack depth, psychological impact, the capacity to reach across the screen into the movie theatre and convince the popcorn-guzzling customers that this was real, this was a life they could relate to, however bizarre, however stupid, however unbelievable. It was real. That's how the fiction of a movie becomes acceptable to the punters: it becomes part of their lives, believable, tangible.

At the opening of this film, Sophie says, "I'm not afraid." How wrong she was proved to be. To *be* her, N had to say to herself "I'm not afraid," but to project herself into Sophie, as she had done in every film of hers I had seen, projected her also into a darkness so much more malevolent than *An Other World* because she put herself in the way of danger that she had not realized could be so overpoweringly, so unforeseeably, evil. The pitch at which N had to work in *Love, Fear, Hate* was so intense that, if she had been a mechanical engine, everything would have blown sky-high. That's what she meant when she exclaimed, in agony, in the privacy of our suite, 'I'm in bits.' N was, at heart, a fun-girl. But there was no fun in *Love, Fear, Hate*. And the girl was lost.

Watching her in rehearsal, my heart bled for my belovèd. I wanted to jump onto the set and scream "How can you do this to such a beautiful woman?!" but immediately the thought, the impulse, came into my head, I realized that it was *because* N was so beautiful that she had to suffer. '*Il faut souffrir pour être belle*' is all wrong. '*Il faut être belle pour souffrir*' is right.

Danolič would, of course, convince you that he was a "good guy," a 'nice guy' (huh!), but only by wearing down your resistance, killing you mentally until you would sign any confession in order to be relieved of the pain and the degradation. That is what I saw him doing to N.

Seeing him touching her off-camera, I wanted to exclaim, "Pervert! Take your lascivious, dishonest hands off my woman!" but – on one occasion only just in time – I remembered that I was there as N's "consultant," not her bodyguard, not her lover. To shout like that would have been pure melodrama, but that is what all cinema is, and its creatures: the actors and actresses, the extras, the crew, the director, are all servants of implacable masters – the producers – whose job is to ensure that you collectively deliver melodrama to the screen. Sensation, emotion, triumph and disaster, beauty (N) and ugliness (Danolič) and every point of feeling and unfeeling in between. And I was provoked to think that, whatever our reservations about Solly and Mart, this wouldn't be happening if they had been the producers of *Love, Fear, Hate*. You'd hardly expect them to hire Mel Brooks to direct *Love, Fear, Hate*, but there had to be a middle way.

It's well known that, when Billie Whitelaw was rehearsing Beckett's *Not I*, with the author directing, she was under so much pressure that she suffered what she herself called 'sensory deprivation' and a near breakdown – to Beckett's dismay; but relentlessly the rehearsals went on. Henry James wasn't available to be dismayed by what was being done to his heroine, but dismay was the last thing evident in either Hampton's or Danolič's behavior as N's deprivation of almost all faculties wore her down. There was no expression of regret, no compassion. To put it crudely, a duo of 'Gotcha!' as N eventually came through and delivered a magnificent performance as Sophie.

Like Billie Whitelaw, N persisted in acting her way into a solution, so that she could create herself, and her rôle, from the ground up. Danolič used to say that as an actor he never asked 'Why?' Just do the lines. But N *did* ask 'why?' That was where Mr Guffaw, in what seemed light-years in the past, had gone so very wrong. She was incapable of working, of becoming Sophie, or Kamila, or Jessica, unless she used her innate intelligence to complement her beauty, to know *why*. Thus, she acknowledged her vulnerability yet retained some dignity, and, for her, a professional integrity that would eventually be greeted by the critics as another triumph.

11

Windmill

Only one thing was certain: that neither of us had been unfaithful to the other. God knows, there was temptation enough, even for a humble scriptwriter – starlets and so on. For N, of course, there was always the bed scene with her opposite number – Brad Pitt, Michael Douglas, Warren Beattie – but that wasn't for real. Except that it did get real in the lives of so many Hollywood stars. But not in N's case. And I had no qualms when I watched her in the screen-bed with any of them. Not even Brad Pitt. Faithfulness was the imperishable rock on which our partnership and our parenthood were built. But my loss of faith lay elsewhere: in the shock I experienced when I saw the draft of *Windmill*. It horrified me, more than if N had slept with Richard Gere or Sean Penn or whoever.

In a way, I could have accepted that. As part of the Hollywood way of life, sleeping around was in the DNA, the woodwork of the movie mind. It would have been unpleasant and hard to believe, after the promises we had made to each other, *my* woman with another man, whoever he was, but to see her doing what in my opinion was unforgivable – an icon losing her charisma through the pursuit of bad taste – was like sleeping with the Devil. If she was a fun-girl, this was a girl taking fun to macabre and disgusting depths.

And I held this view not as N's lover, which I was, or as a film critic, which I wasn't, but as a Joe Soap who would have reached the same point of disillusion if he had still been at home in Croydon, watching it on the box. Like so many millions of his fellow stargazers, the scales fell from my eyes, and an untouchable goddess of the imagination had become a painted whore. All our jokes about Meryl Streep and the word 'whore' in *The French Lieutenant's Woman* had come to this point of reality.

This didn't happen all at once. I've said that N gave me her scripts to read, and I think she genuinely took my advice. I certainly know that in a couple of cases she asked for scripts to be changed when I had made what she accepted as a correct assessment. But when she had shown me the initial script of *Windmill* I had said, as if the whole thing was a joke. "You're not seriously going to do this one, are you?" She had looked at me with her most rebellious face:

"If I like it, I'll do it. The money is good."

"You don't need the money," I protested.

"But I need a good part for this year."

"This isn't it, Nicole, this will do you no good. Please drop it before you get in too far." We left it at that, because I could see the face growing cloudy as I had never seen it before, on or off screen.

The film plummeted in the ratings, and N's reputation with it. Although I sat in on rehearsals, often with regret. I never saw the finished job until the première. In fact, few stars ever saw the finished product until that point. N was one of the few who stipulated in their contracts that they had to approve the final cut. So she knew full well the way they – and she – had mis-cast her beauty *and* her intelligence, and she seemed unrepentant. As we left the première, I knew that something terrible had happened. Not only would N fall away, but she would pluck my heartstrings as she went. I knew, that night, that the world of beauty, the world of deepest love, the world of unbreakable commitment, was now a fantasy, a make-believe, that love had been defeated, that our commitment lay in shattered pieces on the red carpet.

It wasn't until two days later that I felt able to confront her.

Knowing how much resistance I was going to encounter, at first I very gently and cautiously said – it was after dinner but before bedtime – that I was not surprised that critical reaction had been so negative.

"What do you mean?"

"I think you know what I mean. I tried to persuade you not to do this movie, but you shot me down. Now, as we English say, you've been and gone and done it."

"Done what, exactly?"

"Let yourself down."

"How?"

"Oh, Nicole, do I really have to spell it out? Everything I warned you about has proved me right. This is a disaster. I don't care if it's a flop at the box-office. Your failure is there for all to see, for all time."

"*FAILURE?*"

"Yes, failure. You've done a lousy movie, you've shown yourself in the worst possible light, artistically speaking. When you do those promos that they use to boost sales, you won't be able to tell the truth – you'll have to lie if you want to convince anyone that you've enjoyed making the movie, that it was a *great* movie, that the director and your co-stars are terrific people to work with, that you *loved* the script."

"Well, Andrew, I *did* enjoy making it. It may not be my best movie, but I gave it my best shot. I *do* think it's a very enjoyable movie and I *do* think it's genuine, and yes, I *do* think it's a terrific script. And" – she glared at me, worse than I have ever seen her, even in a pretend-temper – "I *loved* being a whore. I *loved* every moment of my wickedness, my depravity. I *loved* deceiving men who thought they were hurting me. *Loved* it."

"And that's what it's been all along with us, hasn't it?

Deceit, acting – you can't stop acting, can you? And when you find yourself in a rôle as bad as this one, you're too much driven by your acting demon to realise what a WHORE you really are!"

Oh god how I have wished, every moment of my life since that moment, that I could have cut out my tongue rather than saying those words. Meryl Streep, French Lieutenant, come and save me.

"I can play *any* part. It's a challenge. And I can get on top of *any* challenge. You know that. You saw what I could do with *Love, Fear, Hate* – was I a whore then? I was a child, innocent, lost. And that's me in *Windmill* too, finding myself. And you're too much Mr. Stuckup Brit University Shithead to recognise it!"

"Bullshit. You've made a huge mistake and you can't acknowledge it. Let me ask you one basic question: how could you betray your art? When I advised you not to do Hamlet, I thought you respected my judgement and that was what decided you against the part."

"You know perfectly well, Andrew, that I turned it down because I was having Oscar and Lucinda."

Suddenly I was shocked into numbness. A numbness that hurt. Oscar and Lucinda were *ours*. She carried them for *us*. Ten years ago, she wouldn't have said 'I was having Oscar and Lucinda.' She didn't. She said 'We're going to be parents.' Now it was just her and just me, and Oscar and Lucinda in the middle, as a reason for not doing Hamlet.

But I tried to recover some ground. "That Hamlet was all wrong for you. You knew that. What was so different this time round? I gave you the same advice as before."

"But this time I *wasn't* having twins and I *wasn't* in any doubt that this part suited me. Your opinion just doesn't matter." She clicked her fingers as if to indicate the emptiness of my existence as far as her movie life was concerned. "How could you betray *me* by asking such a thing?"

"Can't you see how damaging this is to *you*, the real Nicole?"

"Who is the 'real Nicole'? Do you think you know her? Know *me*?"

"Aren't you my lover, aren't you the woman to whom I've given my life?"

"If so, how could you ..."

And so, the circular arguments continued, revolving around the one unasked question because we dared not to risk the unspoken, the unspeakable, answer: who were *we*? *Why* were we? Was this simply a matter of professional pride, of career moves, of ambition? Or was it a matter of faith in art? Of the search for the truth that – I had thought – lay at the heart of N, the heart of N-and-me, the heart of lovemaking, home-making, child-making?

Almost like a referee in a prizefight, tiredness separated us each into our own corner to recuperate, to see if the damage we were causing one another was justified. Did it have a basis in N's work or in her life? Were her work and her life all one? Wasn't I a part of that oneness, that immaculate congruence of the great actress and the great lover, the beautiful, the true?

The irrational, which had provided much of the excitement of our life, now became the subject matter of our separation. It was time to explain the inexplicable, to attempt, like the Irish or the Palestinian peace processes, a meeting-place where the two imaginations, the two memories, could explain to each other why this problem seemed so intractable.

So we went back into the ring for round two: two submissions or a knockout to decide the contest.

Of course there was a succession of the "Yes you did," "No I didn't," "Don't talk to me like that," "I'll say what I want, how I want to" kind of lovers' cliché. Criminations followed by recriminations. Her fictions and my facts; her facts and my fictions.

"What are you trying to do to me?" I'm so punch-drunk, even in recollection of that horrendous night, that either of us could have said that to the other. Maybe we both did, so destructive, so wounding, were our exchanges, our belief that each was being betrayed, that each was being torn apart by the other's stupidity, obstinacy, ill-will. Ultimately, torn apart by our overdraft in the love-bank to realise what we were doing, to know how to stop it, to help each other to heal.

"I'm just trying to show you how wrong you've been about all this." (This was definitely me meeting myself on the return from the ropes.)

"No you aren't. You're trying to tell me that it's *me* that's all wrong, a dollar-grabbing bimbo who'll take any part with any kind of script. Isn't that it?"

"Well, if you insist on showing yourself in such a bad light, I *do* think it *is* you who's all wrong."

"A bad light? *You* are the only one who's saying I'm showing myself in a bad" –

"Yes, me and a hundred critics."

"No, Andrew, You and a few cretinous begrudgers."

"First, you're not a bimbo. That's almost the whole point."

"Almost!"

"Don't interrupt me, please." How polite was our lack of tenderness!

"Don't tell me when to speak *my* mind."

"Second, you're certainly not dollar-grabbing."

"Well, I'm glad we've cleared that one up."

"But you *have* made a mistake." How many times would I make this pointless accusation? It had no future. "Just in this one case."

"Who on earth are you to know whether it's a mistake

or not?"

"I'm only putting myself in the seat of the ordinary punter who admires you from afar and hates what he sees you doing in *Windmill*."

"And that's where you ought to be – in the cheap seats voicing your cheap opinions. If you can't stand the movie, get out of the cinema! Ask for your money back."

"You say I don't like it. *Of course I don't like it!* Do you think it gave me any pleasure at that opening night to see you disgracing yourself and" – I surpassed myself in saying this – "your profession, by prancing round like a common whore? Do you think I liked it when people around us were sniggering and nudging one another? If you'd been doing a love scene, they would have been riveted into silence by your serenity" –

"Don't give me serenity. I don't do serenity! I do *me*!"

"Oh no you don't, Nicole. You may not aim for serenity, but you give it. And that woman on screen was *not* you."

Love had taken us beyond the edge of reason, and now it threw us back again, threw it in our faces, made us repent that we had ever trusted one another with the most precious prize in the world – ourselves. Was I anything to her at all? Was she, or was she not, my whole world? Could we trust each other again? She had shown me that I wasn't really the "me" I thought I was, and that I certainly wasn't the 'Andrew' whom she thought she loved.

I, for my part, had given her the idea that she wasn't "my" N, that she meant nothing to me. Because ... because ... because. I give up. There was no "because," because there was no reason, no logic to the questions we were asking ourselves, asking each other. From the intimacy of pillow talk we had passed in a moment to being strangers. I no longer knew who this woman was. She wasn't N – not the film star, not my lover, not the mother of our children.

For a few glorious, fantastic but ultimately unreal years she had been all of these – screen goddess, bed goddess, nursery goddess. Now she was just a question mark punishing my conscience.

Was she merely a mannequin? Is that what actresses are (thank you, Mr Guffaw)? A clotheshorse? We write their lives for them and drape them across their minds. Now, the life I had written for N was rejecting me, even though it wasn't in the script. The script was empty.

And for her, I was a non-entity whom she had probably always suspected. Maybe she even thought I was the gold-digger, an unprincipled charlatan feeding his misplaced vanity by worming his way into Hollywood and persuading a gullible young girl to hang on his arm.

The need to resolve these pounding questions inside her head and mine, or at least to see them through to a conclusion, brought us back into the ring for another round of mental and emotional pummelling. Round Three.

I knew that this was "championship point," that the moment or, rather, the long night of punishing moments, strung together by a remorseless deity that increasingly took on the appearance, in my disordered mind, of "Solly Sullivan," was make-or-break time. But I still persisted in thinking that I could win – not the match, but the trophy that our love represented, if I could only persuade N of the rightness of my argument. If I could achieve that, she would see that the mistrust and distrust and enmity between us was the result of two stupid people believing they were sufficiently intelligent to have a normal conversation. And therefore I poured out, not my angry opinions, not well-argued observations, because I knew already that they could not even begin to find a way into her defences. So I made an approach to the love that I was sure – and am sure to this day – was there at the heart of our being, our reason for having this row in the first place.

We wouldn't be tearing each other to pieces if it were not for our love, and our life, if it were not for Oscar and Lucinda.

But I began to realise that if either of us was going to retire from the ring, punch-drunk, it wasn't N. This woman, whose strength I had seen at close quarters, whose resolve was indomitable, was pushing me against the ropes of our love. To protect that love, I had to retire from the fight. We had punched each other beyond endurance.

In the end, the art that had brought us together forced us apart. That's a very saccharine and escapist way of saying that if we had not met on a film set, we wouldn't have got into this mess. But it was our own private, individual irresponsibilities which betrayed each of us, made us incapable of finding the love to sustain us through what we both later admitted was an unnecessary tantrum. Unnecessary in the sense that it needn't have happened, but necessary because it made apparent to us both that love was based not on the love of art or the love of the movie – even if at times those two things might coalesce (as they had in *Hotel Shanghai* – which, as they say, is where I came in) but on love itself, simple, unadorned, uncomplicated, and that kind of love was not enough.

I've known young innocents who were dumbfounded when they discovered that their premature love had come to an end. Margaret and me, for a start. Like a favorite movie ending, but you can't believe that there is no more of the magical story. Like the child at bedtime who doesn't accept that "they lived happily ever after" is a satisfactory way to say goodnight. There would be no more 'tell me a story' because the story was now unbearable.

But for two seemingly mature "grownup" people to fail, as it seemed to us the morning after, was so much greater a failure. It called in question whether we are ever "grown-up," or whether the love thing is just part of that growth and that one never gets to the top of the learning curve. Was it a fault in each of us, or in the unholy alliance between us, that was fatal from the outset? Was it an error of judgement? Yes! Love *is* an error of judgement. It's a leap into the dark that you have to take – as Petronius says in *Satyrikon, aut tunc aut nunquam* – the 'now or never' is the essential part of finding out, of the growing, of the coming together in hope and fear and longing and destiny. Take it, and you're signed up for bliss-on-hot-coals. Ignore it, and you'll die wondering, but in a lifelong death where wonder never comes, even for the briefest of visits.

That's the tragedy of life with N: that love, however utterly powerful and encompassing, wasn't enough. We could work for it. We could gorge ourselves on it. We could die for it. But we couldn't *live* it. Fuck love.

You could say we spent eleven mistaken years in a wonderland of our own making that was completely irrational, unrealistic and unsustainable. Well, yes, it *was* irrational, that's what love *is*, inexplicable, totally beyond the authority of reason. Unrealistic, because there was no 'reality' against which the strength of our passion could be measured. But unsustainable? The fact that after eleven years it came to an end doesn't mean that during those eleven years it was unsustainable. It was self-reliant, and its secrecy was the bond that made love into something very different from the public face that couples and their children conventionally offer to the world. Mr and Mrs Right and the 2.5 little Rights.

And of course it *was* a wonderland. Love that doesn't include wonder is a pedestrian and futile thing. N and I wondered about each other before Snow White; we wondered what love might bring us as we went through the process of *Intimate Letters* and in the course of working it out we found each other. By the time N came to make *Love, Fear, Hate* we no longer needed to wonder. We *knew*. But that didn't end our need for wonder, because, however much two people, especially so different in background and temperament, love each other and wallow in each other's personalities, they still need to *wonder*: about the past, where this love came from; about the present, what this love means *now*; and about the future, where will it take us, what *if...*?

So those eleven years were full of wonder, full of the inexplicable, full of the *merveilleux*, full of an unreality which we commuted into the real. And those passions and wonders and exciting questions sustained us. But maybe they didn't sustain our love... Not enough to transport us through that awful night to the other side. Yes, we went through that 'dark night of the soul' (sorry for the cliché; in fact, the dark night of *two* souls) but when it brought us out the other side it was the other side of love, not one we recognized, not one we could face with any confidence. You don't need confidence if you still have wonder. But the wonder had gone.

After we had exhausted ourselves with the fight, and after we knew it was all over, the extraordinary thing, for both of us, was that we went to bed together with the dawn; our crepuscular love-making was as exciting as it had been at the beginning – tender, searching, finding, such as we hadn't experienced for a few years. It was as if the release of tension, the removal of the burden we had, unknowingly, been carrying, was taken from us and we were left once more, and for the last time, with a 'boy meets girl' situation in which the delicacy of touch and tremor was an excitement all in itself. 'For one night only – in a bedroom near you.'

And then she was gone.

12
Afterlife

If you've had unprotected sex and don't welcome the possible consequences, you take a 'morning-after pill.' N and I had had unprotected, violent, eviscerating exchanges which left both of us as naked as Adam and Eve and horribly aware of their nakedness. And I didn't want any of the consequences, but couldn't avoid them. There was no 'morning-after' solution. We had been having unprotected love.

In theory, it should never have worked; *could* never have worked. In practice, it did work, spectacularly, for eleven years, until theory reasserted itself and proved it had been right all along, and reduced the spectacular to what it was: infatuation deceived by respect. It imploded and exploded all in one cataclysmic moment.

My whole existence would now be a 'morning-after-life' – not an attempt to wipe out the effect of ecstasy but to obliterate the way that ecstasy had been wiped off the slate by the acrimony between me and N that had revealed so much that was hurtful and hateful and could never be healed.

Any creative life seemed barred to me, either in film scripts or academic work. Back to an obscure academic life was out of the question. Even if there had not been the magical eleven years with N, a university English department is no place for an Oscar winner. I had no ambition at all to continue with anything remotely to do with film – even a lucrative screenwriting project would be ashes in my mouth after the nectar of N. I had had all the writing I wanted and needed. The one act of creation was that of parenthood: Oscar and Lucinda were little works of art, more important than anything I had ever written or N would ever act.

The children: did we ever think of them during that night of panic – for I now see that panic was the grim motor of our row? *No* – the row took no thought of anything except *Windmill* and the recognitions it provoked in N and me. It was only after I realized that N had gone that I also had the horrifying thought that we had just ruined the lives of Oscar and Lucinda.

After N and I calmed down, enough to talk sensibly about the children, we had to face the future realistically – perhaps the first time we had done so as man and woman, as parents, as people who loved each other but were now irrevocably going our separate ways. She, back to her Hollywood life, me, to ... what? N was sufficiently calm to say quite clearly that there was no question of shutting me out of the twins' lives. If we couldn't live as a family, at least we could make it possible for me to see Oscar and Lucinda as often as possible, and to know if anything of importance needed to be discussed.

Since then I have been unable to live either with or without myself. As for N, I can't tell, although she assures me that her 'life' is a happy and successful one. She can live with *it*, where she couldn't live with *me*. As long as Oscar and Lucinda continue to love and respect their mother and – I hope – understand her, as long as they have some residual affection for their absent father, I'm not too disconsolate. At least, I don't think so. I can recapture that wonder in memory.

Once the split was acknowledged by both of us to be irreparable, I had only one choice. I had nothing in the world except what I thought was the extinct volcano of love that had kept N and me together, and the twins whose future had been blighted by our adult tantrums. I had more than enough to live on, but nowhere to live.

It was James who came to my rescue. "But you have the house on Karponisi," he argued. "You can make a life there." It seemed a dubious idea, but, short of being footloose or returning to Leeds, it held a germ of possibility. With M, there was no question of a reconciliation, she was dead.

There were two villages on the island, the main one, Agios Paraskevi, to which the harbor and its accoutrements belonged, being at the island's southern tip. Since the main facilities, few as they were, were to be found here, this was where Margaret and I had bought our house. From the harbor a steep road led to the *plateia* or village square, which featured the church and the school.

Karponisi was home to approximately 600 people, of whom 400 lived in the main village, clustered around the harbor and on the hill above, and 150 in the north, with another fifty in scattered cottages, mostly along the spinal column of the road. There was a school with fifty students, some of whom I gladly tutored in English. There was a bakery which served many purposes: bar, grocery, and post office and the communal oven.

Karponisi also had a quayside taverna-cum-kafeneion, which stayed open all year for the islanders, some of whom still pursued the ancient work of fishing, and for the few resident foreigners such as myself; locals played interminable games of backgammon, which seemed to be the national pastime, and a card game of impenetrable complexity. The mail boat came once a week, doubling duty as the ferry and carrier of groceries, paraffin, and anything else that supported island life, which could be ordered from the stores on the mainland.

I had always been more than fond of both the island and the small house. If I were to live there full-time, I would need to ship everything – all my books and papers and a few bits of furniture – to the island, and this in turn would necessitate building a new wing to the old house. When that was done, the life of solitude replaced the life of the Hollywood crowds. But there was one similarity. So often, on the studio lot, I had felt like an extra. Here, too, on Karponisi, I felt that I had only a walk-on part. I hadn't belonged in Hollywood and I didn't belong here.

And so began my life of isolation, of reminiscence, or self-chastisement for what I increasingly realized had been an arrogant outburst that had, quite understandably, invaded and insulted N's professional life. I should have sat squirming through the première and sat squirming through the slating it got at Cannes and sat squirming through N's tantrums as she herself realized that she had, indeed, made a professional mistake. But I didn't. I had provoked that row while she was still on a high from the glamour of the opening night – the house full of flowers, the in-tray piled high with telegrams of congratulations from sycophantic hangers-on. And the children quietly reserved to the care of Jessica.

I suppose everyone thinks that I just sit in my room, watching and watching her films. But I don't. I don't need to. Her still incredible presence is with me, in bed, at table, walking in the olive groves above the village, taking the ferry to the mainland, inside my mind at every moment, day and night. If I want to watch her films – which I *do*, occasionally – I can bring them to the mind's eye quicker than the DVD player can present them. I can run them and re-run them in my memory as clearly as if they were on a twenty-foot screen such as the villagers still stretch across the village street for the weekly picture show.

Yes, of course I run her films. But it isn't an obsession. Just as I sit staring at the Annigoni portrait, and talking to it, to her. Or looking through the album we lovingly put together. Not just the photos, but the sentimental little keepsakes, like ticket stubs from some of the opera nights which so strongly brought us together. And, because I was known to have worked with her, I'm occasionally asked to review books about her. I reviewed David Thomson's so-called biography, which turned out to be a long essay on the nature of the cinema, showing off Thomson's prodigious knowledge of the subject, with the occasional bits of N thrown in to keep the story going. And, of course no mention of the hiatus in her career and my part in it.

And I write these pages, which James will find when I am gone. I feel it strongly, that I must do what every writer does compulsively – put it down on paper so that it can have a life in someone's memory. I want to do that before the inevitable end.

Talking about the experience of filming *Love, Fear, Hate*, which I have already described in some detail, N had said "When you have to overcome adversity, whether it is making a film, or in a relationship, if you can get through it and it doesn't destroy you, then something beautiful can be captured." During all the days since we parted, I have recited it like a mantra, knowing that, whatever happened between us, it didn't destroy us, it *was* adversity, and we *did* get through it. Something beautiful was truly captured, brought home, found within us, made into our own secret mystery. The remembrance of that beauty sustains me.

James Esposito: Those were the last words Andrew Dalton wrote – at least, they are the last pages in his memoirs which I was able to find in his well-ordered file of memoirs when I began to edit them. There is no date, but, as he seems to have continued putting his memories on paper until his final illness, I have assumed that they were written late in 2013. Even if there were more pages to be found, what he says here is a striking expression of the continuing presence of 'N' in his life, and the love and comfort that he continued to find in those memories – a fitting epitaph to a love that 'dared not speak its name.'

I last saw Andrew a few weeks before his death. He was seedy-looking, but one would not have thought that 'the end' was in any way imminent. There was no point in trying to persuade him to drink less. He found it the only other prop in his life – the life in which 'N' was the main pillar, inspiration and helpmeet. When I left him, he was sitting in front of the Annigoni portrait, in the same mesmeric state that he often records in these memoirs: a spiritual intoxication with the ghost of a life lived elsewhere.

13

Epilogue by James Esposito

In later years Andrew, while respecting N's privacy and protecting the identity of the twins, would sometimes talk in the village bar, the *Kafeneion*, to some local cronies, about his days in the shadow of Hollywood. They called him the "*skiafilmo*," the shadow film man. The fact of his Oscar could not be hidden or denied, and he was proud of it. Occasionally a visitor he might meet as a fellow guest at a friend's house would ask, "Are you *the* Andrew Dalton?" In this way, the fact that he was – or had been – famous, a "celebrity," was gradually revealed and his reputation as a reclusive scholar would be replaced by one commanding much more popular respect.

It was only when he began to drink deeply that indiscretion took over and N's name was mentioned. The affair, deepening into a relationship, the birth of the twins, all became public, but only locally. Because Andrew did nothing to substantiate his story, except for the presence of the twins once or twice a year, the idea of his life with N was transmuted in popular legend into fantasy. Andrew was living in cloud-cuckoo land. Not a word of his drunken rambling could be believed. It was just the village dipso, trying to impress folk who had heard it all before. When sober, he didn't give a toss what they said or thought about him. When drunk, which was increasingly often, he just sank back into the memories to which his fellow villagers had no access. If he had insisted on telling them more they would have rejected it, with polite and not-so-polite sniggers, just as he himself had rejected with indignation so many versions of his script as rubbish, make-believe, nothing to do with "real life." For Andrew now, sitting staring at the Annigoni portrait (which he kept hidden away from curious eyes), or re-running N's films over and over again, these were the only realities. It's probably for the best that Andrew didn't live to see the *fracas* which N caused by her bio-doc *American Princess* – it might have resuscitated his feelings over *Windmill*, but he was able to feed for as long as possible on the story that was no longer a story except in his memory.

The villagers were agreed that *something* must have happened to him. The Oscar on his mantelpiece was undeniable. But the general verdict was that Hollywood had turned his head. Yiorgos had had an uncle who was so deranged in his youth by the single kiss of a pretty girl that he had become a monk and spent all his subsequent life talking to the birds. That's more or less how they rewrote Andrew's past, as Hollywood had so cynically and brutally rewritten his future. And they would have been partly right, since, as Andrew told me when we were together in Long Island, N's kiss was 'a transfusion.' Not just a transformation – which it was – but a transport into an 'other world.' He'd gone from a quiet, sedentary existence amongst his books into a world which had fascinated him and, in the end, turned his head so far that he didn't know which way it was facing. Now he was back among his books, in a world which offered him nothing unless he unlocked its closet with a couple of bottles of Nemea wine or, on very bad days, Metaxa brandy.

He was, they said, "*ilithios*" – meaning "loola," "dopy," "away with the fairies." But they loved him, and, secretly, they loved his daft story, a romance that had never happened, but one that made them laugh and, occasionally, cry. He was certainly a wordspinner, even if the words came out of his deranged imagination. What he said was all makey-up – never real, never true. Just stories.

In the bar, when the more brash and intrusive drinkers felt like making fun of him, one would raise his glass and shout "Here's to Nicole!" and another would respond "Here's to the twins!" "Here's to Andrew!" was the kindlier way of greeting his storytelling, and "Here's to fantasy!" became a not unwelcome conclusion to his recitations. They meant it good-naturedly, because fantasy has been part of the Greek mind – its way of facing down realities – for millennia. And Andrew took it that way.

It was only after his death that the villagers, who had laughed behind his back and sometimes to his face, were told by his executors that in his library they had found the cache of letters from N and photos and other remembrances of the twins, lovingly inscribed, which confirmed his "fantastic" story. The letters, up to the point where they abruptly stopped, were passionate and endearing, the poured-out emotions of the woman who really had loved him and who trusted him never to disclose their contents during her lifetime. A poignant close to a life well-lived, its high point a "fantasy" in which only he believed, but which the suited, sombre lawyers read with increasing emotion and respect. Nothing in *Tosca* or *Traviata* or *Manon* – those favorite works which had helped to ignite their passion and sustained it for so many years – could match their intensity or their pathos.

Andrew's funeral was a very quiet affair. I had been at hand during his final illness, and had alerted "N," asking her if she and the twins would wish to be present. She replied that she was committed to filming and wouldn't be able to get away, and she would prefer to tell Oscar and Lucinda in her own time. So it was just me, the British Consul, a couple of friends from Karponisi, a couple from further afield on the mainland, and a few of the villagers. I am tempted to say that, on the outskirts of the small crowd and at a distance, a mysterious woman stood, her identity shrouded by a voluminous hooded cloak. I am tempted to say that it was "N." I approached her and spoke a few words with her, before she moved away to a waiting car. Who she was, I have never discovered, but it wasn't "N." Anyway, I don't think so ...

THE END

THE THIEF OF REASON

The memoirs of
George Manners

Edited by James Esposito

CONTENTS

I

George

He was tired. Very, very tired. Tired because, although he was only sixty-five years old, he easily became exhausted physically, but it was the mental fatigue, the spiritual lethargy, that saddened him most – made him, as a writer, desperate, in fact – because he was tired of life, tired of living, burned out. Life ... Living ... Was there a ....?

Tired of being him, George Manners, full-time author and critic, sometime lover, father and friend. Spy. Both kinds of tiredness had contributed to the enormous sense of *ennui* and lack of purpose which he now felt, having only a few weeks ago, shortly after his uncelebrated birthday – not even a card from either Vicky or Al, but why should he deserve even so token a greeting from his children? – dispatched to his publishers a study of modernism: *Brahms Our Contemporary*. Here, in his home on the island of Karponisi, Brahms seemed a trillion miles away.

Although he was neither a musician nor a musicologist, the enigma of Brahms, as an unfulfilled, inhibited and frustrated genius, had haunted him for decades. The fascination with this composer, whose work, he was convinced, predicted and preoccupied much of the *angst* and panic of the twentieth century, had colored his whole life or, more honestly, had brought the monochrome to the surface like a pustule that mirrored the anxiety of the age. It had run parallel to George's work as a literary critic that had earned him his international reputation: the studies – three of them – of John Fowles, on whose work he was acknowledged worldwide as the greatest living expert; shortly, perhaps, to be the greatest dead expert. Working on (and with) Fowles had been a lonely and solitary existence, whereas, with Jessica, there had been a kindred spirit with whom to share his passion for, and obsession with, Brahms. All these identities, all these pasts, no present, little future.

Now, he had risked all his reputation and the éclat that mention of his name occasioned in academic and literary circles, by this one throw on zero, as if he were prepared to toss away all his carefully garnered kudos just to indulge a whim, a gamble on his personal skills with a gesture. *L'enfant abdique son extase.* Although undeniably weighty – the typescript checked in at the post office at three kilos – it could so easily be dismissed by reviewers far more qualified than he. In fact, he had brought to Brahms merely his critical acumen and his subjective insight into the mind of his subject – and, his ear: the ability to hear, within the music, as he had "heard" Fowles's voice within his novels, the true story of modernism, the genealogy of despair.

Up to now, his work had been acclaimed for its objectivity, its refusal to enter into speculation and its insistence that only the facts, based on documentary evidence, were available for interpretation. Now, he had abandoned all pretence at the critic's objectivity and had plunged, fully clothed, into the vortex of subjective, heartfelt professional suicide. There *were* no "facts" – even the symphonies, if read as literature, did not reach him as the novels did. Brahms was a closet coward, hiding far more than he revealed in his 'written' work, terrified, perhaps, that the world would discover, prematurely, what was in store for it, as his music led inexorably towards Mahler, Schoenberg and the world wars. But that is for another day and another chapter.

Today, George Manners remembers confiding his tiredness to a close friend – James Esposito, who had been his only confidant since their days together in college – and James had replied: "But you're not old!" Yes, that may be true, but, especially on an island where many lived well into their nineties, it wasn't difficult to realise that he had only a fraction of the energy of the elderly men and women of Karponisi, who hadn't had to live through the stressful episodes that come from living in the 'real' world, whom the world war and even the civil war had passed by.

For any author, the post-parturition (or was it post-coital?) feeling of having just given birth was a time for either jubilation or despair, and the sense of exhaustion accompanied both sentiments. And, of course, this gnawing apprehension about the fate of the book: first of all, whether it would pass muster with the publishers, and then, how it would be greeted by the critics. George was weighed down with the kind of worry and lassitude that he had not experienced with any of his previous books, and on this day he realized that it wasn't due merely to his relationship with Mr. Brahms, but residual anxieties about his lives with Margaret and his children, with Jessica, especially "the Finnish woman" as he distantly thought of her, because he knew so little about her and therefore there was so much more to think about. But he couldn't even remember her name. It had been a one-night "wham bam thankyou ma'am" sort of night.

It was as if all the ghosts of his past – many of them still doing what ghosts are not supposed to do, screaming and kicking – were making their way up the hillside from Karponisi's tiny harbor, where the weekly ferry had just docked, ready to smash down his door and demand a proper place in his book-strewn life.

Finnish? George was finished. He had gradually closed down all the exits that had allowed him to escape from one hell-hole to another: Woodlawn, academe, marriage, family life, even fame of a sort, until today here he was, in the waiting-room-for-death, with everything shut down except, of course, authorship. Because of his medical history, not even a drop of alcohol was permitted to endanger his already fragile liver. He had closed a door on that, too. So, only authorship remained. Why? The compulsive writing that every writer dreads every morning of his life, which will never let go. Once you are a writer, of any kind – poet, novelist, historian, critic, or the anonymous source that George became in his 'dispatches' to an equally anonymous destination in, he supposed, Whitehall – all these preoccupations take over, and become the life itself. Of course. A course set not by him but for him, by who knows what malevolent power. Today George, despite having written his last book – or so he had proclaimed to anyone willing to listen, most of whom had replied derisively that it was unthinkable and out of character that he would ever stop writing – remained obsessed with the problem, the near impossibility, of self-expression. After four books, published at steady intervals during his totally unspectacular university career, and now this thing on Brahms, he had nothing more to say, yet knew that he had no choice but to go on saying it.

Was he simply a silly old man, refusing to quit while he was still ahead? – making the same mistake as his namesake George Steiner, persisting in churning out work of increasingly unconvincing and uninteresting *ennui*, merely for the self-congratulatory tone of "I'm still here! I still have something to say! – well, almost," without in fact knowing what it was he wanted to say or, indeed, how to say it.

The books on Fowles, designed to explore his works and then to explain them to a wider audience which, thanks to the university reading lists on his set courses, would reach, at the most, a few thousand readers over their (the books') lifetime, had appeared over a twenty-year period, after assiduous research in libraries as disparate as Monaco, the British Library, Exeter, Spetses and – horror of horrors – Austin, Texas and, even worse, Tulsa, Oklahoma. Fowles, up to his death in 2005, had been a personal friend, even though his reticence meant that he seldom made explicit confessions to George and, like Brahms, had remained an enigma, so much so that, by way of farewell to his friend, George had, somewhat unwisely perhaps, entitled the last volume *The Enigma of John Fowles.* But by that time Fowles was dead and, whereas he had read and, according to his own admission, enjoyed George's first two books, *An Introduction to John Fowles* and – predictably the most acclaimed of the three – *Sexuality and the Double in the Work of John Fowles,* he was beyond both reticence and the right of reply. And he would have been saddened, even shocked, by that book. How he would have regarded George as having betrayed their friendship with his revelations about his character!

But wasn't that what George did, also, in his spy 'dispatches' – betrayed his friends, his ideas, his country perhaps? Why should Fowles be any different?

As he looked down from his library window to the harbor of Karponisi, sheltered by its walls like the claws of a scorpion, George knew that in a sense tiredness was no disability: it signalled a finale, a sense of completion. His body had already been destroyed by alcoholism, so much so that if his constitution survived another bout of heavy drinking (and now, *all* drink was forbidden, absolutely out of bounds) it would be a miracle. He was in sight of a welcome terminus, but still not yet ready to get off the train he had carefully constructed to get him this far and to footle around for, perhaps, a few more years of idleness – except for the "dispatches," of course.

There was no point in complaining of tiredness, either to the island doctor (who spoke excellent English and was a superb diagnostician) or to the retired English psychiatrist who lived nearby, who might in earlier days have provided some sort of guidance as to where his single-mindedness was leading.

Yes, he was drained of energy, both physical and intellectual. But, much more fundamentally, he was drained of meaning and hope – those two elements without which man cannot live. Woman, maybe. Man, not. It wouldn't be accurate to say he was demoralized because he had never had either morals or morale.

He had spent all his life making sense of other people, Fowles especially, finding *their* meaning, but, now he realized, never his own. And as for hope, it just didn't arise as a factor in his present life. A man devoid of meaning is a man of no qualities, a cipher. In his case, a conduit for the ideas of Walter Pater, Fowles, Brahms, and all that was left now was making sense of the world's puzzles and dichotomies in his 'dispatches' – those letters from the watchtower of his desk which might, for all his recipients knew, be a mixture of fact and fiction, or even pure fiction. Pure speculation, in any case, which its recipients referred to as 'insight.' Like his own unfulfilled life. His life without meaning, without hope, without insight. One would be fine without the other – meaning *or* hope, hope *or* meaning, but to have neither, or to have lost both, looked like carelessness. George called it "sperectomy" – the excision of hope; a hope that had definitely been there, but had been cut out by some psychosurgeon intent on reducing him to a state of *nihil*.

He recalled that as a teenager he had met someone his own age – a farm labourer's son on the Woodlawn estate – who had asked "Wot's the poin' of anyfink? Nuffink" – a true *fainéant*. But it had taken him fifty years to work out that it was as true for him today as it had been for that forlorn teenager all those years ago. And, if he had thought about it at the time, for him too. But at the time he had thought – well, he may have nothing, or nuffink, to look forward to, but, with the family heritage and his public school background, and just off to uni, he had had evryfink to look forward to. That great adolescent adventure into the unknown. He would go far. Now, he knew differently.

Given its tiny size, you couldn't go very far on the island, but some of the sea-views from the cliff tops, and the focus in the narrow, central valley, were exhilarating and challenged his sense of humanity. George recalled what Fowles had written about the neighboring island of Spetses, and even more so about his ascent of Mount Parnassus, that the landscape afforded the solitary walker an almost mystical experience, of being 'in touch' with some otherness that was somehow no longer available in the modern, mechanized, over-populated world. Isolation – again, that sense of being an island – could offer that mystical experience.

The mail boat from the mainland was nosing into the harbor and preparing to tether at the quayside. It was early days yet for his publishers to be sending back queries on the Brahms book, and it would be several months before the bulky package of page proofs would arrive. Yet every week, the anticipation of some contact from the outside world kept George, and one or two of the island's other foreign residents, alert to the fact that there was, indeed, another, very different, world out there – one on which they had turned their backs for whatever personal reasons they may have had; and while they may all have had the island in common, they were divided by the fact that each had his or her own reasons for becoming a refugee from their previous worlds.

As far as his publishers were concerned, they had tried

to resist his insistence on page proofs, but they had had to capitulate. No proofs, no book, he had declared. Almost all proofs these days were sent, and returned, electronically, by internet, but George had successfully stopped this on the grounds that, although he could use a computer as a word-processor, the internet and everything to do with it remained a sinister labyrinth into which he refused to be drawn. As a boy he had read Forster's story 'The Machine Stops," and had taken completely to heart the idea that the world would become totally subject to the internet for all communication and, indeed, sustenance of every kind, and that it would eventually collapse, taking mankind with it. So it was actually a childhood phobia, like the fear of snakes or needles that formed his early revulsion at the thought of what the internet could do to him.

He did have a phone in his house – a landline – which was seldom used. He never phoned out, and incoming calls were limited to the weekly chats with Vicky and Al – one on a Saturday, the other on Sundays. During his 'Russian affair' Aleksandra had pestered him until he threatened that if she persisted he would go completely incommunicado and have the thing disconnected. In fact he had changed the number with OTE, the telephone company, and only Vicky, Al and James, knew the new number. If Margaret wanted to phone, she could get the number from Vicky or Al. His 'masters' or 'minders' or 'control' in Whitehall, or whatever or whoever they were, did not need to know it. Jessica, he now realized, would never call him.

So it was that George Manners lived a limbo, suspended almost literally on his cliff top between sky and sea, and figuratively between a life on which one could only look back in some trepidation and a future which hardly existed at all.

How could one live in trepidation of the past? Because

memory – that unoriginal sin with which we are all cursed – dredged up all the detritus of his failures with three women, and his well-deserved sense of his shortcomings as a father. About his university career he had no regrets, no nightmares, no sense of guilt. He had done his job, keeping up the college's reputation for research while providing some form of education for oiks who were born with two ears only so that the gems of academic wisdom could go in one and out the other. It was as a person – and in this, perhaps because of his enduring relationship with his father, who had died over forty years ago, he included the fact of being a writer – that the gong of memory rang false, created and stimulated the sense of worthlessness.

What, in the three books on Fowles, had he achieved that could possibly survive even one generation of readership... if there were readers at all? What could any reader – even the most studious of students – find in those books that was in any way more enlightening, or rewarding, than reading Fowles himself – his novels, essays and journals? It's true that he himself, George, had had to acknowledge that the later Fowles was a disappointment compared to the early work: a prick-tease like *A Maggot* could not hold a candle to *The Collector*, *The Magus* or *The French Lieutenant's Woman*, novels which were assured of their place as great works of the twentieth century, great explorations of truth and untruth, fiction and reality, time and space. So he had been expected to make a brave effort to be pro-Fowles in that last book, making a case, in which he did not really believe, for *Daniel Martin* and *A Maggot* and doing it not very convincingly, he had thought then and he thought now. Among the later work, he regarded only *Mantissa* as having any lasting merit, and that probably because it gave him an intellectual, as well as a sexual, thrill. Not a bad combination. But in this last book he had succumbed to the terrible temptation to tell the truth, a quality feared by novelists as much as any 'normal' person, a storytelling as accurate as a camera, exposing Fowles's weaknesses, not least the mess of his private life.

But otherwise, the academic life had, however humdrum, been unremarkable as far as mistakes were concerned (except for the early *faux pas* that had nearly cost him his career and sent him to the salt mines of Scunthorpe) and so he had no regrets. Recurring nightmares he had aplenty on the other parts of life. The festering memory of the break-up with Margaret, the long, rewarding partnership with Jessica, the fact that, like his own father, if in a different way, he had been absent for Vicky and Al, and never there at all for 'the Finnish girl' as he called her, all had their catastrophes which returned to admonish him on a regular basis. In this sense, the island was no escape route to amnesia, and he had never expected it to be such. But it did enable him to shut certain doors that need never be opened again.

Were there recurring dreams? In some ways, escapees to an island dream constantly of what life might offer, rather than seizing the day and actually diving into the dream as one would dive into a swimming-pool (if one had been sufficiently bourgeois to install one). The island itself was, of course, a dream. But yes, George did have recurring dreams, dreams that he knew could never be realized, not only because there was so little time left to him, but because with sperectomy had come the inability to follow the dream. Dreams required faith, a need to be fulfilled, whatever the consequences. George had long ago ceased to care one way or the other. But he still dreamed.

We are tragic cowards, he wrote in his diary. He was thinking of the ways in which people respond to the calamities, catastrophes, upheavals in their lives which go commonly under the name of "tragedy." The big ones were easy to understand – death of a loved one, marriage break-up (or -down), getting the sack – and what people did in the wake of those enormous milestones was completely understandable.

But there were also what he called "quiet tragedies." He was sure that Thoreau's idea of people leading "lives of quiet desperation" applied to those who had become aware of the mundanity, the emptiness, the pointlessness, the lack of meaning in their lives and relationships. They were the most likely to take a savage revenge and to move out of an impossible situation into one which, however challenging and seemingly dangerous, offered them some chance of survival through discovering, and being, themselves. There may not have been any violence, any sudden imposition of a cruel fate; merely a recognition that life has not exactly been a comedy. So they embarked on the journey. They started to move beyond those quiet tragedies. And in noting these thoughts in his diary, George was thinking of his own jump into the known unknown of Karponisi. And behind that thinking also lay the notion that, while it had not happened in his own case, many of his contemporaries, in the generations coming after the Cambridge spy group, had had that Damascan revelation that they had undergone a hurtful period for which the future would be a search for compensation. It would haunt him all the way through his own recruitment to 'Whitehall' and his subsequent reflection on the nature of betrayal, in men he knew and, he suspected, in the case of Margaret.

In his diary he wrote: *Few, of course, have the courage to make that journey into the unknown, but they do so in response to the quiet tragedy that up to that point had determined the course – or lack of it – of their lives. Aut tunc, aut nunquam – it was "then or never" – wrote Petronius in his Satyricon. To defy the odds, to jump, to*

135

throw away the givens in exchange for what one might make of oneself. There is an even more troubling journey, for example when Lawrence Durrell told a journalist "Je suis un refugié de moi-même," a flight not only from the source of tragedy but also from the self, a flight in which one carries both the tragedy and the self within: a seemingly insoluble dilemma which in his case remained unresolved. We are so troubled by the "ordinary" frustrations of life that we have reached a point where they can no longer be tolerated. We have reached a caesura, a point beyond which life must be lived according to different measures. One thinks, at various stages of life – such as the milestones of college graduation, one's first job, marriage, the births of children, one's first published work – that these cardinal episodes have a meaning that is intimately associated with freedom, whereas the more jaundiced among us will masochistically say that they are, more likely, inhibitions on one's freedom. The Greek expression "the full catastrophe," of marriage, children and a house, brilliantly placed by Nikos Kazantzakis in the mouth of Alexis Zorba, expresses what most westerners would recognise in their mortgage, the school fees, the skiing holiday, the time-share in Marbella, the weekly trip to the shopping centre, mowing the lawn, and changing the car every two years. Forty years between one home (Woodlawn) and another (Karponisi) seems a strange way to live one's life. In retrospect that's the way it seems from where I sit today.

He had in common with these refugees the fact that like them he was not running away from something but running towards it. He was, like them, in revolt and despair. A world-renowned critic, in revolt and despair, with neither hope nor meaning. And, in Karponisi, he hadn't found it. Perhaps some of his own restlessness had been a subconscious response to what he saw all around him as the pointlessness not only of academic life but of most forms of life in Britain, where a combination of vile Thatcherism, followed by an equally vile succession of spineless Labour governments, had made most people's lives unbearable. He was lucky in that he had the courage and capacity to quit, an alternative life to go to. Life?

It was not due to a lack of purpose that George had walked away from university and come to the island, nor had he been 'driven' there by supervening forces. He had made no conscious decision and, as far as he was aware, it was entirely his. And yet...

He looked at it again, asking himself "But who was 'I'?" *One's relationships with lovers, children, books, friends and associates suggest more questions than can be answered, questions about honesty, responsibility, knowledge of them and knowledge of oneself that, in a case like his, make one uneasy and, ultimately, unable to co-exist with them unless one sets a distance between them and oneself. It needn't be a huge physical distance, but a space needs to be inserted between the real and the imagined selves until they can be satisfactorily accommodated within the same test-tube.*

And so, in his journal, George came to examine the odyssey that had brought him here: *All journeys – whatever their apparent purpose – are journeys in search of the self, including the journeys we undertake when we set out to write a book. And all journeys are potential exiles, all departures a leaving behind of one part of the self, all arrivals a part of renaissance, of rediscovery. To leave 'home' is to seek "home," or a clearer understanding of what "home" is, or might be. The flight from our background is also a flight towards a place which may be known or unknown. The cardinal point about our destination, known or unknown, is that it is irreducibly* different. *It may offer the possibility of accommodating us, as that previous background had not. A foreground, a prospect, another chance at "home." Samuel Beckett wrote of life as "a setting out without the coming home," and, for those who have made an irrevocable leap, the limbo between two homes may be the best for which we can hope. To step outside one's known world – whether it is a safe and accommodating world or a harsh and threatening one – is to become an exile. For the writer, life, as I have always known, is permanently exilic, so that the journey away from 'home' is always known. It is not necessary for the writer to go consciously into exile, because he is already there: the writer-as-exile is a mismatch between himself and society, and indeed a mismatch between himself and himself. A writer lives always at the border: he can never go back, and the next step is a permanent adventure into the unknown. And when you reach a border that you don't want to cross, someone, something, call it "fate," kicks you up the arse and propels you, however unwillingly, across the next no-man's-land towards the next set of puzzles and problems. The writer lives between the written and the unwritten, the one a source of dissatisfaction, the other a source of wonder, apprehension and fear. For some exiles, those who have made the irreversible journey outward, the sense of not belonging predominates. For those who proceed towards a goal, there is the chance of belonging again. For the writer, neither of these experiences is available. He has never belonged, and he will never belong. He is the ultimate* xenos, *the stranger who is also the guest.*

George, reading this in Karponisi after the Aleksandra débâcle, had thought: "I have had family at Woodlawn, and family with Margaret (god knows about Pirkko-Liisa), and the adopted family of academe, and in all of these I have been a stranger, a sovereign ghost."

Footloose exiles may develop the art of not belonging. To the writer, it comes naturally – in fact, it may be the only natural condition of which he is capable. So the exile learns to be at home in exile. Thenceforth, he is at home only with and to himself. All else is elsewhere. The exile has abandoned 'real' life. One is effectively abandoning, saying farewell to, loving and belonging, in order to attempt peace with oneself.

This is why he had been able to turn his back on the life he had known up to that point. Rewrite that: this is why he had been pushed into an unknown life. Margaret hadn't left him. He had left Margaret. Jessica hadn't walked out on him for another man; he had abandoned life with Jessica in order to embrace another ... idea, another ... anxiety. And he didn't even begin to understand the word 'farewell.'

What is a secret? A secret is a dark space that punctuates the process of transition from private ritual to public drama. In all societies, individuals, groups and ideas are carried across from the inner to the outer worlds. Making manifest a hidden truth is to bring together the unseen and the public worlds, to create an identity for one and all. And a secret can either facilitate or impede that transitus. When we try to cross a threshold – into a new house, a new life, a new relationship, a new set of ideas – the success or failure of the movement will depend on whether the secret which empowers that movement can be spoken, whether we have the skill to speak it and whether it is ready to be spoken. It is this problem of speech, involving self-knowledge, honesty and relations with others, that bedevils all our journeys. We stutter our way towards freedom.

A secret may be a very tiny fragment of reality – or

unreality — but its meaning can vastly exceed its significance as a mere fact. Most people with a secret have a dread of discovery. If the discovery can lead to the healing of lesions, it will be welcomed and the dread can be overcome, but the fear of exposure, of ridicule, of exclusion, of being found to harbor a secret thing, makes most keep silent. I have no such fear.

Oh, wasn't he the intrepid voyager, with, deep inside, an abiding admission that he did, indeed, know fear, that it was fear that fuelled his flight, that the secret thing would undo him, as it had come close to doing with Jessica and would come dangerously close during his short liaison with Aleksandra. His secrets began with his childhood fears and nightmares, never divulged, not even to himself or Nanny Conneely; secrets from his second life, an intimate life with Margaret and then Jessica; and the secret of his work in "dispatches," beside which the others were open secrets. And his early life-secret, the hushed-up one.

He recalled that in Evelyn Waugh's *Brideshead Revisited* the character Charles Ryder speaks of finding 'that low door in the wall that others, I knew, had found before me, which opened on an enclosed and enchanted garden.' Reflecting on this, George wrote: *I think we all seek the discovery and the security of a 'paradise' that is no longer lost, that has somehow been restored to us, that we are now safe in that enchanted garden, the* hortus conclusus, *even though it may contain beasts other than ourselves, and challenges to our identity which we could not previously have imagined.*

He had done the right thing in choosing the walled garden of Karponisi, rather than the cosmopolitan Spetses or the multicultural Corfu. A smaller, less significant island with less character, a lesser name, less enchanting, perhaps, was the answer, the necessary test-tube.

The diary continued: *The twin questions, which maybe will evolve into simultaneous equations, if answers to them can be found, are: Who am I? What is this island? And of course 'what do they have to do with one another?' The journey and the secret become one.*

II
Woodlawn

George was born in the family home, Woodlawn, which had been built by his great-great-great-great-great-grandfather in the early 1700s after the family – the Dukes of Rutland – split in consequence of a rift which sealed the fate of a younger brother and created the Woodlawn inheritance. His mother had died within a year of his birth – of "complications," the nature of which were never explained to him, except that Uncle David used to joke, playfully and not at all maliciously, that he, George, had been the complication. He even said, many years later, that her death certificate should have read: 'Cause of Death: George, followed by complications." It was the only unkind, unthinking words he ever spoke. Then there was Nanny Conneely, who had come initially to nurse his mother who, he later discovered, had been Irish. Nanny came from the same part of Ireland as his mother, Connemara. She supervized his childhood and adolescence. She was his mother.

His father, Henry, was a historian, obsessed with family history, which was unfortunate for him as he had no one with whom to share his enthusiasm. No one in the family except him had the slightest interest in history. In fact Henry's grandfather had once written to his distant cousin, the seventh duke of Rutland, claiming relationship and asking some detail of their common ancestor, the ninth earl who had become the first duke, and had received a grudging reply which told him, politely but emphatically, to bugger off.

Uncle David, Henry's younger brother, used to say

that their grandfather had been passionate about the past, and could tell you the seed, breed and generation of most people in the county. "He could even tell you who was your real father" David once announced to a startled neighbor. Well, it was all part of the agricultural mind.

For the main branch of the Manners family, their life centred almost exclusively on Belvoir Castle which they had occupied since the early sixteenth century. It wasn't in fact in Rutland at all, but in the neighboring county of Leicestershire. (Uncle David had joked that there wasn't much kudos attached to being a duke in England's smallest county, especially when there probably wasn't enough to provide the Manners with all the land they needed – 15,000 acres just for the main part of the castle demesne at Belvoir.)

It was at the point when the ninth earl got his promotion to a dukedom (as a *mari complaisant* for facilitating the King in access to the ninth countess) that he had kicked out his younger brother, Arthur, ostensibly because Arthur had become a Catholic. In the early 1700s, just after the emphasis on Protestantism had been incorporated into the central tenets of the British way of life, being a Catholic was not a popular option, and Arthur had done it in order to marry a Catholic heiress, Charlotte Gainsborough. Luckily for the family, their children had shown no serious adherence to any form of religion, and had lapsed back into the Church of England.

Arthur and Charlotte had been given a handsome pay-off by the duke, on condition that they never darken his doorstep again, and, together with Charlotte's family fortune, they had been more than rich. And they had been if not thrifty, then not prodigal either, and the family wealth had come down to successive generations, along with the house that they had built at Woodlawn, an estate of a few hundred acres in the western part of Norfolk, which, like their wealth, had remained intact and to which Arthur had taken with gusto as a hands-on gentleman farmer. They might have built the house in the 'Queen Anne' style, or an early Georgian mansion, but, for reasons their descendants never knew, they had chosen something much more modest – a long, low house suitable for a farmer rather than a lord, with extensive outbuildings appropriate to its status. They had become major employers in the area, breeding horses and sheep, but the main element in the farm economy in recent decades had been the dairy herd.

In later generations the enthusiasm for farming had diminished so much that the head of the junior Manners had eventually employed a farm manager and, later still, appointed someone who, effectively, took the business out of their hands and simply delivered a bi-annual account and a share of the profits, pocketing his own considerable share which he had earned by contract: a lieutenant.

This suited George's father, who had no interest whatsoever in milking cows or even in the excitement of the turf which went with the business of breeding horses, even though he remained an *ex officio* patron of the local hunt and owned racehorses for which the lieutenant was responsible. He, Henry, was always sequestered in his study. He was utterly joyless. When George passed into adulthood, he saw a dramatization of *Brideshead Revisited* with John Gielgud playing Charles Ryder's father; it would have been a perfect caricature of his own father, if Henry Manners had had an ounce of humanity, but Henry made Gielgud look like a lively, compassionate, with-it barrel of laughs. He even had his meals served in his library, so that he was seldom seen around the house.

Almost his only contact with the household was to scrutinise the accounts with which (suitably doctored) his steward presented him every quarter. The only occasion on which anyone could recall Henry Manners having said anything relevant was when he queried expenditure on an item listed as 'Milton.' Thinking it must have something to do with the great poet, he could (and quite rightly) make no connection between the author of *Paradise Lost* and his accounts. Had someone been making regular purchases – and, as a miser, he regarded them as extravagant – of books of poetry? And if so, where were the volumes to be found? He was little less enlightened when he it was explained that the item in question referred to nursery expenses for Master George. A bit soon for the boy to be reading – he was, what? (he consulted his family history) about two or three years old. Nanny Conneely explained it was for sterilisation. "Would have thought he was too young for that, too" was Henry's reply. "Must talk to the boy when he grows up."

Writing was a confessional life. But old Henry Manners must have had nothing to confess, since he never published anything in the course of his studies, except, in *Proceedings of the West Norfolk Antiquarian Society* vol. xlvii, a slim account of the building of Woodlawn and his ancestors' custodianship of it, down to the time of his own grandfather, who had died at the end of the century (it might as well have been the eighteenth, although rumour had it that it was around 1900) having, in his turn, achieved absolutely nothing during a long life. In fact this branch of the Manners family had almost nothing to redeem it from utter obscurity until George became a world-renowned critic – but by that time his father was in the family mausoleum on the Woodlawn estate.

He had once spotted his father emerging from his study and had tried to engage him in conversation – anything more elevated than "Good morning, Father," "Good morning, er, George" would have been a major breakthrough for the communication skills of the human race. He wanted so much to tell his father about his plans for his thesis (surely a nineteenth-century subject would have been acceptable as a talking-point, as long as he didn't let on about Pater's "inclinations"); he wanted, god dammit, to get some words of meaning, of understanding, of *love* out of the old man. He stood at the study door. "May I please come in? We have much to talk about, Father." The door shut in his face, silently and without response. He never saw his father again.

So Henry was a remote figure for everyone, especially for the motherless George, who was practically an orphan. And yet George had followed his father into the practice of writing. Not that old Henry took the slightest interest in his son's ambition, since he was utterly contemptuous of modern literature. His father died while George was still studying in Dublin, preparing for his post-grad. It was some time before anyone noticed.

Because George's mother had died so young, he never had to witness any relations between his parents. As an only child, he could neither bully, nor be bullied by, his siblings. And his father was a sovereign ghost. His life consisted of Nanny Conneely and his Uncle David, which meant a happy childhood. Not an insecure or miserable one. Nothing, in fact, in his background pointed towards the writer living out the traumas of childhood. Until, that is, his assignments in 'Intelligence' liberated traumas that he had hardly suspected to exist. But in another sense, George had had no childhood. In later years he would think that he had been robbed of it by his mother's death and his father's negligence. Nanny Conneely was the only parenting he had ever known.

And yet George, like many writers before and since, was not secure or happy. If he had been, he would not have become a writer. It had to be ideas, since he had almost no personal feelings worth writing about. Not a novelist, then, nor a poet. He couldn't have written an *Oedipus* to save his life, because he had never known his mother, so he could never have said, as all little boys do, who come from normally abnormal families, "When I grow up, I'm going to marry Mummy." And because his father was so uninteresting, he couldn't feel any patricidal longings. No one wants to kill a bore.

George didn't have any feelings until he got to Dublin, at the age of eighteen, and discovered that the world consisted of other, real, people, with bodies and emotions and feelings and securities and insecurities and alcohol and nicotine and bodies and bodies ...

The sole redeeming element in George's family was Uncle David, who would later take over the running of Woodlawn and, in his turn, pass it on to his son, Alex, George's one and only cousin. George would have preferred to live with his uncle, who had married Elvira Tollemache, a woman as unorthodox as himself, a relic of some family equally as ancient as the Manners, and she looked it. But that option was not open to a one-year-old, despite David's sincere offer of a home with affection which Henry Manners could never offer the boy. His childhood was in fact worse than being orphaned, even though David's much-anticipated visits, which were, thankfully, frequent, brought life and love and laughter into the mausoleum that Woodlawn otherwise resembled.

When, in the course of his career, he moved from Leeds to Lincoln, George was staying very approximately in the same 'neck of the woods' as Woodlawn. He enjoyed the occasional visits, sometimes with M, more often alone, since M didn't really get on very well with Uncle David. After D's death, things were different. The property passed to D's son, Alex, the same age as George but without any of George's interests and without D's sense of humour.

Alex was committed to making a go of the estate,

'small changes' as he put it, rather vaguely. But even if he had decided to turn Woodlawn into a safari park or a Disneyland, there was nothing George could have done about it – nor cared, if he thought about it at all, which he didn't. Alex, in fact, had developed the place very intelligently, not to say imaginatively, turning the bloodstock side into a riding school that rapidly became a huge success in the region. But on one subject Alex was adamant. He had no interest whatever in the library and no intention of retaining it, so, to prevent it being sold, and, as George later realized, to give himself the excuse that he still carried the corpse of his father on his back, he agreed to take it over and install it in the house in Karponisi.

The death – at a much later date – of Uncle David affected him far more severely than that of his father. Henry had been an absence, a silence, in his life that, after one half-hearted attempt, he had never tried to explore. David, on the other hand, was a lively presence: even when he wasn't there, he was there. When he died, a light went out of George's life. The cliché was "a great tree has fallen," but, if he had heard that, D would have produced a string of deletable expletives that would have sent a nunnery – and a nunnery dedicated to blasphemy, at that – into terminal shock. But that was the measure of the man. A legend in his own lunchtime. Equally at home in a palace or a brothel. George once told D that he'd read a piece in *Private Eye* about a visit to a strip-club; an old man sat in a corner, tears streaming down his face, shouting 'Huge!' There was a pause. An apologetic cough from D and a slightly sheepish look that was unusual for him. "That was me, old chap. But you won't tell your aunt, of course – ha ha."

George grieved for David as he had never grieved for his father. It was David who had taught him his first 'naughty' rhymes: "Little boy stands in front of the loo. Old man's showing him what to do. Splish, splash, into the tank, Christopher Robin is learning to wank. Ha ha." Later he would add, rather more sagely: "self-abuse isn't the worst, my dear George: abusing others is far more culpable."

Many writers on psychology stress the importance of "keeping in touch with the child within" – but what if there is no child within? Someone writes in a novel of a character lacking 'a properly constituted childhood.' Childhood did not happen to me in the way that a "properly constituted childhood" should happen – at least, in one's imagination. If childhood is not "properly constituted," it gives rise to a "buried hunger," the novelist says. That, when I read it, immediately struck me as a definition of the absence of my young life. An emotional void? An emotional impasse? No one writes about a happy childhood, or if they do, they are lying. Perhaps I should settle for the idea that, on the day I was born, I got out of bed on the wrong side, and I've been trying to find the right side ever since. Most of us, at some stage in our lives, like to imagine that we are schizophrenic, that there are two of us. I myself am quite convinced that there are in fact three selves: the me in the world, the me at variance with myself, and the between-me, the me-as-if whom we are trying to become. I was far into my life before I realized that, in Rimbaud's "Je est un autre," there are three beings. The third self is the elusive character who may hold the answers to the continual dialogue between self and self, between self and world. And we may not be a person in our own right until that third self is apprehended, comprehended and occupied. Without him or her, there will always be a certain sense of unreality, of not having really lived.

But in another sense he had never left childhood: he

had locked himself away in a world where he could keep at bay the insecurity; it had driven him into isolation, the world of books becoming his escape valve and his make-believe. Access to modern novels was difficult, since his father, while not prohibiting them, would never countenance their purchase out of George's meagre pocket-money. So childhood reading, much of which was directed from a distance by his father through the conduit of Nanny Conneely – perhaps the only caring act his father had ever undertaken towards him – consisted of Scott and other historical romances of which there was paternal approval. "Begob, Master George," Nanny would complain, "Here's another of them Scott things. How you can read all that Scottish guff I don't know, when you have your mother's Ireland to read your way through." Even Jane Austen was grudgingly admitted to the highly restricted canon of legible authors. Curiosity about "modern" authors made him enquire, only to receive a contemptuous snort: "That stuff? Filth and rubbish, most of it. Russell, Huxley – a disgrace to his family, that chap – and the vile muck dished out by that Lawrence fellow! You won't go near that stuff in my house!"

Because of his father's implacable objection to anything modern, he was left to the mercies of what Uncle David brought along to fill in the gaps, or rather, to embark on the reading that would fuel his life's work. Sherlock Holmes and P.G. Wodehouse in the early years, *Lady Chatterley's Lover, Catcher in the Rye* and *À Rebours* as time went on, or what he could borrow or steal from the local library.

Because the Woodlawn library contained few books published after 1820, and none at all from the twentieth century, these modern authors became his own province, his secret and private territory. It was a world that was his alone, George's world, as sacrosanct as the impenetrable study where his father sat continuously, making pointless notes on a topic on which he would never publish a word. Hidden indeed, for, if his father were to be believed, it would be treason followed by a bonfire to be caught with such a stash of 'filth' and 'rubbish.' So he had to make a hiding-place, far away from his father's eyes, where the reading might be done. Not for him the torch under the bedspread in the long night hours after lights-out. It was as if, in his mind-space, he had a door, locked, to which only he had the key, to which he had affixed a notice: 'Out of Bounds to All Beneath the Rank of George. By Order." Forgive him. He was only five years old.

The fear of being alone, of not being able to buy a book to read or a pen to write with, no sense of belonging, no sense of direction, have made me an emotional orphan, psychotically afraid of travel, of association, of chance. This is my 'fault' – a mismatch between the tectonic plates of my character. I am made of books, not feelings. I am a machine for reading and writing, rather than for living and being a person capable of emotional involvement. George had written this long before he met Jessica Mausch and found his buried self – liberated by her love.

In a later diary he writes: *For decades I believed that I was conceived during the longest night of the year – or, if you like, the shortest day. The dark has always been my enemy. There has never been sufficient light in each day. One thinks of Beckett: 'They give birth astride of a grave, the light gleams an instant, then it's night once more.' I have lived with depression for over sixty years, and I know how to deal with the black dog. Much more pervasive is sheer unhappiness, and it is with that that I find it difficult, if not impossible, to live. Unhappiness, rather than depression, is the condition, akin to bewilderment, which makes it impossible for an individual to function in society. A depressed person can continue to have relations, to perform a job, to write books; an unhappy person cannot relate, cannot find expression, without looking almost compulsively, obsessionally, for compensations. A depressive does not need to look for explanations or escape routes because he knows they do not exist. An unhappy person, especially if the unhappiness has been genetically transmitted, looks for them all the time.*

III

Uncle David

According to Uncle David, who had some slight knowledge of his elder brother, Henry Manners' whole life, if one could call it that, was a craving for recognition by the senior branch of the family. His unpublished – and unpublishable – tome on 'The Manners of Belvoir Translated to Woodlawn' was his mute tribute to the Dukedom and an *apologia* for the lives of the junior Manners since the family split so many generations previously. Because it remained unseen, it received no recognition whatsoever, from his immediate family or from the senior Manners, who remained oblivious to his desire for recognition. Uncle D had without regret decided that such hankering after an irretrievable past was a waste of time, and George, too, had adopted the same realistic attitude: if the junior family was so hopelessly pointless, what benefit could there possibly be in signalling the senior branch to throw it a lifebelt?

George could have legitimately referred to "my cousin, the Duke of Rutland," but he didn't. Uncle D certainly did, but only to take the piss, always following the remark with a disarming smile and "not really, of course."

George's father was humorless. On his rare appearances in the house he had never shown that he even knew what a smile might be. By contrast, his younger brother seemed to do nothing other than to smile disarmingly and to tell jokes. He was never without a joke, a smile or a happy face. In life, George thought, the smile is all.

When Uncle D told a joke, recited a dirty limerick or a

155

bawdy lyric, he never did so in a smutty way. One might almost say that he made such remarks, told such jokes, in a dignified way. The intention was still there – to amuse, to shock, to offend if necessary, but never to cause harm. *Épater les bourgeois* was certainly offensive, it was a way of saying, "I won't be bound by your conventional *mores*, I respect your life but I won't live that way myself, I'll say what I want and as long as it doesn't start a world war or an outbreak of *koro*, I do no harm." A pause. "Actually, a dose of *koro* might do wonders for our over-populated planet, ha ha."

D had a completely idiosyncratic way of adding "ha ha" to almost every remark he made. The fact that most of his remarks were humorous was entirely fortuitous. "Ha ha" wasn't intended to acknowledge that the remark had been a joke, simply a nervous exhalation to indicate that it had ended. But it was generally taken to mean, "I've just made a joke," even if the company couldn't actually see a joke therein, so that if Uncle D happened to greet a newly-widowed woman with the words "Sorry to hear about Freddy, ha ha," it might easily be taken the wrong way.

When the local MP toured the constituency, D was wheeled out as one of the local dignitaries. D took a poor, if not penniless, view of politicians of all persuasions ("Worse than bumboys, if you ask me, ha ha"), but he agreed to be one of the reception parties. It was a great relief that he kept his mouth shut until he met the minister's wife and advised her to "stick your head up a dead bear's bum, ha." "Ha ha" did not, unfortunately, on this occasion, mitigate the offensiveness of the remark, or translate it into a joke from the genuine advice which D had intended – especially when he added "neither of you will be able to tell the difference anyway, ha ha." The wife, of course, smiled inanely at this gratuitous reference to the ursine anus. The story got back to Westminster, where several other wives admitted the appositeness of the remark. Uncle D was never again asked to appear at any such event, which had probably been his motive in voicing the advice in the first place, but, if he had wished it, he could probably have won the seat for the South Park Party at the next election and even found his way to a whoopee cushion in the Cabinet.

You either loved Uncle D for the endearing, sincerely gratuitous gentleman that George saw in him, or you despised him for the insulting degradation that he brought to the civility of a noble family. Or perhaps you were just aghast at his sheer, unabashed outspokenness.

D was frequently given to crude or, one might say, obscene language in the delivery of a joke. But because he spoke his obscenities in such a gentlemanly manner and voice, he never – or only seldom – gave offence. His Limericks were perhaps his strongest line:

> There was a young plumber called Lee
> Who had a young girl by the sea
> Said she: "Cease your plumbing,
> I think someone's coming."
> Said the plumber, still plumbing, "It's me."

Which David, with some assistance from George, could also render in French:

> Il y'avait un jeune plombier d'Artois
> Seduisa une jeune fille dans le bois
> Dit-elle "Quitte mes reins,
> Quelqu'un vient."
> Dit le plombier, encore plombant, "C'est moi."

Even George sometimes wondered how he could tolerate D's crudity, especially when it became too coarse.

The family was well accustomed to his "fuck," "bollox" or "arse," but drew the line at "cunt," especially when he used it not in connection with the vagina but in relation to people he didn't like. "He's a ... he's a ... he's a *cunt!*" he would say, after due deliberation; it was his way of saying "he's not a gentleman" but it never occurred to him that by calling a man a "cunt" he was in any way diminishing his own gentleman status.

Once, his long-suffering (but, as she was so ugly and boring that she seemed it) wife got up the courage to say "How can a man be a cunt?" The room went silent. Well, it only contained D, Elvira herself, their son and George. The silence suggested that, by asking the question, Elvira had forfeited her right to be a lady, rather than questioning D's own honor.

Uncle D was never vulgar. "Manners makyth man," he punned on the family name, adding naughtily "And a few women, what? Ha ha." It was probably because most of the family disapproved of D (a "black sheep") that George had a great affection for him.

D even subscribed to a charity which he jokingly referred to as "a hostel for disused nuns – or is it diseased nuns? Anyway, they're all the same – dicky-dodgers the lot of them, ha ha." George never actually discovered who the beneficiaries of this charity were, but he was sure that it was a worthwhile cause. Otherwise this outwardly facetious and iconoclastic man who peppered his talk with words like "niggers," "wops," "bolshies" and other terms of endearment would not have committed any sum of money, however derisory. It was well meant, as was everything Uncle D did in life – or, it turned out, in death.

David was the innocent child who George had never been able, or allowed, to become. Just to *be*. To greet the day with a smile, knowing that, whatever the day might bring, at its end the smile would still be there. D could be serious, of course, but he wore it lightly, so much so that many people thought he was merely a buffoon. When D did, on rare occasions, speak seriously, George realized that the jocund exterior was not his true self, but a mask, beneath which was a man who felt deeply about the world but knew that there was nothing he could do about it, and had therefore adopted this mask as a means of getting through life less scathed than he might otherwise have been.

D wasn't in the slightest snooty, as his disparaging remarks about the senior Manners had proved. But he *was* a snob. When he declared "Oh, my god, *very* NQOCD!" everyone wondered what on earth the initials could represent. "Never question our colleagues, duckie?" "Normally quiet on Christmas Day?" "Normal quota of clumsy dwarfs?" – that one made D chuckle. One of those present suggested "Nice quietus of consenting death" – to which D responded "Thinking of topping yourself, are you?" "Nifty queer or cunt-dodger" provoked a "Knew a few of them in my time. No hard feelings, ha ha." But the real meaning, when D consented to divulge it, was "Not Quite Our Class, Dear." And everyone took it from there until, if you disapproved of anyone, for any reason, you simply turned to your neighbor and whispered – or, perhaps, shouted out – 'NQOCD!'

He once dressed in his wife's clothes and went into his local pub, a traditional, village-green free house which had been gentrified into "Ye Olde Widdershin" and demanded, in an old-school tone of voice, "My good man, a jug of your best wallop, and chop-chop." When threatened with eviction, he retorted "Is this how you treat a lady? A lady impersonator? You, who impersonate a proper landlord with your striped weskit and demmed Cockney throat disease?" When the local plod was summoned, he merely, and respectfully, asked Uncle D to go home and get changed, and warned the startled publican that not only had he offended the lord of the manor but had broken the "Freedom of Impersonation Act."

When George came to live on the fringes of espionage, he thought how easily David could have done it, fooling everyone with his apparent nonchalance and irresponsibility, but inside, a shrewd and contemplative man. Short of being gay, D filled the stereotypical image of the perfect spy, the outer and the inner man. Something of the Scarlet Pimpernel about him – a fop who could suddenly become the man of action, a man who seemed to live entirely for pleasure and the *mot injuste*, but was really a man of principles.

Largely uneducated (since reading was hardly encouraged by his and Henry's fox-hunting father), D was, like his brother, sublimely ignorant of most literary figures. But in his case he cared, whereas Henry had turned his back on it all. D had heard of Dickens, but he thought Trollope was a whore, and if others could recite the "Charge of the Light Brigade" or Kipling's "If," or other rousing jingoistic ditties, he was more at home with "Eskimo Nell"; he'd never heard of "The Ballad of Reading Gaol," but he was thoroughly familiar with "The Ball of Kerrymuir," which he considered "a fine poem," superior in most ways to what they had tried to inculcate at the school which he had left as soon as possible.

Some of Uncle D's malapropisms were pure mischief. Only a joker, and a crude one at that, could come out with the expression "Put the catamite among the stoolpigeons, ha ha." And he had failed to master even the most elementary aspects of foreign languages. No one was ever sure about David's knowledge of French. He seemed to think that *suivez la piste* meant "follow that drunken woman" which, on reflection, George thought was not entirely wide of the mark. And, again, when he referred to

Keats's *La Belle Dame sans Merci* as "yet another ungrateful woman." And he scored highly on George's Davi-scale with his offhand translation of *"Je deviens immortel dans tes bras"* – "I could live forever in your underwear."

But he was not devoid of a flirtation with his own language – that is, his version of English. He insisted that a bastard was "born out of bedlock," rather than "wedlock." "It's obviously wrong. The place was bed, the ahem was locked, the deed was done. Wedlock be damned." Similarly he loved the word "bed-raggled" – "So she was raggled, was she? Well raggled? In whose bed, ha ha?" He would never have accepted "intercourse" as a polite version of "fucking"; intercourse was something that happened between the soup and the fish, or between the beef and the pudding – and often did. As for "liposuction," D hit the roof – "just be honest and call it a blow job, dear boy – ha ha."

Once he'd been buttonholed by some feminist who shouted: "Why is a woman's world dominated by men? *Men*struation; *men*opause; *guy*nacology; *his*terectomy. Huh?" To which D had instantly retorted *"Her*pes, m'dear. *Her*pes."

When he heard the word "transvestite," having no idea whatever what it meant, he thought he had heard "a tramp's vest," and wondered why the cabinet minister who had been thus outed should want to wear such a thing – and where had he acquired it? In a shop? or from a tramp? And when one of the distant cousins had been appointed to a senior post at Cambridge, D genuinely believed that Albert Manners was "Professor of Morbid Theology."

One of D's ideas might have taken him far – even as far as Hollywood – if the circumstances had been more favorable. He had a bee in his bonnet about St Paul – Saul of Tarsus – the gamekeeper-turned-poacher who gave up collecting taxes and went over to the Christians, who didn't. Paul, as everyone knows, had written many "epistles" to people like the Ephesians, Corinthians, even the Romans. But, as D pointed out one day, he never got any answers. D's idea was a book which would include the real epistles and the answers the Ephesians etcetera might have written: "Bugger off and let us lead our own lives." The Corinthians would have told him: "Look here Paul, it's one thing to say we must either marry or burn, but the tendency in these parts is to get it where you can find it, and devil take the hindmost. And as for saying women should keep silent in church – have you ever tried telling a woman to shut her mouth?" When the Corinthians got his next one, they gave him some home truths: "Faith, hope and charity? Come off it mate, we have NO faith, we have given up on hope, and you know as well we do where charity begins. Right?"

The Galatians saw through his hypocrisy: "Yes we know you feel great about getting converted but we think this holier-than-thou attitude is bullshit. Get off your high horse and stop lecturing us. Who do you think you are? Jesus Christ?" The Philippians were almost touched by his own problems, being imprisoned by the Romans and losing his job: "Look, we feel very sorry for you, giving up the tax collection and all that, so you miss your 30% sifted off the top, don't you? Well, here's a hundred shekels for your troubles but please don't write again." The general tone of the book would be a sort of "Empire Writes Back" with the ultimate message "Get lost."

At one stage, encouraged by a despairing family, D tried to get a job in an advertising agency. He proposed that a client calling itself a "one-stop baby-shop" selling everything a mother could need, should extend its horizons: "Take 'em in as virgins. Nine months later, push 'em out with a bonnie baby, a pram, two years' supply of nappies and a gallon of Milton." That idea had all the characteristics of a lead balloon – even his brother Henry could have seen through the Milton proposal.

His copyrighting abilities were, to say the least, negligible. "No jobs small enough" was one slogan which the client, a building contractor, rejected out of hand. Another was for a specialist in outdoor flooring: "Decking the garden? Let us do the planking." A d-i-y hire-all company was not at all impressed with "Master Bates has all the tools." "Mills and Boon puts the 'sigh' into 'psychology'" was another disaster. Another foray into the book trade was his proposed title for Christine Keeler's memoirs, "A Hard Day at the Orifice," but it went the way of all his other bright ideas. Uncle D left after a week, with "Botox for Buttox" his only contribution to the industry of persuasion.

IV

Ireland and Margaret

Ireland was her country – his mother's. It was only in his teens, when applying for a passport, that he discovered from his birth certificate that he was, properly speaking, St. George Manners. His mother had been Grace St. George, from an ancient but depleted landed family in the west of Ireland. As no one had ever mentioned the matter of his 'real' name, he could only guess at why he had always been called "George" rather than "St. George," but he had to admit that, although he was proud to be carrying the name of his maternal ancestors, it was more practical to be just plain "George."

He did have a friend called "St. John," pronounced "sin-john"; needless to say, Uncle David had a crack about that. But why anyone would want to name their child after a Baptist who got his head chopped off at the behest of a sex-crazy princess was anyone's guess. Or why they should want to pronounce it the same way as that arch prat Norman St. John Stevas (steev-arse, Uncle D called him). Come to think of it, why couldn't people either spell their names as they wished them to be spoken, or pronounce them as they were spelt? His cousins, for example, had a beautiful, historic castle, Belvoir, meaning "beautiful view," and they had bastardized it into "beever." Featherstonehaugh became Fanshaw; Colquhoun was Colhoon. Why not simply omit the 'q'? English baffled most foreigners: why was a "yacht" a "yot" and not a "yatchet"? Maybe the Americans had a better system: say it like it is. Noter Dame, Dez Moynes. Funny lot, the Americans, almost as funny as the French and the Italians.

United with the English, as Wilde said, by everything except language. Or was it Shaw who said they had everything in common except language? An Irishman, anyway.

But he was, at least in theory, proud to be a St. George, and he went to his mother's country with a feeling of belonging, and also one of being in pursuit of something – his Irishness, her Irishness? His four years at Trinity College, Dublin, might show him the way. In the outcome, they showed him the way to lots of very pleasurable things, including Margaret, but not much in the line of either Irishness or mother-place.

Like all his family – well, the menfolk – since the early nineteenth century, George had been sent to Rugby, one of England's second-league public schools. For a budding academic, it was the wrong choice, but no-one could possibly have known that the young George would break the family mould in pursuing a bookish career. Arnold might have been headmaster a thousand years ago, but the school boasted no academic record of any kind, its *alumni* going mainly into the army, the city, the church or the family farm, all, as they say, by a prior arrangement. Since most of Britain's future soldiers, financiers, vicars and farmers were incapable of independent thought, such predestination seemed a sensible *modus operandi.*

Uncle D had succeeded in getting sacked when he was sixteen. George had to undergo a further year, since it was imperative for him to sit his exams for university entrance. In those days there was a statutory body, the University Council on Central Admissions – at least, he thought that's what the acronym UCCA stood for, but there was hardly a student in Britain who didn't know the application paper as the FUCCA-form. You listed the universities and colleges you wanted, in order of preference. There was no point listing Oxford as no. 1 and Cambridge as no. 2, or *vice versa*, as both would feed your FUCCA-form to the college cat, so you put down far-flung destinations like Exeter, or Bristol, or Loughborough if, that is, your supervisor, aka your career guidance officer, permitted it. Dublin was outside the FUCCA system, and when every choice on George's form had declined the honor of offering him higher education, it was to TCD that he gladly went. It was, in any case, his only possible fall-back position.

George's sex life had got off to a slow start but proved exponentially better and better with each succeeding encounter. The girls in – and out of – college were, like himself, trying it out, finding themselves, and the steep learning curve had been a pleasure to climb. The girl to whom he had given his virginity – and she to him – was another offspring of the same farm labourer at Woodlawn, young and not so innocent, but still retaining some semblance of originality. It was only when he went to Dublin ("You flew Aer Cunnilingus, I suppose? Ha ha" was Uncle D's only comment), free of parental or any other form of control for the first time in his life (for the college rules were very lax) that the eighteen-year-old's testosterone was allowed to kick in, and sex became a fascinating, almost totally unexplained, possibility.

On a visit home, he'd mentioned that he'd found a student flat in an unsavoury Dublin suburb called Kimmage. Uncle D was genuinely hard-of-hearing, but he sometimes exaggerated it if he could turn it to effect. Mention of Kimmage went in the wrong end of D's metaphorical ear-trumpet, and he assumed it was a new slang word. Within a few seconds he had translated it from a place-name into a raunchy verb and noun. "Did you kimmage her, my boy?" and, without waiting for an answer, "Was she a good kimmage? Worth the kimmage?" – as if he'd been a guidebook, *'vaut le détour.'* Nanny Conneely hardly knew where to put her own ears.

So here he was, half-Irish and half-Catholic (at least nominally so) in a college which was half-British and wholly protestant in the centre of a city which had been the crucible of Catholic, nationalist rebellion against everything that both sides of his family had stood for. Did he feel at home! A hyphenated man, in what had been called a petty-minded parochial town-within-a-town that thought it was at the centre of the world, when in fact the position of its walled thirty-acre city in the busiest part of town caused traffic problems which some nationalists contended could be readily solved by replacing this last outpost of the Anglo-Irish with a traffic roundabout.

TCD in those days was still able to offer to the inner world, if not to Ireland at large, a collection of eccentric dons whom George later remembered with affection: men and women who wore their learning for the most part easily, some of them with European reputations (for example, in arcane areas such as papyrology and applied mathematics), but whose presence in the college – from which they seldom ventured forth – was valued more for their eccentricities than their scholarship. Mossop, the professor of metaphysics, was one such: he believed himself to be a bicycle, and he rode one around college convinced that *it* was riding *him*. As he was the world's leading expert on the philosophy of the Irishman George Berkeley, and was capable of *proving* his belief entirely by philosophical argument, there was no gainsaying him. At High Table, his colleagues didn't call him "Mossop," since he had convinced them by rational argument that Mossop was leaning against the railings outside. They referred to his various parts as 'handlebar' (his arms), 'crossbar' (his spine), 'pedal' and 'tyres' (his legs and feet) and 'chain' (his nervous system). As he careered round college, students and staff were given to wondering which was the saner part of the contraption, the bike or its rider. Or whether, as in the case of Flann O'Brien's *The Third Policeman* (a novel George had read with enormous enjoyment) an osmosis had taken place by means of which the bike was more philosopher than bike, the thinker more bike-like than the sophist between his legs. He was eventually retired on the grounds of ill-health, which was the Provost's euphemism for 'off his trolley' – an epithet which Mossop himself, who was by this stage beyond cognition might have welcomed as a valid description of the broken leg he had incurred as a result of mistaking a lamppost for his wife.

Janet Acton had been perhaps George's first 'serious' encounter at TCD. All the time, he was sowing wild oats as fast as they would grow, husks and all, and, if he was lucky, every party was a score. Intimacies that would later make you wake in the night in a cold sweat. Did we really do that? And has she told anyone? He thought it was Woody Allen who'd said 'Sex without love is an empty experience – it's the best empty experience I've ever had.' For three years, that thought was meat and drink to George.

As in all other areas of life, Uncle D gave his invaluable advice. Leaving out the cruder aspects, which made even him blush to recall, he thought with amusement of D's words about love-bites. "Hugely over-rated. In the days when cannibalism flourished, they may have served a useful domestic purpose, but that, I'm told, is a thing of the past except in places like Scunthorpe and Glasgow." Little did he know how Scunthorpe would figure in his nephew's professional future.

Unlike J.P. Donleavy, who, by his own account, seemed to have passed through TCD whoring and drinking, George had concentrated on drinking, with only the occasional whore thrown in. He was all too conscious of the dangers of syphilis from the whores... One of his college friends had confided in him that, in the previous generation, his uncle had acquired the clap – "spotted dick," Uncle D called it – from a lady of the night, and that, when this became known to his contemporaries, the men closed ranks to protect their sisters' honor and health; he was thereafter excluded from the marriage mart that college really was. George himself had avoided some particularly manky specimens who may not have been whores-for-money but were certainly willing to part with their virtue after a good many drinks. They had all the appearance of it. 'The college bikes' was the generic term, because everyone had ridden them. And he also avoided girls who 'did' drugs. A proper Little Lord Fauntleroy. Butter wouldn't melt in his mouth. Or would it?

But Janet came "of a good family" – in fact, her family had owned thousands of acres in County Wicklow which had gradually been taken away by the legislation that transferred land ownership from Anglo landlord to Irish tenant. Fair, perhaps, as long as it didn't happen to oneself. But the Acton family had lost everything except the now deserted ancestral mansion, Kilmacurragh, where, after the change of ownership, the Botanical Gardens in Dublin had taken over the maintenance of the feature which gave the place its international reputation: the arboretum. George's great-grandfather had had the same idea at the same time as Janet's, but the soil at Woodlawn was unsuitable for the cultivation of what was then sweeping the fashion boards throughout the British Isles: rhododendrons, which had been introduced from the Himalayas by collectors since the eighteenth century. In particular, Kilmacurragh was home to some of the world's finest specimens of *Rhododendron delavayi, Rh. Roylei* and *Rh. falconeri* and the Actons had even bred their own hybrid, *Rhododendron actonensis* At Woodlawn, great-grandfather's ambitions had led him to have a huge section of the land beside the house dug out, and an equally huge amount – many thousands of tons – of suitable soil imported. But George hadn't really appreciated it, despite family pride in the damned thing, and it was only when Janet persuaded him to travel down to Kilmacurragh to see the Actons' arboretum that he began to take an interest, and to discover that this one was markedly superior to that of the junior Manners.

Trinity: that was where, besides truly getting his rocks off, George's incipient alcoholism showed that its roots were thoroughly embedded in his genetic soil. Without control, he flexed his freedom unrestrainedly, and the steady course towards serious – one might even call it professional – drinking had begun. He would never call it a 'slippery slope' although he did love the homily given out by the Catholic missionary (yes, they needed them in holy Ireland too, perhaps more than darkest Africa) who began with "The family that prays together, stays together. And the family that drinks together, sinks together." What a crowd-puller! How convincing! By his reckoning, every family he knew was well and truly sunk. The Irishman's capacity for 'the jar' was such that it would break even the chains of Sampson, let alone the apron strings that bound him to little Molly and the three screaming brats. And thus George discovered the Irishman in himself. Didn't he?

Up to the point, years later, when chronic liver failure and imminent death announced themselves, he made no excuse for his consumption of Guinness and the wines available from M's father, who was in the business, with extensive interests in Bordeaux, supplementing what he had already learned from the always plentiful and exceptionally well stocked cellar at Woodlawn, to which Uncle D had the key.

A marriage mart? Most students, of both sexes, waited till final year before making any serious moves towards marriage. Margaret was much sought-after, as she was known to come from a wealthy, if *nouveau*, background, so she was at the top of a lot of lists. Very *cherchée* and very *trouvée*.

Yes, then there was Margaret. She was reading history and political science, when most of her fellow undergraduettes had taken the soft option of French and Spanish, or Greek and Roman Civilisation; he was reading English and Irish literature, but you'd never have guessed from their behaviour. Meeting in third year, there was an immediate attraction, but both were still sowing wild oats, so that it wasn't until their last year that they were bonking each other stupid, in spite of – or maybe because of? – which they both got firsts. She had an apartment in town in a block owned by her father, whose other business interests included a couple of multi-storey car parks and a chain of billiard halls. Margaret at this stage was unsure of what she wanted to do after college, but George knew that a First was essential if he was to gain access to an academic career.

His always disorganized handwriting became, under exam pressure, almost totally illegible, so that he was recalled by the Senior Examiner and required to record them, under supervision, into a tape machine that was then transcribed by a secretary. It was a success, unlike his second, and last, experience with a tape recorder. He apologized to his various lecturers for this mishap, but one, who was responsible for his most vital paper, and who ultimately held George's fate in his hands, had replied: "Well, my dear Manners, I didn't actually read your exams, as I'm thoroughly aware of the excellence of your work, so I just gave it a first as a matter of course." For all this don had cared, George might have written "William Wordsworth was a pugilist, a serial adulterer and a pervert; his affairs with Shelley and Tennyson were legendary; his relationship with Queen Victoria can not, even at this remove, be revealed." He would still have got his First – *summa cum laude*.

Before M's father would give permission for their wedding to go ahead (since, holding the purse-strings, he would not pay for it until he was good and ready), an interview had to take place. When they had announced their engagement, it had not seemed necessary for George to do the needful thing and have a talk about his 'prospects.' But with the wedding looming old O'Brien wanted his pound of flesh. So George was summoned into the O'Brien company offices and shown into the sanctum. There was little small talk. None in fact.

"Well, if you're going to marry Margaret" –

"Yes, I am" –

"Don't interrupt me please." Wait for it. "Margaret's mother and I need some idea of what you think your life is going to be? I've already agreed that, until Margaret finds a suitable job (little did he know!), I'll give her whatever support she needs." That made it clear: "she," not "you."

"Thank you."

"Yes, but I'm taking a longer term view. Where do you see yourself in ten – twenty – year's time?"

There had been no secret of the fact that he and Margaret would be going to Leeds for postgraduate work and there seemed to have been no difficulty in old man O'Brien giving them financial help to do so. Think, George, of the best way to put this.

"Well, after I get the PhD, I would expect to move on to a larger, older university and get a lectureship there."

"Teach, you mean?"

"Yes, that would be the basic job, but the responsibilities of being a lecturer" – here he was brusquely interrupted.

"Responsibilities? You just go into a lecture room a

few times a week for about twenty-five weeks in the year, trot out the same sort of guff that you've been ingesting in Trinity for the past four years, and then head off for holidays as long as your arm! Responsibilities? Pull the other one. The only responsibility you have, George – or should I call you Mr. *Saint* George? – is to my daughter."

George was afraid the next thing he would hear would be along the lines of "If you can't show me that you can support my daughter in the style to which she is accustomed..." but the cliché died unspoken. Instead, he swallowed hard and went on what he thought was the attack.

M and George had never discussed his family's financial affairs, so Owen O'Brien could hardly have known that the Manners' 'old money' could buy and sell his newly minted wealth several times over. George didn't want him to know that he would easily be able to keep M in style, not the style to which she had been accustomed, but to the Manners style of living, once the family trust had released the share that was due to him on this twenty-fifth birthday.

"And in addition to lecturing, there's research and, of course, publishing."

"Research? Poking about in dusty old libraries, digging up stuff that's best forgotten? And publishing what, exactly?"

"I'm already at work on a book on Pater" –

"Your father?" George didn't know whether to faint, ignore the question, or break his shite laughing in O'Brien's face. The thought that he might be writing a book about his father! A slim volume? A pamphlet? A single page inscribed with a few empty words? He decided to grin and bear it.

"No, Walter Pater."

"Who?"

"It would take a while to explain. A nineteenth-century aesthete" –

"I don't give a tinker's curse who he was. What has it to do with my daughter?"

"It's a book which I'm confident will get a publisher, because there's a gap in that market." Here, George thought he was onto a winner, because old O'Brien had made his fortune on the early hunch that the Irish lack of taste for French wines was a 'gap in the market' that he, Owen O'Brien, could very profitably fill. And he had been proved right. George did not anticipate that his thesis on Pater would earn him enough in royalties to build a heated indoor swimming pool, so it was best not to go down the route of how much he might make on top of his meagre uni salary. But he staggered on. "And after that, I'm thinking of doing some work on John Fowles." Another "WHO?" was in the offing, so he rapidly went on "Anyway, I see myself more as a writer than as an academic." A frosty silence.

"A WHAT?"

"A writer."

"Ah, so you want to be a failure, like your father. Is that it?"

This time the frosty silence emanated from George's nostrils, not O'Brien's. And silence remained while he sought helplessly for a reply that would not only show O'Brien that he was going to succeed as a writer – something the bastard never lived to appreciate – but how to expunge this well-deserved insult to his father. Should he draw himself up to his full height (O'Brien was a good five inches taller, so that wasn't really a choice) and declare "Now look here, my good man, I am a St. George Manners and will not be spoken to in that fashion by a jumped up wine merchant. We buy our wines from people like you – people in trade." But that didn't seem like a

great idea either; O'Brien had often expressed his
contempt for the Irish landed classes, as only a self-made
Irish bourgeois can, and when he had learned of the way
George's branch of the Manners family had been kicked
out of Belvoir (and thank god he was sufficiently ignorant
to pronounce it as it was spelled) he added that to his list
of contemptibles, however grandly they remained
connected to the original family.

O'Brien probably went through the rest of his
mercifully short life regretting that instead of selling his
daughter to one of George's precursors – one had been a
marine biologist who was now head of some big UN
commission, another an industrial chemist, a third a
professor of music at Oxford and author of a book on
Janáček – he had actually *paid* to let her shackle herself to
a wastrel, and an aristocratic wastrel at that. George
almost felt sorry for him that he had not lived to see his
daughter liberated from the wastrel when they separated.

They had presented a comical sight at their wedding,
for George was scarcely five-feet-six inches, while
Margaret was slightly more than six feet. The difference
was immortalized in the wedding photos, where the
normally short-statured Mannerses were outstripped by
the towering figures of their new Irish in-laws, upon
whom, therefore, it was impossible to look down. Needless
to say, George's father was absent – it's possible that he
hadn't even read his son's letter announcing his
engagement or seen it in *The Times* – and Uncle D did the
honors, with James Esposito as best man.

When they were married, and George was still working
as an assistant to Derry Jeffares, his income wasn't enough
to support them both, and it was therefore necessary for M
to find a job suitable to someone with her degree (first-
class) in history and political science. There was a regional
office of the Ministry of Information based in Leeds, and

they took her on, at first as an auxiliary clerk. As an Irish citizen, *and* a Catholic, she was barred from more senior rank, so her promotion to other grades suggested to George that there were other regulations facilitating the hiring of 'aliens' when their talents matched the requirements of the post. In fact she had shown such promise that she was rapidly promoted to junior officer. George knew that it was important work, because M was not allowed to talk about it at home. When friends and neighbors asked what she did in her job, she would answer casually "Oh it's just a boring old desk job. Counting paperclips and that sort of thing." She sounded so convincing that people believed her, probably wondering how someone so obviously intelligent could bear to keep a job of such a mundane and mind-numbing nature – so much so that George joked that "she might as well be a spy, for all the secrecy!"

Anyone operating in a confidential area, whether top-secret or graded lower down the hush-hush spectrum would, as a matter of course, be under permanent surveillance by the Special Branch or some other unit tasked with suspecting reds under the beds. The caution was obvious: chemical warfare was hardly the subject of international conferences, openly reported in the world's press. It was something the poorer governments bought second-hand from those which had tried and tested it. If anything was made public, it came not from the experts or the governments which employed them, but from whistle-blowers, and one hardly blew one's own whistle, did one? Unless, of course, one was acting (and that, George discovered, was the appropriate word) as a double- or even triple-agent.

Their straitened financial circumstances (temporary, but real) meant that, however much they wanted them, they couldn't afford children: working full-time on his thesis, which he completed in a record three years, plus acting as Jeffares' assistant, was enough to occupy his time, and Margaret, too, was heavily involved in her own job. Five years later, after he had secured his junior appointment at Lincoln and the family trust fund had been settled, they decided the time was right, and, to their bewilderment and delight, twins were diagnosed. Seven months later, out popped Victoria (Vicky), closely followed, as was only right and proper, by Albert (Al). Their friends' reaction to the names ranged from the jocular to the scathing. 'Victoria and Albert' – really! (We had toyed with 'Virginia and Leonard' but thought better of it.)

She was always 'M' when he mentioned her in his diary, and it had almost, but not quite, turned out that she had actually become 'M' in the secret service. But that is to jump ahead by several years.

Their only extravagance, which was financed by Margaret's share of her father's estate, was a small house in Greece, on the tiny island of Karponisi. It was more George's wish than Margaret's, and, as things turned out, the fact that it had been bought largely with her money was not an issue when they separated, as Margaret was happy for him to buy out her share for a nugatory sum. She had never cared as much for the place as George. As a fifteen-year-old, he had been able to read, write and speak classical Greek, but apart from the vocabulary, which had lived on into today's language, he was unable to converse. Even if he had retained the grammar, it had, unlike the vocabulary, changed radically in the transition to modern Greek. But he had enough to make himself understood – "restaurant Greek," he called it – and in Karponisi had no difficulty in being accepted as a philhellene. For Margaret, that facility was unavailable, since her foreign language from school had been Spanish, and Karponisi was far from

Spain.

Far from anywhere, in fact. Except Spetses, the neighboring island, where George's friend John Fowles had spent his early career as a schoolmaster – a coincidence which may have contributed to the closeness which developed between critic and novelist, and led to George's authoritative books.

They had chosen it for other reasons also. After island-hopping for a few years during their holidays, which for George were lengthy but for Margaret circumscribed by her civil service job, they had decided on a small, unpretentious house, quite different from what the average 'tourist' buyers would want. It wasn't an old schoolhouse (thankfully the schoolhouse on Karponisi was still in use) nor a converted oil-press (all the oil-presses on the island operated as such). It was a basic cottage in the traditional style; the previous occupants had died and their son, who lived on the mainland, was selling. George and Margaret soon filled it with books, modest *objets d'art* – mostly craft pieces acquired locally, along with peasant rugs and household implements. Later, after their separation, George had made a small extension to the house and, later still, after Jessica had left him, and he realized that this was where he should most probably end his days, all the rest of his library was to be housed. But that, again, is jumping ahead.

They had never divorced, due mostly to his lethargy, so they were still married, more than forty years after their wedding and nearly thirty since they had split up. They still exchanged the conventional good wishes at Christmas and on each other's birthday. Once or twice they had both attended family events, although he had given her father's funeral a miss. But it was increasingly unlikely that either of their children would summon them to a wedding, although there had been talk of Albert and his partner,

Tony, having a civil ceremony.

While they were still in touch after they split up, George had never asked M about her job. Quite apart from the fact that they had nothing to do with each other's careers (although he knew from Vicky that M had read his books as they came out) it would have been impossible for him to ask her about her job. Even had they still been living together, her security grading would have made it a total no-go area. Even a clerk in the education ministry who excitedly told his wife, in the security of their bed, that he had seen plans for a new type of whiteboard for primary schools, was technically in breach of the Official Secrets Act, and what M might reveal about her projects would score a few notches above that.

And he had no idea whether, at her level, M was aware of his own "dispatches," which to her would have been "intelligence reports." Perhaps she did see them. Perhaps she was even part of the process which commissioned them, or even acted upon them. Perhaps – even though she bore no animosity towards him – she could, with a pen stroke, remove him from the list of agents. But he doubted it. Money would have nothing to do with it, if the national interest were better served by other means. He sometimes wondered if M had the power to take such a step; she certainly wouldn't have done it to hurt him financially, but then she knew that, with his college pension and his income from the family trust, he was well off in any case.

For all he knew, she and he were both involved in a project which would ultimately see Britain supporting an American *coup d'état* in somewhere like Iraq or Uzbekistan.

What rank she actually held, and what position she occupied, he not only had no idea but could not have discovered even if he wished to do so. Vicky and Al never mentioned her work, and he imagined that they never referred to his 'dispatches' when they spoke with their mother. Even if the two parents were involved in the same line of business, their closets were hermetically sealed both from the world and from each other.

He remembered very clearly the day their marriage had, in effect, ended. He had returned that day from a lecture tour in Finland – the time that, ironically, the 'Finnish girl' had been conceived, although he was not to know that for a few months. When he did find out, it was through the colleague who had organized his lecture tour and who became a very close friend and, as it turned out, benefactor. The woman – and he really did have trouble remembering her name – had not wanted to keep the baby, nor had she wanted an abortion. Adoption by some unknown couple seemed the only possibility, until George's friend, Olli Vuonen, and his wife, who had just lost a child through a miscarriage, had offered to bring up the child as their own, as the youngest of their other four. The miscarried child was to have been called Pirkko-Liisa, so that was the name they chose for this newcomer. Olli and his wife kept George up-to-date on the growth of the baby girl, on her progress at school and university, but at Olli's suggestion and with George's agreement, contact was minimal and George, to his everlasting regret, had never seen her, as he had declined all subsequent invitations to return to Finland, even turning down what would have been a very lucrative professorship at the University of Joensuu. He never again heard anything of the birth mother. Vicky and Al remained ignorant of the existence of their half-sister. George sometimes wondered what it would be like for them to discover the truth; even, what it might be like for them all to be together, but he managed to stifle that kind of curiosity. It was enough to manage distance-parenting between Lincoln and London, after Margaret's move there, without taking on a Lincoln-

Helsinki dimension to his life.

Both knew that there was no further mileage in the marriage. Ironically, it was in bed with the Finnish woman that the realisation came to him that M had also been unfaithful at least once. But it was not a factor in what was probably the briefest conversation they had ever had. "Are we going to divorce?" To which he had replied, "Yes, I suppose so." That was that. There was no problem for M to admit the affairs she had had during the past year, one with a bus conductor, one with a Protestant vicar (so she wasn't choosy, then?) and, as she made the same assumption – ignorant though she was of his one-night stand in Jyväskylä, of all places – there seemed to be no problem over whether she would sue him for adultery or he her.

He had expected that she might give his less than meteoric performance at university as a reason for her disillusion with their relationship. So far he had only the Pater and the first Fowles volume to his credit. In both cases, he was delighted to remark, he had stolen a march on 'that rotter' Andrew Dalton, his contemporary, who had also written his PhD. on Pater and who claimed to be a friend of John Fowles. In retrospect he had feared that Owen O'Brien's prediction "You want to be a failure, like your father" might come into play. But no, M had supported him morally all through those years and, he thought, took some pride in his work. She was not vindictive. Despite the fact that she was clearly "on her way to the top," she would never have regarded George as holding her back professionally.

But much more serious was the fact that she wanted somewhere much bigger and better than Lincoln to spread her wings, professionally speaking. She had her sights set on head office: Whitehall and the MI6 hq on the Embankment, at the end of Villiers Street, where George as a schoolboy used to buy condoms at the now disappeared Ward's Hygienic Stores. The move to London would have complicated matters if they had decided to stay together "for the sake of the children," but her transfer had come after the divorce was finalized, and she seemed to leave Lincoln with some regrets. As far as the children were concerned, they were, at the age of five, well able to look after themselves most of the time, and it was tacitly agreed between himself and M that she would be a good mother and he a hopeless father.

As the children grew, George came to think of them more as people and less like irritants. He began to take an active interest in their progress, in their growing into young adults with all the hopes and fears and misplaced optimism that life afforded. As a teenager, Vicky had a succession of boyfriends – lovers, to be more modern about it – but only one long-term partner in her early twenties, Ralph, a plumber; George, with all his worldly wisdom, predicted that it wouldn't last, and it didn't. Both he and Margaret were relieved, not for reasons of social snobbery but because Ralph hadn't shown the kind of commitment that they felt Vicky needed and deserved. He spent more time under the bonnet of his jalopy, attending to the health of his "rad," than he did in sharing a home with Vicky. Eventually, after four years, she kicked him out.

Their relationship had seemed to fit in with Vicky's socialist idea of improving the lot of the working classes (as they used to be called, before work became a thing of the past) but relationships don't function just because one partner feels sorry for the other, which is what George thought Vicky felt for Ralph.

So she was once again single and, it seemed, content in herself. Her work was the fullness of her day. Despite the strong possibility of following George into a high-flown academic career, and a successful first book on the metaphysical poets, Vicky had chosen to follow her beliefs, and to work in the area of juvenile education, at a technical college which was the educational arm of what had been the Bristol Borstal. She shared with George (although in his case it was a tangent to his main work) the task of introducing 'literature' to minds that were far from serious reading. She had sought – successfully, it seemed – to have circuited this problem by giving them adventure stories and, more particularly, crime thrillers, such as Wilkie Collins' *The Moonstone*, supplementing the books with the television adaptations which they enjoyed. Similarly, the gentleman-burglar Raffles, played on television by Anthony Valentine, was a roaring success, and she told George that just lately she had tried out Baroness Orczy's *The Scarlet Pimpernel* – again, the books read in parallel with viewing the films. She was able to justify these choices of material to the head of the college (who had assumed that she would be teaching Jane Austen, Dickens, George Eliot and other classics) by pointing out that these, too, were classics in their genre, and that their authors were highly regarded by the literary world. The fact that the head had never heard of them convinced him that Vicky was doing the right thing. Secretly, he sought out the books himself, and was soon engrossed in their exceptional storylines.

Albert had been far less interested in literature, quite probably because it would mean following his father's career and competing with his sister who was, after all, several minutes older than he, and therefore more experienced and worldly-wise. But he had taken to the other arts – painting, drawing, sculpture, photography – like a duck to water, and, after a course at art college, had become a successful interior designer, getting quite annoyed if anyone called him 'a decorator.' Al was also in a long-term relationship, and this one had lasted and seemed likely to continue. His partner was a photographer called Tony; sometimes they worked together (which had brought them to each other's attention in the first place) but mostly they led separate lives, professionally speaking. Neither George nor Margaret had any reservations about their son being gay; in fact, George hardly gave it a moment's thought. As long as his children were happy, honored and loved their mother and remembered him occasionally, that was all that mattered, and all that George was entitled to expect.

V

Lincoln, Pater and Fowles

He was not your average academic. He didn't wear a tweed suit, preferring the cream linen concoctions that made him look like something out of a second-rate Graham Greene movie. He didn't shuffle around, looking for things he had accidentally mislaid. In fact, he could be quite aggressive and assertive. Once, at a traffic lights, he was annoyed by a motorist in front who seemed undecided about the lights, which had been green for some time. "Get a move on, you dozy wanker!" George bellowed. Unfortunately the object of his abuse was an off-duty police officer. Because he was off-duty, George was lucky and got off with a caution. Another time, when in similar circumstances he shouted "Lily-livered lager lout!" it wasn't a policeman. It was a professional boxer and George was lucky to get off with a nose that would never look the same again. His ribs still ached with the memory.

Supervising his students' research, and conducting his own, were the enjoyable aspects of college work. Teaching was not. Teaching was boring, unproductive and stultifying. In fact, George thought it was immoral. And as for the non-academic side of the job! The interminable departmental meetings, when they talked more and more about less and less until they had everything to say about nothing, and nothing to say about everything.

He'd read somewhere – he thought it was in a story by an academic masquerading as a writer of detective fiction – that the typical university college was populated by 'moral and level-headed men, who do nothing aberrant, nothing rashly or in haste. Their conventional associations are with learning, unworldliness, absence of mind and endearing and always innocent foible.' Bullshit, George exclaimed. *His* colleagues were mean-minded, viciously contemptuous of others' success, fanatically secretive about their own area of study, and, as far as haste was concerned, so slow that they would put even Henry Manners to shame with the decrepit slothful progress, or lack of it, in their job of improving men's minds and adding to the (useful?) sum of human knowledge.

George was nothing if not irreverent. He habitually set exam questions with tongue in cheek, in such a way that they *could* be taken as straightforward opportunities for his students to display knowledge, intelligence and initiative. At school, he had had to answer a question 'Is this a question?' to which he had written "Yes, if this is an answer," which, apparently, was the *wrong* answer. Now he wanted to get his own back, and in this there was more than a touch of Uncle D's mischief, who had chortled when George bluffed him that he was contemplating a book entitled *Proust's Foreskin and Other Drawbacks*.

One scholarship question he set was "We derive the orchid from the Greek word *orchis* means *testicle*. Does this explain why Miss Blandish had none?" That got him into a lot of trouble with his department head. Another posed the question: 'Travel narrows the mind. Discuss." That one passed muster with his superiors, mainly because they themselves had no interest in travel, believing that "foreign" was a nasty place. Others, which he justified on the basis that they stretched the students' powers of imagination, gave them something to think about, were: 'What would you expect if you read *Tess of the d'Urbevilles* by Sherlock Holmes?' or 'Did Conan Doyle write *Women in Love* – and if not, why not?' In some questions, such as 'What is romantic poetry?' or 'What is literary criticism?' he was more on the straight and narrow, but it was the deviant, not to say zany, answers he received that got the alpha marking. He was pleased with the response to: "Write a story that either starts or ends with the words 'That was the first they knew, that their mother had a bicycle.'"

He was particularly pleased with "What would George Orwell have made of it all?" which, he hoped, would elicit not only something about Orwell but, more importantly, what the respondent thought "it all" might be. He was rewarded, and punished, when he met the author of the most interesting reply, since it brought into his life, for a delicious and nearly devastating half-hour, a seductress who, unknown to George, had brought into his study not only her very promising body but also a tape-recorder. His defence, that she had made him a present of her body because she knew it was his birthday, or his fall-back position (how Uncle D chuckled at that expression!) that she had done it in order to get a better exam grading, was laughed out of the disciplinary hearing at which he was humiliated.

That led to near dismissal. Summoned to the office of the President of the college, George was under the impression that he deserved shameful dismissal and would get it. But the President professed to be a humane, understanding gentleman ("Doesn't it happen to us all at one time or another?") and put another alternative to George, besides resignation and suicide, to which he was equally attracted.

"George, dear fellow. We are, for the good of our souls, and to ensure that we continue to receive our DoE funding, to engage in outreach. Yes, I had to look it up, too. It means, to be blunt about it, taking on the great unwashed. Oh, my dear fellow, not here! Good god no! In Scunthorpe. At the industrial school there. Trying to din some appreciation of the finer points of the humanities into riff-raff who hardly qualify as members of humanity themselves. You'll go there twice a week. Well done.'

Well done? For what? And where on earth was Scunthorpe? "George, let me be blunt again. We are all expected to pull our weight in this ghastly business. I myself will be giving the occasional lecture there. But you, George, because of recent, er, occurrences and the existence of a certain tape recording which a certain student has threatened to send to *The News of the World*, have greater weight to pull in this area than most of your colleagues."

There was nothing more to be said; therefore, no discussion. George simply left the President's office, meekly accepted from the college secretary a voucher for train travel between Lincoln and Scunthorpe, a timetable for the trains and another for his assignments, and slunk out of the building, wondering whether, considering what were now the horns of a trilemma, the other two prongs were not infinitely preferable to Scunthorpe.

George was in very grave doubts as to whether he should be doing this, but it seemed that, in order to rescue the prospects of his career after the mishap, he had no choice. Thank god he and Margaret were separated. She need never know what he had got up to with Miss Exhibit A, as he thought of her. And the worst part of it all was, it hadn't been worth it.

So George's demonstrable lack of promotion was due not only to his own lethargy and lack of ambition (which it certainly was), but also to the fact that there was a note on his file referring, in terms which were instantly transparent to the experienced eye, to his misdemeanour.

Uncle D greeted the news with hilarity. "If Typhoo put the 'T' into Britain, who put the 'cunt' into Scunthorpe eh? Ha ha." He tried to follow it by explaining to George that Cleethorpes had originally been called 'Clee-tori-thorpes' but that common decency had prevailed some time in the eighteenth century – or was it the nineteenth? – to arrive at a more socially acceptable version of the name by eliding the "tori," which the electorate had done dutifully almost ever since, assiduously voting Labour even when they didn't mean to. For a time George had almost believed him, so straight-facedly had D made this statement, because his fondness for D made him susceptible to his foibles, and even after he had realized it was a gigantic leg-pull (thank god there had been no women present, let alone ladies!) he still thought that D's explanation held a lot of water.

One of the lessons Scunthorpe taught him was that you could take nothing for granted. Maybe it was because his class of established recidivists and trainee criminals were so familiar with police interrogations. With apologies to Tom Sharpe's Wilt, he nicknamed them 'Meat Three.' He actually got to like them. Trying to open doors for them into 'his' world was a challenge he never succeeded in meeting, but *they* opened doors for *him* into their mindset: down the pub they ingested Yorkshire Brown, while using Elke Sommer's tits as a darts board, and for hard liquor they relied on formaldehyde which they acquired from their colleagues in Autopsy Two. He, for his part, joined them at the local, Greek-owned caff, 'Kotopoulo Tiganitis, Est. 1989' which they thought was the proprietor's name, when in fact it advertized the perennial special, chicken 'n chips.

They would ask the most searching questions in the most threatening way. For professional reasons they were interested in Carver Doone, but Withering Shites only provoked scorn: "Why don't he just fook 'er, the wanker?" "All that moaning about Cathy'd make yer balls turn to frogs," a nice turn of phrase, George thought, that would for ever endear Meat Three to him.

191

Where, even at such a down-market college as Lincoln, one could still work on the assumption that one's students knew what one was talking about, at Scunthorpe one couldn't. In particular, you had to explain *why* reading literature, as opposed to – or at least different from – the racing page or *Exchange and Mart* or, he supposed, *The Housebreakers Gazette incorporating the Muggers Vade Mecum*, was worthwhile, *why* it had some value, other than the second-hand sales price they could get for their free copies, handed out at Scunthorpe like the NHS handed out free specs and diphtheria injections. This meant explaining, to raucous mirth, "Why I am a Critic."

As a critic, George had no patience with the "Marxist" school of criticism. The very fact that it was a school suggested to him that its pupils were unable to think for themselves – not entirely like the Scunthorpe lads, he thought, although the latter would probably have made better Marxists, believing that what was someone else's should really be theirs.

Of course, we had to take into account what other critics had said, and even had to respect their point of view, their own intellectual background. A working-class boy or girl, from an urban background, especially if inured to hardship and deprivation, will read a text by Jane Austen through different lenses than someone brought up to comfortable living in an idyllic rural setting, however much the emotions aroused by an Elizabeth Bennet or a d'Arcy or an Emma might strike common chords in both types of reader.

George had known this before taking the Scunthorpe assignment. After it, he knew too damn well what a Scunny would say about the prancing and pirouetting and poncing of characters who were largely *nouveaux riches* just as they themselves were the *anciens pauvres*. He'd heard enough denunciations of Austen and so many others to fill a book – he'd even contemplated 'A Down-and-Out's Answer to FR Leavis.' Rather predictably, they had mixed feelings for Dickens, because he had an obvious sympathy with the poor, but didn't do anything about it; for George Eliot (who, whatever George said, was a man as far as they were concerned), they had a grudging respect because s/he had depicted rather well the fortunes of Silas Marner and the family in *The Mill on the Floss*, despite their insistence that *floss* wasn't a proper name for a river when you had candyfloss and dental floss to get it mixed up with. Sometimes he thought the Scunthorpe boys were among the most intelligent students he had ever had, even though he totally failed to teach them anything, or to improve their minds. In fact, *they* had taught *him* and, he thought, had improved *his* mind.

It brought back to him what that boy on the Woodlawn estate had said years before: "Wots the point of anifink? Nuffink." When the Scunthorpe boys said it, it made much more sense.

The larger point was that any Marxist thinking must begin with the absurd idea that all men are equal, and proceed from there to the fact that, because they are *not* equal, they *should* be. Wishful thinking, perhaps, but there was enough of that in modern criticism without using the tools of a theory which was not only over 150 years old, but had been proved to be useless, even damaging the lives of people, in practice. The Scunthorpe boys were well ahead of them there.

Then came the idea that 'all men are born free, but everywhere they are in chains' – Rousseau had got in well before brother Marx. That was spot-on. That was how it was. The Scunthorpe boys had proved that when, while celebrating their freedom one Guy Fawkes night, they had chained up not only all the cars and bikes in the college forecourt but also several of the senior staff.

George had one simple belief, and if it was dogmatic, at least it was his own dogma: that the function of a critic is to read the text and then to offer his reader – a reader who, hopefully, was familiar with the text – some idea of how he, the critic, saw it. A critic, as he knew from his Greek study, was a judge. But who was one man to give judgement on another?

To state that this book is worth reading and that book is not? The critic, in George's view, was there purely to give his honest impression of what he saw, heard, read. And then to sit back and see if the readers agreed with him. Nothing more, nothing less. If he held Marxist beliefs, then he probably would give a different impression to, say, an arch-conservative (or perhaps not); that was more or less undeniable. But, as the example of the Scunthorpe boys always reminded him, you said what you thought. "But sir, it's a load of shite." "But sir, he must be a reel fookin' dipstick to not screw the bird." "But sir, all this prancing around pretending to be a clever dick, what good does it do him?" Oh, honesty, out of the mouths of... But on reflection George would prefer not to remember some of what had come out of the mouths of Scunthorpe.

The Scunthorpe connection brought him and Vicky much closer together, since this was exactly the sort of commitment she had undertaken. Comparing notes, they even found that they had tried to teach the same books, she successfully, he not. The difference between them was, that Vicky *tried*, because she *believed* in it – believed in redemption, believed in the power of literature to soothe the rampant breasts of youngsters who would spend their out-of-class lives robbing and whoring and burning out BMWs as *their* way of showing society the same sort of two-finger resentment of which even the great novelists, like Kingsley Amis, were capable, in a slightly different fashion, of course.

But he also reflected that the Scunthorpe boys and his 'regular' Lincoln students were not a million miles apart in intelligence and their ability to express themselves. They just did it differently, that's all. One of his Lincoln students thought that Monty Python was real, and that *The Fast Show* was a documentary. (Talking to her about her essays, George found himself saying "she could be right," she was so ardent and convinced on the point. Or was that a gigantic leg-pull? At least it wasn't a prick-tease, like Miss Exhibit A.) *Not the Nine O'Clock News* was called that, his student continued, because it wasn't screened at 9pm, but it *was* the News, nonetheless, with all the authority that that hallowed institution commanded. Luckily she was too young to have seen *At Last the 1948 Show*, or she would have wondered why it had got so delayed in transmission. One of her essays had all the appearance of a spoof – a very clever twist to the subject, which was Joyce's *A Portrait of the Artist as a Young Man*, but it transpired that what she had written hadn't been lifted out of Wikipedia but was her own, genuine opinion – and quite well expressed, too. Actually, she should have joined the team of the Harvard Lampoon, considering what an improvement they had wrought on Tolkien's *Lord of the Rings*....

PATER

"Can we, in studying the work of Walter Pater, entirely exclude a consideration of his private life? Or, conversely, can we avoid the question of how far his life created the conditions for his work? Was his deployment of his imagination on Greek topics wholly dispassionate?" This was the opening of his PhD thesis, in which George 'spilled the beans' about Pater, the reclusive, closeted Oxford don whose only claim to public homosexual fame was his temporary friendship (and possibly infatuation) with Oscar Wilde. George, despite his own vehement heterosexuality, had discovered his capacity for noting, and describing, the homosexuality, first, of his college acquaintances and, second, of the authors whom he studied.

Pater, along with Edmund Gosse, Henry James, Havelock Ellis and J.A. Symonds, were closet gays whose fear of disclosure made them run for cover in the light of the scandals caused by Wilde and others of the openly gay community. When a mutual friend had commented to Pater on the giveaway (for gays) in the title of *The Importance of Being Earnest* – "earnest" being a codeword for "gay" – Pater had simply replied, possibly in all innocence, "surely not." And if anyone had muttered "bath-house" he would probably have given up ablutions for life.

Everyone knew at the time that Pater was a closet gay – one of the most closeted queers in academe. No one would have thought he was a sodomite. He probably still thought it was for stirring his tea. But as gays go, Pater didn't. Neither came nor went. There are paedophiles, pederasts, bumboys, rentboys, callboys, ballboys, transvestites, bath-house madames and Gilles de Retz. Pater was the most secluded closeteer known to medical science. But he had 'tendencies.' Nice ones. Tendencies any caring mother would be proud of. As innocent of his desire as a sleeping babe of its most basic Freudian dreams. The love that dare not speak its name? Pater didn't even *know* its name. His 'love' took the shape of marble buttocks, a *putto* caught in *flagrante delicto* with a cloud, a thought overthought because Pater didn't know how to think of such 'things.'

He lauded, and wrote of, the Mona Lisa not because he had been tipped off that the model had actually been a man, but because its author had been gay. He loved the 'David' of Michelangelo not for its erotic strength but because Michelangelo had written those suggestive oh-so-prickteasing, sonnets. Naughty, naughty Buonarotti. He was responsible in his Sonnets for "a certain strangeness," "the penetrative suggestion of life." The fact that they were translated by Symonds added piquancy to their surreptitious seduction.

George reflected that Pater would never have used even a small crudity, like "bum," let alone "arse," and almost certainly had no knowledge of what a cunt was, even if he had heard the word. If a much more worldly aesthete like Ruskin didn't know that women had hair on their delta of Venus, what hope was there for other inhibited Victorians?

But George also reflected that if Pater had had the guts to think deeper into the bland suggestiveness with which he described and honored homoerotic longings, he might – just *might* – have allowed himself to covet his neighbor's arse or to think scrotum-wise. It buoyed him up (pun intended).

But George was the first to make clear the exact relationship between Pater's gay sexuality and the homosexual (sub)culture in his books and essays. The key to the secret of silence had been the fact that at that time, with virtually no gutter press or social media, very few people even knew what homosexuality *was*. If the British public had known that the government – including the Prime Minister, Lord Rosebery – was a gay bunch, or that the Archbishop of Canterbury, his wife and their four children, of both genders, were all gay, the empire might have collapsed.

The fact that they had been caricatured in *romans à clef* like WH Mallock's *The New Republic* (in which Pater appears as 'Mr Rose') or the erotic fantasy *Teleny* – the collaborative sketchbook of buggery to which Wilde had contributed – went unnoticed. *Teleny*, of course, was never published at the time, but *The New Republic* was widely read by respectable pater- and materfamilias who would never have guessed what lay behind the gentle satire. It was just another of those 'country house mysteries' that dear Agatha would make her own. But with catamites and sodomites instead of vicars and spinsters.

Pater might, in fact, have followed Symonds' example by writing, in his closet, "A Problem in Greek Ethics," setting out why it was both necessary and dangerous for his own time. But he didn't dare (and even Symonds had suppressed his pamphlet).

The mere fact that the gays who made up half the audience at the première of *Earnest* understood the code in the title sums up the extent of the silence on both sides. The homosexual underworld was rompant but not rampant – it fucked quietly so as not to frighten the horses. Scandals such as Cleveland Street – implicating a member of the royal family – were hushed away – again, by both sides. Gays lived in terror of exposure – in every sense. While in the privacy of their libraries they might jerk off when ogling photos of boys in 'classical' poses, or the boy-paintings of Henry Scott Tuke, in the reading-rooms of their clubs they were models of masculine propriety.

Pater, through the gayvine, knew all of this, of course. His *Marius the Epicurean* was admired as a somewhat twee paean to the emergent Christianity of Rome – the catacombs providing Pater with his way into the underworld, the labyrinth of gay silence. The love between Marius and Cornelius is pure, driven by religion rather than lust. But what religion? Christ or a Greek god? The chapter 'Manly Amusement' was all that the knowing reader (he who subscribed to *Queer's Weekly* or *Sods*

Monthly) needed in order to discover the key to the whole mystery: a homosexual relationship masquerading as a religion.

Here's a typical coded message:

> The reserve which had puzzled Marius was but an instance of many, to him wholly unaccountable, avoidances alike of things and persons, which must certainly mean that an intimate companionship would cost him something in the way of seemingly indifferent amusements. Some inward standard Marius seemed to detect there of distinction, selection, refusal, amid the various elements of the fervid and corrupt life across which they were moving together – some secret, constraining motive, ever on the alert at eye and ear, which carried him through Rome as under a charm.

Having the code (*reserve, avoidances, intimate, inward, selection, fervid and corrupt, motive, charm*), Pater's gay reader would find that text an open challenge to the invert to embrace charm but at the cost of vigilance. In a pre-HIV world, the admonishment that "seemingly indifferent amusements" might require the exercise of "distinction," and "refusal" before "acceptance" was prescient of modern openness and a subconscious warning by Pater to himself "not to go there." When Pater wrote, in *The Renaissance*, that "art aspires to the condition of music," what he had written in his diary, before coding it, was "Pater aspires to the condition of Wildeness."

And in his essays, Pater betrayed himself more steadily, assuming (George thought) that aesthetics, his ostensible subject matter, would 'cover' a multitude of socio-sexual suggestions. By so doing, he was actively promoting, but subcutaneously, tendencies more acute than anything of which he himself was capable.

Years later, when the Scunthorpe boys spoke of having "a bit of the uvver" or "a bit of strange," George realized how far into human consciousness the idea of 'the Other' had entered. We all encountered, at some stage, the idea of strangeness. Some, like raunchy teenagers, would dive into girls like a new medium, a fucking-pool. But there was a point beyond which it was dangerous to venture, and Pater had, hesitatingly but deliberately, provided Victorian readers with signposts which were invisible to the naked eye but, to those who could 'see' it, opened doors into a different world, an alternative world, where the inmates would call "Welcome home."

The Child in the House is perhaps the most revealing. Many writers have addressed the theme as a form of confessional, an *apologia pro vita sua*, a way of explaining abandonment and loss of love. It was a therapy, a purging of one's childhood fears. For Pater, as George saw it, the essay was an admission that the child in question – himself of course – was available to gay impulses and orientations because his circumstances left him bereft of other avenues to security.

But the culmination of Pater's oppressed eroticism was the essay on Winckelmann, one of the most notorious boy-fuckers of the eighteenth century. Winckelmann's interests were "wholly Greek and alien from the Christian world" (hint hint, nudge nudge) and he wrote in favor of observing "the beauty of men" because their beauty is "supreme" rather than that of women. The more Pater insists that Winckelmann tried to elevate this to a spiritual level, the more we detect that he is pointing innocence in that direction while setting up a signpost for something more tangible, more down-to-earth, "the perfect animal nature of the Greeks." Youth aspired to godliness, yet always fell off its pedestal into the arms of an art critic.

Pater's essay on Wincklemann is in fact his own essay

on Greek love with some reference to Winckelmann's life and work thrown in for camouflage. No one but Pater could genuinely have got off by contemplating the Greek sculptures over which he rhapsodized, unless his intellect were located in his scrotum. Winckelmann is an excuse – Pater's excuse – for these erotic mental acrobatics: Greek art is sensuous but lacking in "any sense of want, or corruption or shame." Oh yeah. So, thought George, it's acceptable because it's shameless but not corrupt.

When he writes in "Athletic Prizemen" of Pindar's "language suggestive of a sort of metallic beauty," Pater was not only making his own suggestive commentary, but alluding discreetly to another gay code word of that time, "bimetallism." The "development of youthful limbs" was a theme often celebrated by classical scholars of a certain disposition, especially when, as in Pater's case, they referred to "two youths in a real incident which had the quality of a poetic ambition turning as it did on that ideal or romantic friendship which was characteristic of the Greeks." Pater's was the sort of mind that would experience an intellectual orgasm at the thought of an unperforated postage stamp. He got off on his own essays, a dialogue "of the soul with itself," worshipping "the irresistible grace, the contagious pleasantness" of youth. "In the presentment of youth," Pater argues, "there will be no place for symbolic hint." How, George thought, could Pater have been so two-faced, when that was all he did: hint symbolically at "the love that dare not ..."?

George had wanted to add, tongue in cheek (his own, not someone else's) that to read Pater in this interstitial style was to find him "in the cracks," but his supervisor was worried that, if he insisted on this, the PhD would fail. As it was, his examiners took 'a dim view' of his subject matter. "The sexual lives of our great writers are not necessarily the quarry of a great critic," commented one early reader, but then compounded George's argument by adding "that kind of exegesis, of what is *not* [heavily underlined] in the text, suggests that Pater was 'not one of us,' which he undoubtedly was." Oh yes he was! QED.

In some essays, every word was suggestive and symbolic of the paedophile's restrained lust. The sculpture of a young man with "fittingly expressionless expression" is "beautiful, but not altogether virile," while one of Leonardo's heads is "the face of a doubtful sex." C'mon Wally babe, get your kit off.

The triumph of George's thesis was that he succeeded in dressing all this up in such academic jargon that his examiners for the most part did not recognise what he was actually presenting: he was outing Pater and outpatering Pater at one and the same time. Only the extern reader, Anthony Blunt, gave George a nod of recognition. Otherwise, George's PhD came with flying colors from an unsuspecting faculty.

Uncle D's reaction, when George told him all about it, was surprising both in view of his opinion of "bumboys" and for its calm appraisal of the thing. "What you said must have made them uncomfortable. I'd say they were probably a load of old poufs like the chap you were writing about, but they gave you the medal to put one over their opposite numbers in Cambridge."

So George had got away with it. A daring thesis, totally incorrect, politically speaking, until it was published, much to George's surprise, with a foreword by Eve Sedgwick. And this was George's second triumph, to publish the thesis *en plein air*, unbuttoned, decoded, explicit. *Pater's Closet* alarmed the gay world still screaming (quietly, of course) for anonymity, and delighted the chattering classes. It actually sold 3000 copies, more than any PhD-turned-into-book can hope to achieve. It got one review, from *The Times Literary Supplement*, which opined that it "filled a much needed vacuum," a view that was both daft and well-deserved. But by then George had got tenure and was happily settled (until Ms. News of the World and Scunthorpe reared, respectively, their lovely and ugly heads) into a cosy lifestyle of lectures, conferences, committees and idle research.

And by that time, too, he had inaugurated the Fowles Industry with the first volume of the 'trilogy of betrayal' as he came to see it.

FOWLES

If Pater was a closet gay, Fowles was a closet shit. He really was a shit. He always had been a shit. George knew that from their acquaintance, an acquaintance that had deepened – regrettably, he now realized – into a trusting friendship. Was it wrong – absurd – to be friends with someone you knew to be a shit? If he wasn't actually shitty to you personally, was his shittiness towards others necessarily a bad thing? George now wondered how far he had allowed himself, for reasons of career advancement, to ignore that side of Fowles, in order to write about the novels. And when it came to his third volume on Fowles when, as in the case of Pater, he had "spilled the beans," was that a betrayal? Yes, of course it was. But wasn't it also a final arrival at honesty – a realisation that, unless he exposed his "friend" for the unprincipled, misogynistic, cavalier bastard that he was, he would be untrue to his readers, those innocent generations of readers who trusted what George had previously written from an undeniable position of authority, and therefore accepted his praise of the novels without knowing the real character of their author? Was it the same kind of betrayal that George had somehow – he didn't really know how – incorporated into his 'dispatches'?

"It has been my privilege, as a critic, to know intimately one of the greatest writers of the twentieth century" George had written in the preface to *An Introduction to John Fowles* (volume 1). "My friendship with John Fowles has enabled me to occupy a privileged position as an interpreter of his works" was the opening of *Sexuality and the Double in the Work of John Fowles* (volume 2). "All through my career, until recently, I have extolled John Fowles as a great writer. Now, I am forced to acknowledge that I see him in a new and distressing epiphany, as an author empty of all but the most disloyal sentiments" was how volume 3, *The Enigma of John Fowles*, began.

At the time of volume 1, George genuinely believed *The Collector* and *The Magus* and *The French Lieutenant's Woman* to be works of genius, and he still did: original (within obvious limits), thoughtful, important essays into the state of the psyche and of contemporary culture. Massive works for our time, bla, bla, bla.

A few years later, trying to do the same service for *Daniel Martin* and *A Maggot*, he realized how dishonest he was in his critical acclaim. Taking Fowles seriously was so much harder work than 'discovering' the truth about Pater, and George had accepted that what he had written about Fowles was a fraud.

He had known for many years that the Fowles-Elizabeth marriage was an empty one. The passion and the compassion had gone out the door. Fowles had frequently said, while she was alive, that Elizabeth was the *fons et origo* of all the women in his novels – especially, George knew, the enigma of Sarah Woodruff, but also the Collector's Miranda, Alison and Lily in *The Magus*... Any woman who could inspire Woodruff was a very special person. *All Fowles's women were aspects of the one enigma, and that enigma was in itself a falsity, as the public would discover when Fowles's Journals were published and his biography written.* But if Elizabeth was no longer an enigma, there were no more women asking for a place in his novels and, therefore, no novels.

George had declined inclusion in Dianne Vipond's collection of "Conversations with John Fowles," even though he had a scorcher of an interview on tape, its contents, in his reflective mood, taking on a striking similarity to the stuff he put into his secret service 'dispatches.' Revelations, diversions and searingly honest statements – he was astonished that Vipond had wanted to print them. He thought it would have completely wrecked the book, destroying the carefully modulated contributions of the other contributors in identifying Fowles as a great novelist, a great storyteller, a great explorer of mind and morals. A Great Charlatan. A Great Liar. A Great Cheat. A Great Whore. Someone who appeared to love his fellow men, but in private proclaimed *Odi profanum vulgus, et arceo.*

When he came to write *The Enigma of John Fowles,* he repudiated the friendship by revealing what he knew about Fowles – facts and viewpoints which he had suppressed earlier in order to... well, to bolster his own academic reputation as an expert Fowlian to the detriment of his integrity as a person. Once he began to understand Fowles the man, he should have backed off. Made a clear and conscious decision to retreat from his proposed study, issued discreet warnings to fellow Fowlians, even to that other shit, Andrew Dalton, and to explain to his publishers and to an indifferent faculty (who basked vicariously in the fact that they had such a distinguished and authoritative Fowlian in their midst) that this was an avenue of research which, despite his being on the inside track, he no longer wished to pursue. Wouldn't that have been the 'honorable thing'?

But no, for the sake of advancement in the faculty, which never in fact materialized, he had persevered with the white lies regarding the mind and art of Fowles, lies which became grey in the second volume and impossibly black by the time he came to write the third – a book which was almost certainly unnecessary in scholarly or critical terms, but which became necessary if he were to redeem himself, firstly, from the whiter lies and, secondly, from the inferno of Scunthorpe. He wrote entirely without conscience up to the point where conscience, lack of advancement, and a surprising acceptance of what Scunthorpe actually entailed, persuaded him towards honesty.

Was he ashamed of what he had written? Well, there were two conflicting questions here: was he ashamed of the white lies of the first two works, or ashamed of his treachery in the third?

How have I prostituted myself in academe by writing that final book? Can we truly separate the man and the work? Not in Pater's case and not in Fowles's. I extolled the novels without giving any indication whatever of the character of the man behind them. Just an appraisal of the artistry, without an appraisal of the man. How could he have written such fine novels and then such appalling ones? Well, Fowles was revealing himself in the first novels, yet we didn't realise at the time how predictive they were. That's my excuse anyway.

Spilled the beans. Blew the whistle, In the cases of both Pater and Fowles, a whistle had been posthumously blown; they weren't alive to defend themselves, and while Pater scholars accepted, with considerable demur, my elucidation of Pater's erotic weaknesses and obfuscations, Fowlians deplored my statements about a literary hero whose private life and personal attitudes they believed to be above or beyond the responsibilities of criticism.

Pater himself of course would never have responded; he would have retreated even further into his closet, while gay London would have tittered, had a good wank and looked even more favorably and clandestinely at their private paedofiles.

Fowles, on the other hand, lived in a much more public world, to which the advent of television documentaries, talk shows, gossip columns and tabloid papers had brought the gaze and ears of the moralistic voyeur. And, while Pater had his coterie, Fowles had a circle of anxious 'friends' and a wider and more vociferous industry – which I myself had established.

George wasn't proud of himself, but could he justify what he had done as 'in the public interest'? His opinion of the later novels had been bowdlerized and adulterated in order to get the second book into print. That was unprofessional, and unworthy of a true critic. How many of his colleagues had produced books in which they did not believe? How many of them read up their subject not as a compelling, consuming passion but merely as a stepping-stone to a full professorship? It was so easy to find a neglected writer (like Maurice Baring or Charles Morgan) who wrote second-rate novels or, worse still, *belles-lettres*, out of a sublimated private life, and boost them into a major study that no one would ever read but which looked good on a c.v., especially if one had access to the private papers mouldering in some obscure American university.

George himself had the excuse that he knew Fowles personally and could claim him as a friend, thus growing his reputation as a Fowlian with direct access to the Master on a basis of mutual respect: *the* Fowlian, in fact; father of all the Fowlians.

And to himself he would argue that he hadn't gone to

Fowles in a spirit of betrayal, but that that betrayal had become necessary ... once Fowles was dead and beyond caring. There was the problem which George, neither to himself nor to the Fowlian world, could not evade or deny.

But justify himself he did, by a clever strategy: the dearth of invention and imagination and the irrelevancy of the later novels was directly due to Fowles's innate shittiness. Up to the stories in *The Ebony Tower* he had kept faith with his art, had suppressed his baser nature in order to put before the world books which were exhilarating, probing, and *honest*. After that, he had revealed his 'true self' by works that were deceitful, devoid of love or care, and flippant with regard to the feelings of the characters. A cruel man, an unashamedly sensual man whose appetites and increasing egotism turned him from the writer who loved the French lieutenant's woman into the man who preferred the French lieutenant. Uncle D, having rather surprisingly picked up *Daniel Martin*, declared after a few pages "The man is a SHIT!," while Jessica, who was as ill-read as any of the Manners, took one look at *The French Lieutenant's Woman* and said "Anyone who can write about women like that deserves to be castrated." (She'd said it about Lawrence Durrell, too, who was incomparably the greater writer, and she was right about him as well.)

Fowles's first two books, *The Collector* and *The Magus*, were beautiful books, noble books, brave books. They took basic terms and played with them so improbably that one saw the world in a new light. That, George argued, is what a novel or story should do. Not to make us into better people or to portray social conditions or class warfare – all that Dickensian bollox that that Catholic bastard Evelyn Waugh had spent his horrible life doing – but to turn you, the reader, inside out and reassemble you into a new person, more capable of dealing with your own emotions, your own view of the world, and to present challenges which were both intellectual and emotional, spiritual almost. Frederick Clegg, the protagonist in *The Collector*, was only a vampire rewritten, but his stature as a monster was not diminished, and we were asked to choose between him (and his rather disgusting hobby) and his heroine(s), colorless and empty women who deserved little better than what they got.

"What I fear in you is something you don't know is in you" could have served as George's own verdict on Fowles. But it was more subtle than that. Maybe 'Miranda' never existed, except in Clegg's imagination; maybe their conversations were simply his conversations with himself. After all, we all did it, didn't we? Invent others in the process of inventing ourselves? When he makes her say "Why do you take all the life out of life? Why do you kill all the beauty?" he's reprimanding himself for his emotional incapacity to recognise love and celebrate it. Again, Fowles himself. More to the point "He's not human; he's an empty space disguised as a human."

The Collector is a starter, showing Fowles's promise but not capitalising on it. He was beginning to experiment with the power of language: "You can get away with murder with words," and in his heart he would, indeed, murder women but with silence rather than words. It made a better film than novel, with Terence Stamp and Samantha Eggar. *He saw his own life as a pen on paper, and he knew that his own imperfections would eventually come clear and explicit.* In *The Collector* they were sublimated, a jerking-off of the inconsistencies which troubled him as an adventurer taking another man's wife as a hostage, taking the butterfly beauty within her, and thus killing within his own self the path to beauty. "Nobody understands" was not Clegg's appeal but Fowles's, and the world would have to be made to understand through novels that would deceive but never reveal, never tell the truth, nothing but sidling up to truth and then fucking it senseless, abusing truth instead of abusing himself. And thereby abusing his readership in general and literature in particular. But that was volume three, not the self-serving adulation of the first two books.

In between the first and second novels came *The Aristos*, a collection of aphorisms greeted by sycophants as a profound and eloquent exposition of the human condition. It was a lot of hot air, disguised as Heraclitus, and it was a taste of the emptiness to come.

The French Lieutenant's Woman was more adventurous, the positioning of the idea of dualism, of querying the time-space continuum, back into an historical past and set in a landscape which Fowles knew well, using the techniques of alienation as a way of digging into his characters and into us, the readers. Again, it owed much to the eighteenth- and nineteenth-century fictions, with their palimpsests and their disturbing route-maps. George Eliot had done it better, but she wasn't around to compete, was she?

One of the best lines in *The French Lieutenant's Woman* – in the film version anyway – is when Meryl Streep, alias Sarah Woodruff, says "whore." Generations of voyeurs have relished that "whore," the brilliant way that Streep, as a dedicated and assiduous student of the voice-coach, could so perfectly say such a very English word.

With the exception of the surrealist phantasmagoria and supercharged sexology of *Mantissa*, Fowles's creative life ended with the short stories in *The Ebony Tower*. There were, in fact, only two novels after that – *Daniel Martin* and *A Maggot* – both of which were lazy, voluminous prick-teases of pseudo-intellectual drivel.

If *Daniel Martin* and *A Maggot* were prick-teases, intellectually and artistically sterile, *Mantissa* teased the prick on the prick-level, while also, George had to admit, posing worthwhile artistic questions. It did much – but only temporarily – to redeem Fowles's sinking reputation. The idea of individual identity versus multiple personalities, and the intermingling of ideas, emotions, sexual orientations and sense of purpose among several characters, which Durrell had perfected, were here addressed in a beguiling fashion, and there was considerably more sex – of a titillating if frustrating kind (but what other kind is there?) – than anything in Durrell.

But there was also a layer of persiflage as, for example: "Your true evolutionary function as a rule is to introduce your spermatozoa into as many wombs as possible." George reflected how much better Durrell had put it.[3]

Everyone in *Mantissa* was a part of someone else (especially when the fucking is under way) and this, George thought, was reassuring. It smelt of Kretschmer, Bergson and the Marquis de Sade, which was, of course, outrageous borrowing (or plagiarism of a higher kind), but nevertheless effective. Yes, *Mantissa* would win some sort of prize for invention, especially if there were a special award for an author redeeming himself from previous lapses and lassitude.

And there was a personal element in *Mantissa*, between George and Fowles, which, in retrospect, provided George with another excuse for spilling the beans about his friend: George had told Fowles about a dream he had had, which, to his not entire consternation, surfaced in *Mantissa*:

We have at least one thing in common: a mutual

---

[3] Editor's note: Manners was thinking of the passage in *The Alexandria Quartet* when Capodistria pronounces: "the world is a biological phenomenon which will only come to an end when every single man has had all the women, every woman all the men."

incomprehension of how your supremely real presence in the world of letters has failed to receive the attention (though you may regard that as a blessing in disguise) of the campus-faculty factories, the structuralists and deconstructivists, the semiologists, the Marxists, academic Uncle Tom Cobbleigh and all, that it deserves.

George never saw Fowles's two volumes of Journals. He didn't need to. He knew them intimately without having to read a word. He could have written them himself. After his wife's death, Fowles had an affair with an Oxford undergraduette. Her letters to him revealed what George already knew: that his persecution mania and his belief in the rottenness of the world were the fuel of all his behaviours, the hallmarks of his imagination – or, rather, his imagination consisted of nothing except these mania. But he also pursued her as Charles Smithson pursues Sarah Woodruff (the French lieutenant's 'woman'): "I love you because you are fluid, uncertain, changeable, restless" – in other words, a *femme suivable*, a Miranda-like butterfly still pursued by a Clegg who wants to kill her beauty in order to put his own terrors to rest.

VI

Dispatches

It usually happens at uni, or shortly thereafter. Or so we are led to believe by the popular literature which suggests that Cambridge, in particular, was a hunting-ground for members of the secret service on the track of disenchanted young men (why was it always men, and homosexuals mostly?) who saw the future of the world in terms of the defeat of communism or the Yellow Peril or other anarchic or corruptive influences. Or, conversely, those who thought the opposite: that 'England, my England' was a sham, no longer home to anything other than class distinction, self-righteousness, hypocrisy, cant... and lacking the moral fibre for which 'England' was supposed to be famous – at least, as a cloak for the imperial ambitions which led to suppression and rape of vast continents of what we used to be able to call "natives," "niggers," and "coons," but now had to settle for "non-white indigenous peoples."

British India and most of Africa had been built on the foundations of such a sham, and you either decided that that had been worthwhile – a *mission civilatrice* it was euphemistically called – and still required some sorting out, or you found it revolting and went over to the other side. From George's experience in Ireland, that had meant either clinging to the "Anglo" part of the hyphenated "Anglo-Irish," or throwing in one's lot with the IRA. That was a harsh juxtaposition of the political choices, but it brought home brutally the idea of where one's loyalties, responsibilities and inclinations lay. It was always "either/or," never "both/and" – unless, of course, one took the *via media* of dual compliance.

Well, it hadn't happened to George that way. Maybe the fact that he went to Dublin, rather than Cambridge, meant that he had escaped that sort of approach. No-one at Trinity had spoken to him in such a way that he felt he was being drawn into a discussion designed to establish just how dissident he felt, especially not to ask whether he had communist, or anti-British, feelings. After all, this was TCD! No one sidled up to him in a Dublin bar to slip him a message about a rendezvous "with some sympathetic friends" which might have led to his recruitment into MI5 or MI6. Nor did it happen in the Royal Irish Yacht Club, to which his future father-in-law ostentatiously belonged; it didn't happen at a cocktail party (which was, apparently, a favorite place for such assignations) because he didn't go to cocktail parties.

Sometimes he wished it had. Sometimes, once he had started work for "them," he fantasised about people "sidling up" – it wasn't difficult to create a fantasy, since they were two-a-penny in the thriller books, from le Carré downwards, which George absorbed with a now professional interest. There were clandestine meetings, dead-letter boxes where one dropped one's message – hardly the post office in Nafplion![4] – and there was always the wonderful moment when he met himself face-to-face in the Athens Plaka, each greeting the other with a knowing look and passing with hardly a flicker of contact, but with the 'drop' well achieved.

Sometimes he craved that kind of life, presumably because it offered an excitement unknown to academe, but mainly because he was on the fringes; he saw himself reading the latest le Carré with a jaundiced eye, making

---

[4] The main town of the Peloponnese, to which islanders were obliged to travel for commercial, banking or other official business – *Editor's note.*

mental reservations about the 'reality' of the scene. Even though, by his own admission, le Carré knew this business from the inside, there were times when George thought that perhaps he had strayed from the paths of unrighteousness for the sake of spinning a better yarn than personal experience could furnish. But that was, indeed, a view from the fringe. And it was "academic" because George, despite his lingering wonder and, perhaps, longings, was never a spy, never an agent, never a traitor. He was merely a viewpoint that was paid to view, not to take part.

The simple fact was that George harbored no anti-British feelings at all, other than those exhibited by like-minded writers such as Anthony Burgess or Lawrence Durrell, who found Britain – and England in particular – an unappetising, even inhospitable, place to live. Others might be content to write stories of "tepid adultery in Hampstead," as Burgess had put it. Not a great topic, but it rang true for the kitchen-sink bourgeois English mind. The *great* topics were...

What George *did* have was a natural curiosity about the world outside the claustrophobia of university, which impelled him towards the (as it now seemed) inescapable destination of British 'intelligence' – a world in which the greater powers organized the destinies of the smaller ones. That didn't make him anti-British, partly because he knew, as did most Brits, that Britain was no longer one of the Great Powers, which had ruled the known world throughout the nineteenth century and built their empires accordingly.

When the contact *did* come, it came through his old TCD friend James Esposito, who one day simply relayed a message he'd received from an acquaintance in London who wondered if George "might be available for a spot of lunch" – at his convenience, of course.

It was intriguing, even though for the rest of his life he wondered what could possibly have recommended him to the faceless faces he met at those two meetings when some kind of deal had been struck. What that deal consisted of was even unclear to George, but it seemed to be of some interest to someone somewhere who reckoned George was a perceptive critic who could put together a coherent and convincing argument to support his critical viewpoint. It seemed that having a house in Greece had been quite a strong contributing factor. George wondered if Fowles had done any similar work on the same pretext, but when he asked Fowles about it, the novelist clammed up and changed the subject, which to George was as good as an admission. Would Fowles's posthumous papers yield a "Journal of a Spy"? Or a "Secret Diary of a Mole"? Anything was possible these days. Some of the greatest writers in history had been "spies." The Elizabethan world seemed to be populated by little else. Perhaps the second Elizabethan age was just repeating history. It was tiring even to speculate, and it was as much as George could manage to compile the imaginative dossiers that passed for 'dispatches' when they were requested.

He was relieved to learn, early on, that he would not be required to defend any of his reports. He felt acutely vulnerable to being caught out in the act of using too much imagination and too few facts. He was very aware that, like Alec Guinness in Greene's *Our Man in Havana*, or Geoffrey Bush in le Carré's *The Tailor of Panama* (like most people, he hadn't read the books, but he had seen the films), he spent his time – and British government funds – concocting phantom intrigues to keep some Whitehall mandarin on the edge of his seat – or, if it were M, her seat. But M was far too astute, and knew him far too well, to have fallen for what she, with her Irish lilt, had called his "guff."

It was in fact George who had felt the pull towards what one might call "our British interests." If M was, as he suspected, enrolled in some area of the intelligence services, she must have known about his self-styled "dispatches," thinking of them as messages from a non-existent, or at least imaginary, war front. There was almost certainly a file, if not on George specifically, then on those who, like him, had shown youthful signs of dissidence and who were today involved in what, for want of a better, more euphemistic term, was known as "intelligence work." In Soviet Russia they would have ended up in the *gulag*. Here, they were kept within the system and, unless they strayed grievously, were tolerated, even played with by an establishment, which kept them on an elastic string, like wayward puppies.

No, it wasn't the "Philby factor" or anything like it. It is something of a commonplace (and we owe it to spy-thrillers such as those of John le Carré) that when one senses betrayal – believes that one has been betrayed by forces against which one has no resistance – the result is often to make a traitor of the betrayed. To strike back at the attacker with the only weapons available to the humiliated but still resilient victim: in James Joyce's words, "silence, exile and cunning" or, in George's case, verbosity, exile and cunning. Many of the most famous double agents have suffered a fractured childhood and/or a lost home. What is at stake, essentially, is *identity*. *Something has been taken from me, which could have made me what I ought to be. Therefore I pursue that self of which I have been deprived, until I feel capable of taking it prisoner. My self. But always – and this is where the duplicity enters the mind-set – there is the sense of being other, of never quite repossessing that elusive self, of the need to pretend to be what I think I am, but which I know I am not. Above all, I betray myself, perhaps because there is no self within.* George's diary is explicitly secretive on this point, but what we know of his childhood could be construed as embodying loss and, possibly, in his father's presence – or non-presence – a betrayal of paternal authority.

George's greatest sense was that of emptiness, of a space and a silence that needed to be filled. He wouldn't turn against his country, like Philby, Burgess, Maclean, Blunt and all the others. He would go as far as them in their accommodation within the system, but he wouldn't turn the other way and sell his soul to the other side. Apart from ethics, that would be too exciting.

The crux of le Carré's extended thesis on the life and identity of the double-agent comes when we are told the gist of the 'book' (*A Perfect Spy*) in which he is struggling to encapsulate his own life story and his own identity: "We betray to be loyal. Betrayal is like imagining when the reality isn't good enough ... Betrayal as hope and compensation. As the making of a better land. Betrayal as love. As a tribute to our unlived lives ... Betrayal as escape. As a constructive act. As a statement of ideals. Worship. As an adventure of the soul. Betrayal as travel: how can we discover new places if we never leave home?" George had practically memorized that passage as a way of understanding and explaining his decision to undertake intelligence work.

That "central lack," occasioned by a lost childhood and fuelled by 'buried hunger' and emotional impotence is perhaps what confronts us all if we take that 'low door in the wall' – the danger that the hortus conclusus *may be empty of everything except our own empty self, the realisation that the naked, deserted garden is an allegory of our own meaninglessness, a mirror in which we realise that within us is an empty space – the 'central lack' – which may or not have once been occupied by a core, a being, that may or may not have been stolen, and may or may not have been oneself. Loss underlines the fact that one is a husk without a centre, merely an appearance, a disguise without a real presence hiding behind it. The more intensely conscious of this 'loss' we become, the more painful becomes the burden of emptiness. And it makes us create imaginary worlds in which to find ourselves and which we can populate with characters acceptable to us, if not to the "real" world.*

In his youth it had hardly mattered. George had done nothing reprehensible, nor had he exhibited anything more than the youthful exuberance of rebellion. It was during his first senior college appointment, when he was hard at work on his first Fowles exploration, that a few conversations with James had indicated to him that he knew so little about the 'real' thoughts and feelings of his friends and colleagues. Chitchat in the Common Room and at high table seldom touched on the world outside, and the fall-out from the apparently never-ending series of revelations about the third, fourth, fifth and now even sixth, man were merely gossip.

Partly because, despite his half-Irish blood and half-Irish education, George still felt that he belonged to England, or at least a small and deeply cherished part of it, when the 'call' did come – would he be willing to meet a senior chap in the civil service? – he went to the luncheon out of that same sense of curiosity, and came away tempted to believe, but not entirely convinced, that there might be a role for him to play in the compilation of reports on international politics – a topic on which, he had been at pains to insist to his genial host, he was almost entirely ignorant. That didn't seem to matter, and in fact what George wrote in his diary was exactly how it turned out: *And it makes us create imaginary worlds in which to find ourselves and which we can populate with characters acceptable to us, if not to the 'real' world.* He didn't go as far as 'our men in Havana and Panama' but, as 'our man in Lincoln' and then 'our man in Greece' he *did* create those worlds and he *did* indulge in make-believe that almost convinced him, too, that he was writing lucid (which it was), coherent (which it was), informed (which it certainly wasn't) reports on whatever situation it was that they had suggested, or had come of its own accord to his mind. He saw the Booker Prize coming up. "And the winner is ... *A Clown in Greece* by ..." – no, not George Manners, how about 'James Esposito'?

The first conversation, after the usual pleasantries, including his host's polite inquiry after Margaret's wellbeing (but without any mention, of course, of her own place in this affair), took an insipid line.

Host: "We've become aware that you take quite an interest in international affairs."

George: "Well, a bit. Nothing to write home about, you understand."

Host: "Actually, it's about 'writing home' as you call it that we would like to talk to you rather more seriously."

George: "If I'm not being too rude or inquisitive, what the hell *are* you talking about?"

Host: "My dear fellow, this won't happen overnight. I'd like you to meet one or two of my colleagues who have been following your career with interest. Believe it or not, what you've written about Fowles does not go unnoticed, and we feel you may have something to contribute, based on your natural inclination" – George wondered at the use of this word, delivered with what he had heard of, but never actually seen, 'a knowing look' – "for research and interpretation. That's why we feel that you might like to have another conversation – at your convenience of course. We appreciate that you've come all this way from Lincoln today, and we wouldn't like to drag you out of your comfort zone too, er, eagerly. But we *are* eager."

George: "Sorry to seem obtuse, but who are "we" and what can you possibly see in a stuffy academic like me that makes you, er, eager?"

Host (slightly hesitant and with considerably less assurance – was he faking it, or had George really offended him? or was this his regular ploy when faced with the question, which he must have heard a hundred times before?): "Could we let the matter drop there for the moment. Look" – George was afraid that "Old boy" would be the next ingredient in this getting-to-know-you rigmarole, but it passed unsaid – "could we meet possibly in a fortnight's time? I'll make all the arrangements nearer the time."

And so they had said their goodbyes on the steps of the club where they had lunched – not a bad lunch, considering it was club fare, George had reflected on the train home to Lincoln, and a *very* good wine, in which clubs habitually invested more wisely than in their chefs. George comfortably expected, and part of him hoped, that that would be the end of the matter, that his abruptness had scored him sufficient black marks to ensure that he was crossed off the list of eligible middle-aged men.

But more was to come, perhaps because his host had detected that another part of George was bemused, if not flattered, by the overture and would respond more positively once he had been given slightly more of a perspective on the work they would offer him (and rather more Pétrus '59), especially when he heard how much his reports would contribute to his bank balance. Enough to buy himself Pétrus and Lynch-Bages *grand cru* by the case.

And he was right about the money. At first, George – English gentleman that he was, or had been – resented what he saw as an insult to his integrity. Taking money for doing something patriotic seemed uncouth. But later, when he saw how his rising bank balance (together with what he inherited from the family trust fund and his not entirely unreasonable salary) could make him far more comfortable than most of his colleagues, he rationalized it as equivalent (or so he thought) to an army officer's pay and, after all, wasn't he fighting some sort of battle, even if it was behind the lines in a cushy doss, and risking something, he wasn't quite sure what, for his country?

At the second and last meeting, George had taken the bull by the horns: "You are presumably aware that my wife and I are separated?"

"Naturally."

"And that she is involved in the civil service in London?"

"Naturally."

"Well, can you please tell me what she actually does?" The response to this was a blank stare. "You see, when we were still together, in Lincoln, Margaret's job appeared to be so secret that she couldn't talk about it at home; neither I nor our children" – a pause – "You know about our twins?"

"Naturally."

"None of us knows what it's all about, except that her move to London around the time of our split was a major promotion for her, and again, something she couldn't talk about." Silence from the other side of the table. "So I've wondered, in these past years, whether it might be some kind of *secret* work – you know" – I faltered, my composure and confidence plummeting rapidly – "the same line of business as yourselves. After all, not much call for espionage in Lincoln!" – this accompanied by a half-hearted attempt at a laugh in the 'Uncle David' style – "ha ha" – to indicate that it was a joke, possibly in the worst taste.

"The same line of business, Dr Manners?" From 'George' we had retreated to the frosty officialdom of 'Dr Manners.'

"Yes," I persisted, "Spies." A man called Bateman used to do cartoons of people who had just made a major social gaffe ('the man who asked for a whisky and soda in the Pump Room at Bath' came immediately to mind).

"Dr Manners." The composure of my hosts would have put a meditating swami or a Buddhist monk to shame. "I'm awfully sorry, but we haven't the slightest idea what you're talking about. We do know Margaret, of course. There would be no point in denying it. She *is* involved in certain types of confidential work, but" – here a genial half-smile spread over his poker-straight face that suggested a crocodile inviting one to a little chat while planning one's immediate extinction – "whatever Ministry she serves is *not* part of the secret service. Nor are we." So M might well be in the hush-hush section of the Ministry of Dog Licences as far as these goons were prepared to let on. They didn't call them hush-puppies for nothing, ha ha. Monty Python had invented the 'Ministry of Silly Walks.' 'Ministry of Silly Talks' would be more appropriate, with John Cleese doing double-speak – two meaningless languages in the same breath.

George could never explain to himself how even a smithereen of his persistence remained, but he soldiered on: "But it does exist? MI5, MI6..."

"George" – the smile became affable once more, less like a school monitor admonishing a misdemeanour and more like forgiving a fool for his stupidity rather than impertinence – "there are such organisations, of course. The tabloid press hasn't got it entirely wrong. But we know nothing about it. Nothing. If you imagine that, you've seriously misled yourself."

"But, but... John le Carré writes about it. *Smiley's*

People – isn't it real? Isn't that what we're discussing?"

"What Mr Cornwell surmises about the world of espionage is his own business. It entertains thousands of readers. Some of it – the Berlin stories – may well be based on some element of fact – his personal experience – but that is what it is – entertainment. Pap for the dispossessed."

The literary allusion (Heaney) took George so much by surprise that he was lost, not momentarily, but for several minutes, for words of any kind. What in god's name was he being recruited into, if it wasn't the secret service? Surely these respectable-looking gents in this exclusive London club weren't just inviting him to join some sex-crazed gang of orgiasts? Surely he hadn't got the whole thing wrong from the start – that James Esposito had lured him into a shady version of a pigeon-fanciers' association? High fliers, indeed.

Spies were covert, under cover. University lecturers were overt – open to their subjects and their students – at least on the surface. So, for George, it was all the same thing, really. Overt, covert, mumbo-jumbo, hocus-pocus. 'Tell all the truth, but tell it slant.'

And how to extract himself from this solecistic lunch with even a smidgen of self-respect? Would they break their holes laughing at the fool he had made of himself? Was it a crocodile or a hamster that he had just offended?

As it turned out, the conversation was steered away from whatever George thought it was about, in such a fashion that two things were clear: firstly, he must never, *never* make any kind of supposition about his freelance work for whoever it was, and secondly he must never, *never* inquire about M's work. They would leave it at that, and the next thing George would know, a letter of some kind would arrive through the ordinary post, asking for his views on certain matters. If he wished to accept the assignment, he would send his reply to an address, which would be separately communicated, to him, and the whole thing would proceed from there.

George only infringed these commandments once, and he did so as soon as he returned to Lincoln: he knew that one of his hosts had been called 'Benedict Griffin.' Of the other's identity, he hadn't the slightest clue. When George looked up the name in the Civil Service Directory it was as he thought. The name was not listed. And when he phoned the club where they had lunched, a bemused secretary had assured him that no, the club had no member of that name. George never saw or heard from them again.

What he subsequently did was not a matter of betrayal in the sense of spilling the beans on political secrets, or classified information, to which in any case George had no access whatever. Ironically, it was something which, if they had both known it, would possibly have brought M and him closer together – George's ability to sum up a situation and to describe it in such a way that his correspondents could immediately apprehend the significance of what he was revealing.

George may have known little or nothing of the Middle East; he had never visited any part of it, except for one guest lectureship at the American University in Cairo, but he nevertheless had the capacity to identify key issues from the papers which crossed his desk and to project, from the information they supplied, likely scenarios which his new 'masters' could in their turn assess. Everything he read and rewrote for them was in fact checked by one of them against those same sources. All they wanted, it seemed, was confirmation from an independent observer that their own scenario was accurate.

He needed to tell a convincing story. If he had but known it, his plausibility had won him the contract and sustained Whitehall's (or whoever's) interest in what he had to say. His masters seemed pleased, although they never said so. 'Masters'? He didn't even know who they were. The two who had 'recruited' him were unimportant ciphers in the 'real' game in which he was now a player. If interrogated by the thought-police, all he could say in all truthfulness (did truthfulness exist in this kind of world of double-speak?) was that he sent his 'dispatches' (officially referred to as 'reports') to an organisation in Palatine Road, Islington, calling itself the Institute for Middle East Research. Occasionally, but with no regularity, sums would appear in his bank account, which enabled him to undertake his expensive research trips in pursuit of Fowles and other projects which, as all literary sleuths know, he would never recoup. He attributed the irregularity of the payments to the notion that, if he were investigated, no one could spot that "£xxx were deposited on the first of every month" or, indeed, that each payment came from the same source, which it didn't. One month, payment would be made by "Beirut International Imports Ltd.," another by "Tel Aviv Insurances plc." If anyone had examined his finances, they would have realized that George had never applied for the funding for his research trips, which was available through the regular channels, and this might have been the one weak telltale point in his behaviour. But, as was in fact the case, this could be attributed to the fact of his having 'private means' – of being, for those who put it another way, 'independently wealthy.' And wasn't that what he was doing? Telltale. Telling one tale in place of another.

No requests for specific information were ever received – nothing of the "We'd like to know what you make of Arafat's U-turn?" or "What are the Chinese doing in the Gulf oilfields?" These days, he didn't have to keep a pair of binoculars to hand, so as to spot the passage of enemy shipping. Even if he did, who were the enemy? And all the time: who were 'we'? All he was expected to do was to read the bulletins sent to him on the weekly ferry (these would pass unnoticed among the many bundles of newspapers and books arriving each week) along with any other information source he found relevant (such as newspapers, journals, radio broadcasts) and to 'translate' them into the sort of jargon his masters would understand. Among the bundles of newspapers and journals he received were *The Economist*, the *International Herald Tribune, Foreign Affairs* and many other similar sources of viewpoint. The Greek newspapers were unknown in Karponisi until George started ordering *Kathimerini* and *Ta Nea*. He could of course have read all of these on the Internet, if he had had one.

It was for the unseen, unheard, unwritten elements in these journals and broadcasts – the news within the news, the news not of today or yesterday, but of tomorrow, that he was paid, yes paid, to seek. He did tell them, occasionally, what he considered to be Arafat's motives in opening talks with the Israelis – likening it to the charade of the handshake between the IRA and the unionists in Northern Ireland, which was possibly another *faux pas* notched up in his log-book. He did make observations about oil exploration, but in doing so he was answering questions they hadn't actually asked.

Much nearer home, he was gratified, but less pleased, when he had foreseen the short-lived military coup in Greece in 2011-12. He had been in Athens some months previously (he knew it like the back of his hand, especially the student bars in Exarchia), and had fallen into conversation at dinner with a couple of young men who might have been journalists, or ... or ... He had broached the subject of "tanks in the streets," only to be abruptly told "That's impossible. Out of the question. Couldn't happen. Unthinkable." He hadn't had the nerve to tell his companions that they should think again – that the unthinkable so frequently happened, as it had done over and over again in the Greek economic crisis, when politicians and civil servants had denied, for as long as possible, the undeniable.

When the news came through to Karponisi that a coup had taken place in Athens, there was far less dismay than had been shown at the advent of the Colonels in '67 (when George had also been on the island). In fact, most people just shrugged their shoulders and said it would soon be over. As it was. television pictures of protesters in Athens being brutally dispersed by riot police ignited international outrage, but in Greece itself it seemed like business as usual. The last so-called democratic government had done the same things. The state broadcaster, ERT, was taken off the air and replaced with "NERT," a strategy so transparent as to be obvious even to the Minister for Social Protection who had ordered it.

The only sign in Karponisi that there was a military régime was the single soldier who was billeted on the island policeman, exactly the same as had happened 44 years previously. Only the identity of the two was different. The soldier had nothing to do, all day, and did it. Alexis, the policeman, carried on as usual; when he wasn't out pretending to catch drug-smugglers in one of Karponisi's little coves, or intercepting boatloads of asylum seekers (what was the difference?), or watching with a hawk-eye for money-laundering at the post-office, he was out catching something far more profitable: lobster. He didn't have to pretend to do it, it was his main occupation and it more than quadrupled his official pay. This income he laundered, happily ignoring the responsibility of his official function. 'After the lobster' became village *argot* for 'a blind eye.'

Luckily, Alexis' lobsters were immune to military

control, so after selling most of his catch to restaurants in Athens, he could share a few with his soldier-comrade and one or two other cronies – the post-master-cum-baker, whose fire was needed to cook the animals, and Spiros the taxi-ambulance-driver. And of course the priest, who did an "after the lobster" to Alexis' incursion of civil and, no doubt, sacred law.

Within months, due to a threatened expulsion of the country from the EU (which in the opinion of many, including George, would have been no bad thing), the military capitulated, leaving in power a semblance of democracy while the ringleaders were sentenced to punishment in a luxury villa complex on Rhodes. So nothing changed at all.

Life in Karponisi had not been affected, and neither in a sense had George, except that he won additional kudos for proving that one could indeed think the unthinkable, just as some iceberg had proved that one could sink the unsinkable. Rather nice, George thought: the unthinkable in pursuit of the unsinkable. Wish I wrote fiction when I get a line like that...

But was George an iceberg? In a sense he was, because at least seven-eighths of him was below the surface, undetected, but not so, in the sense that he suddenly loomed out of the icy darkness and sank unsuspecting ideas. That, in fact, was what nearly happened to *him*, when Aleksandra floated into his life – but that is to jump ahead.

As a result of his sleuthing, he had predicted, with some satisfaction on his part, the collapse, first, of the Albanian regime of Enver Hoxha, then the break-up of Yugoslavia and, more recently, of Egyptian society in the maelstrom following the removal of Mubarak. It wasn't only the bulletins that helped him to write the dispatches. In this case, the novels of Mahfouz, Alaa Al Aswany's *The*

Yacoubian Building, even Albert Cossery, and especially *The Future of Culture in Egypt* by Taha Hussein, were sources providing invaluable background insights which his "control" would never suspect. The Levant was, and always had been, ever since the time of the Crusades, if not before, a place where a word was a word was a lie.

It wasn't only reading; George (and maybe this was another factor in his being hired for this job) had traveled a great deal in his academic work, usually at conferences but also as a guest lecturer; Tokyo, Delhi, Manila, Belgrade. It was during a visit to Belgrade, in what was still the Yugoslav federation, that he had, quite fortuitously, been present, or overhearing, a hush-hush meeting at the monastery in the mountains above Novi Sad, where it was clear to him that a top-level political plot was being hatched. As the meeting broke up, he asked his interpreter who was that man leaving the room – clearly not a Serb – and was told "That's the Cultural Attaché at the US Embassy" which George, with his limited knowledge of the secret service, knew full well meant that, in the absence of any American interest in culture, the man was CIA. That had pleased his own spymasters very much.

He demurred on the subject of the 'Arab Spring' because it was too vast a topic and, again, he had no data, physical or metaphysical, on which to base a dispatch. Someone had written that the spy world was 'a miscellany of soldiers, consuls, scholars, journalists and travelers in general.' And that 'Arab' was such a moveable term that its ambiguities and complexities confused almost everyone, especially the Ay-rabs. Well, he would absent himself, the so-called scholar, from that menagerie and leave it to the others, even though it also meant absenting himself from the felicity of that month's pay cheque.

He learned that his commentaries on the Greek-

Turkish situation, due partly to the ongoing Cyprus affair and partly to the newer factor of oil and gas exploration in the eastern Aegean, were especially valued by some faceless gnome in 'Whitehall' who, for all he knew, was his wife – a gnomette, as he thought of her when penning his dispatch.

Why did he do it? Ideology? No. It was the fascination in the challenge every novelist, biographer or critic faces, of making sense, of presenting a story that would sound well if read as a bedtime story to the head of MI6. He didn't actually care if what he wrote was accurate or not. In his view, it was pure speculation, but, whenever he had voiced this in one of his extremely rare conversations with "Whitehall," there had been an ingratiating insistence that what he supplied was 'informed' and therefore acceptable. If there were to be a war, he didn't care which side won or lost, provided that, especially now, it passed over Karponisi unnoticed.

He never subscribed to the belief that fact was fact and that fiction was, well, not fact. It was all made up as far as he was concerned. All the 'freedom fighters' – the IRA, Osama bed Linen, the Israelis and their mirror image, the Palestinians – these were merely the foot soldiers, the frontispiece to whatever was really happening. It was like a jigsaw puzzle: when you had located the last piece – usually a bit of sky – and put it into place, you stepped back and, with a satisfied "Aaah" you saw the whole picture for the first time. Then you saw that somehow, before your own eyes, there was still a piece missing. It had always been missing, and it always would be.

Even though nothing George did in preparing his dispatches could by any stretch of the imagination be construed as espionage, either pro- or anti-British, he could not shake off the feeling that what he did was cognate with the spying activities. The material he provided could, ultimately, reach a spymaster whose reading of it might set in motion a string of events leading to the defection, or extermination, of a foreign agent.

That was *hard* intelligence. What he did was so soft that it wouldn't have to melt in your mouth. No intercepted documents from foreign governments or agencies were involved as far as he knew, but then he never asked. What arrived by the ferry looked innocuous enough, although he did realise that, like a film script, it had probably been worked over by a dozen hands before being sufficiently blandified to be presentable to George. But this spying – agents and double agents out in the field – it wasn't a million miles from what he had done with the novels of Fowles, or, before that, the gay subtexts of Walter Pater. Not even a hundred yards distant. And this gave him an idea that chilled him to the bone – if one can be chilled in the steady annual temperature of 20-35° in which Karponisi basked – that what he did, or had done, was in the same bed as what he was doing now, looking for secrets and weaving a story around them in order to make them intelligible and acceptable fictions. Even what he had written about Brahms was not only a commentary on his work and on its influence on the twentieth century, but a revelation, to those equipped to see it, of Brahms's unspoken emotions and passions.

Was he 'one of them'? Yes, he must be one of them, his brain and his feelings told him so – that he had been drawn into a brotherhood (with a sister or two thrown in, if one counted M) whose business was the so-called 'intelligence network' which subtly morphed into the Killer Unit whose offices were further down the corridor of power, or so it said on the door. But how could he be "one of them," since he didn't even know who 'they' were? If the faceless goons he had met at his two recruitment interviews were anything to go on, they were plain – very plain, despite their membership of the Travellers and Brook's clubs – civil servants in some Ministry of Disinformation. Where did Whitehall end and MI6, or whatever it was, begin? George didn't actually know whether he was working for MI5, MI6 or MI99 – the one with the stick of chocolate flake.

There was no one he could ask. If he enquired of the 'Whitehall' people, they would almost certainly tell him he was asking the wrong question in the wrong quarter. "Have you tried your MP?" And the recruiting goons were quite likely dead, or living in discreet retirement in Woking or Cromer, cultivating vegetable marrows and reading dirty magazines in the potting shed, or pretending to take the dog for a walk, or whatever brings a thrill to the mind and loins of a superannuated spy. MI6 would deny all knowledge of him, even *to* him. Especially to him. M, if he asked her, would refuse to reply (or be ordered to do so) and that was going on his unfounded assumption that she was, in fact, in the same line of business.

He had no knowledge of where his dispatches went after they arrived at the accommodation address in Islington. He didn't even know if they were forwarded from there to anywhere at all, although the payments to his bank suggested that their receipt and acceptance were recorded by some paymaster somewhere. But hardly the Accounts Payable section of MI6. He recalled a Monty Python joke: 'don't throw away your used bottle-tops, send them to Mrs Betty Pickering of 5, The Cuttings, Bolton, and *she* will throw them away.' Was there a Mrs Pickering in Islington who fed his dispatches to her dog? And if so, how was the dog's health? And *what was his name*? He often wondered what he would find if he turned up, unannounced one day at Palatine Road and said to the bewildered, beturbaned housekeeper, "Hello, I'm George. Did you get my letters?"

But the simple, the mere fact that he received regular bulletins, followed them up with his own dispatches, and received payment, told him that without doubt someone, somewhere held him in the web within which views were formed, plans made and acted upon.

I had always regarded the 'dispatches' as something entirely separate from my academic work, and the connection between them – an analytical, critical mind applied to realpolitik *– was one cherished (and rewarded) by my employers but not one to which I myself would be subverted. This, of course, had nothing to do with the motivation of double agents like Philby, Burgess or Maclean, whose university careers had displayed no academic bent. (Well, they were all bent, but that's another matter; the predilection of homosexuals to communism is a closed book to me.) Of that group, only Blunt had any academic distinction, and he was not really cut out to be a spy.*

No, I couldn't see any necessary connection between what I did unofficially and what I did professionally – or vice versa. Then, I suddenly realized that what had attracted them to me was precisely the fact that there was *such a connection, an osmosis between what I was doing in my academic work and what they wanted me to do. I had displayed my capacity for exercising a dirty mind.*

They, too, saw me in that same light. I was a brain capable of seeing, however slightly, into the minds of the 'enemy' (whoever they might be), probing their moral and tactical weaknesses, outing their nefarious ambitions and intentions. I was untrustworthy, and therefore I was *trustworthy and earned a natural place on the payroll. I was dependable-expendable.*

Do I get a thrill from the fact that what I do is not only underhand and overpaid but is also against the law? Is it natural to relish the fact that what one does is, strictly speaking, not merely unethical and immoral, but also, more importantly, an activity above and beyond the law? From that, I go further and say that if I am above the law, I am acting against the law.

One day all this will come back to haunt me, when the hour-glass is full at the bottom and someone reverses it, and we all start again, except that in the re-run everything will be upside down and seen not in the mirror in which I today regard myself, but in full horrible Technicolor.

The cynic would say that whoever pays the piper calls the tune, that we dance to their rhythm and that therefore the dance and the tune are the norm, and all else is wrong, perverse, antinomian. You get paid, therefore you are merely a piper with the right tune. The others are wrong, not you. Go out of tune and you're dead meat. You are paid, therefore you are. Descartes eat your heart out.

But even the most accomplished novelist-fabulator, and perhaps because he is so accomplished, knows that he is a liar, living and peddling falsehoods for cash. He looks in the mirror and sees a traitor to reality, making others believe in his 'truth.' Compared to that, what hope is there for a mere critic?

When he thought about it, the relative insignificance – or so it seemed to him – of what he was doing, compared to the high affairs of state which led to surveillance, espionage and assassination, was not an issue. It was the inescapable fact that he was in that same system, that web, however marginal, however slight, that made him realise that between himself and a 'James Bond' type was only a matter of degree. "I put the petrol in the Aston Martin, or maybe just the air in the tyres, and he does the rest" he told himself. "I'm not the revolving number plate, I'm not the ejector seat, I'm not the sat-nav gismo – although maybe what I do helps to draw the road maps. I'm not even the .... And I'm certainly not the defibrillator in the glove compartment. But I do have one thing in common with one of those cars, or at least the one designed in the film by John Cleese. I can be – and for most of the time I am – invisible. A retired professor of Eng. Lit. on a tiny, remote Greek island – what could I possibly have in common with the forgers and killers of the underworld and the overworld?

"But that's maybe just where you're wrong, George" James admonished him on one of his occasional visits to the island. "Half the retired professors living on remote islands (and what would be the point of an island if it wasn't remote?) are probably spies of one kind or another. And anyway, Karponisi isn't all that remote. You can be in Athens in four hours, ferries and weather permitting, and from Athens to Whitehall in another three. Half a day's traveling to take you to the coalface. Not remote at all, really."

So yes, he was. Or wasn't.

Why did it trouble him so much? It wasn't like a golf club, where the steward might politely ask a newcomer "Excuse me, sir, are you a member?" Or a secret society where you declared your membership with a masonic handshake. It was like being a tadpole in a huge aquarium, the only occupant, yet knowing that either there were thousands of other aquaria, each with its singular tadpole, or goldfish, or piranha, or barracuda, or, more likely, that his own water closet was populated with thousands of invisible amoebae, each oblivious of the others.

If he had been in London, traveling home to Lincoln on the train, he might have looked at some of his fellow passengers and wondered "He could be one." Or as a pen pusher on the Tube from the outer dormitory suburbs to a pointless desk in the City, looking at the equally unimportant commuters, with rolled umbrellas and briefcases containing their lunch: a slice of quiche, an apple and a Mars bar. But in the post office in Leonidio or Nafplion, there were no likely suspects, although he did sometimes wonder whether he might not be under observation. The Russians or Al Q'ueda would hardly send a man to report on his movements or try to intercept his post, but he did know that a few of the older people in Nafplion had been sent to the Soviet satellite states during the civil war and might, just might, conceivably harbor pro-communist or pro-Russian feelings, enough to make them into reporters as insignificant as George himself. His 'control' could be the Dutchman who had recently retired to the island, and who seemed to be studiously avoiding his company. But then all Dutchmen were like that.

But on balance, he doubted it. A Walter-Mitty-type existence, where he believed himself to be under constant surveillance from enemy eyes, requiring him to look round every corner (even the ones in his own house) and to speak to no-one, not even in his dreams, had its attractions, but he thought that, on the whole, he was content with the caution involved in making these occasional trips (camouflaged as they were by other genuine business), and the routine of an almost non-existent home life, uninterrupted until disturbed by Aleksandra.

But first, we have to see him in a new life, with Jessica Mausch.

VII
Jessica and Brahms

They had met in Prague, where she was performing the Tchaikovsky violin concerto with the Czech Philharmonic, and he was a guest lecturer at the Charles University. She was a concert, recital and recording artist of considerable renown. She had won the Queen Elizabeth competition in Belgium, and had crowned her success by winning the Sibelius competition. Austrian by birth, she had studied at the Hochschule in her native city of Graz, but had left Austria for London when it seemed that her career was taking off so rapidly that she needed to be more in the centre of things. Now, *she* was the centre and there seemed no end to the possibilities of a glittering career, with contracts for recordings stretching years ahead, and her agent was besieged by promoters anxious to secure her for concerto performances with the world's top orchestras: the Leipzig Gewandhaus, the Vienna Philharmonic, the Berlin Phil, New York, Chicago, Los Angeles and, of course, all the British venues... the list went on and on, with engagements for at least the next three years. Jessica Mausch was *it*: one of the world's top ten violinists.

They were introduced at a party after her concert, for which he had been lucky enough to get a ticket and even luckier that one of his university hosts had an entrée to the reception in the backstage area of the concert hall.

There had been no sex that first night in Prague, but an obvious and immediate attraction had been there. A couple of months later, he was in St. Petersburg at a conference on an immediately forgettable topic, and saw her name on posters for a performance of the Berg concerto with Valeri Gergiev. He immediately felt jealous of the Russian, assuming that he and Jessica would end up in bed together after the compulsory champagne reception. Tickets were part of his conference pack – the best part – and so he could seek her out after her performance, at the interval, while Gergiev was still gearing up for his big show – predictably, the Tchaikovsky 'Pathetic.' The rapport between Jessica and George was as strong as that between her and her del Gesù and, at her suggestion, they went to bed together. It was exploratory, tentative, but superb.

George asked if he could see her in London and she said yes that would be very pleasant. He pretended to be attending a conference, but in fact went specially to London about three weeks later, just to see her. To maintain the conference pretext he had to take a hotel room, but they met at her apartment overlooking the Thames and that is where their next intimacy took place and where they spent as much as possible of their time together thereafter, George practically commuting between the day-job in Lincoln and the nightlife with Jessica. Because his working week was quite limited – fifteen contact hours per week, including Scunthorpe – he was able to spend many days with Jessica, which became increasingly important as she drew him into her professional work, asking him to attend her rehearsals, both with her accompanist and the orchestral work with the British orchestras. She needed reassurance: her hesitancy over every performance was due to lack of self-confidence which assails every artist at the moment when they are about to walk onstage, but she made it very clear that there were also musical reasons for needing George's loving company.

With Jessica in particular sex was rampant and – he

wasn't boasting – twice a day. Well, morning and evening. No discreet fumbling in their pyjamas under the blanket. No coy suggestions about "Let's have an early night tonight." Just clothes off, onto the mattress, and then the whole gamut of mutual pleasures from stroking and licking to animal frenzy and exclamation. They had succeeded in working out how to achieve joint orgasm, something neither of them had experienced before.

One night he dreamt that he was in Hollywood with Nicole Kidman, at a place called the Snow White Café. He had no idea how he'd arrived there, whether or not he was there on business (could he be a guest lecturer at UCLA?), but it seemed that the actress was *au fait* with whatever situation it was. Anyway, here he was, sitting awkwardly on a plastic banquette across a Formica table from one of the most beautiful women in the world. She smiled at me – an incomparably warm, inviting, sensuous smile. "Today, something good happened, George. I met you."

"Look, Miss Kidman" he tried to stammer in reply.

"George, my name is Nicole. On the film set, it's a rule, I'm Miss Kidman, to everyone, including you. But when we are together, I want to be Nicole. Trust me, George."

In George's dream, he tried to cope with the fact that one of Hollywood's top and most alluring stars was asking him to trust her. With what? He awoke in the conventional lather of sweat, panting and wondering where he was, and why. Until Jessica soothed him, asked him what was the nightmare, and, when he said it wasn't a nightmare, it was one of the most frightening dreams he had ever had, laughed it off with "And who does she think she is, anyway? Cameron Diaz?"

George had read a newspaper article (on the agony page, of course) about couples who went to the doctor or sexual psychotherapist because they had sex only once a month, or even less, and suspected that this might be either a reflection of their waning sexual appetites, or a sign that they now loved each other less than when it all started, or both. George had sent this to James, asking what he thought. The reply was apoplectic. "Once a month! Good god, that's atrocious! No marriage can survive on a once-a-month job. Caroline and I would think there was something terribly wrong if we didn't have it twice a day." And George, thankful that James had the same healthy appetite as himself, wondered what these poor sods in the agony column could do to put it right. Watch dirty movies? Tell each other their fantasies? No, probably best not. Find somebody else? And disappoint them as well, most likely. He did know a couple in Lincoln, on a housing estate (she came to his extra-mural classes in the pathetic and mistaken belief that it might improve her mind), who asked her husband, after cocoa, "Shall we put out the light and not go to sleep, then?" – this being a code word for whatever fumblings and misconceptions were about to ensue. With Jessica, apart from their couplings being very direct (and punctual), he found a huge arousal when she had played a really moving concert. Most artists, he knew, were so drained physically and emotionally by their music-making that they simply had no appetite for sex for some time after. Not Jessica, thank god.

It wasn't just the sex, even though that was very challenging, stimulating, fulfilling. It was waking up the next morning beside the belovèd, stretching out and putting a hand on her shoulder, gently tempting her into the day. A quiet tenderness. It was especially thrilling for him because he knew that beside him was not only a woman whose combination of technical brilliance, profound musicality and, let's face it, sexual allure, could charm millions with her playing, but a woman who loved him, who wanted to share all this with him. Later, he missed this part of their partnership more, in fact, than the sexual, missed the intimacy of their close trust and their wanting. Sometimes he thought of Al and Tony – was it the same for them? He hoped so.

With Jessica, George learned late – but not too late – in life, that a sexual relationship, while absolutely essential, was only the bedrock on which a true relationship was built. Regular, good (or better still, top) quality fucking was important, but beside that, the deep meeting between two minds and spirits kept that relationship alive and thriving. He and Jessica succeeded in this through their shared love of music, she, of course, the world-famous star, he merely the man beside her, the man to whom she found she could speak, as to no other, of her musical ambitions, challenges, fears and excitement. It was the excitement in their music-making that matched the excitement of their lovemaking, and created what, for so long, was a precious bond.

She explained to George all the basics of string-playing, how you start by making excruciating squeaky noises that horrify the whole household. If you and your family can last the pace, and if there is really a genuine talent, that phase can pass mercifully quickly. From that point, it's a matter of individual temperament as to how rapidly the true artist begins to show her musicality, to demonstrate that *there* is a talent that must be nurtured and facilitated: the best teachers, the finest instruments, the best possible circumstances for that musician to bloom. A 'daddy's pretty little girl' can wheedle expensive clothes, even sports cars, from fond and doting parents, and there is little difference in the house of a prodigy. "What do you want for Christmas, Jessica?" "A Guarneri. Or, if you can't afford that, dad, I know how hard-up we are, a Strad." Just a few cool million in anyone's currency – well, trillion if you're dealing in *yen* – will keep her quiet for a long time – and yes, her daddy *did* buy her the del

Gesù. Into the house of music come horizons beyond dreams. Jessica used to say "It's like a communion in a church that encompasses the whole world, a fulfilment that takes everyone up into a new world, a sense of partaking in magic, in otherness." With her, George discovered that new world.

With Jessica he met many of the fiddle celebrities of the time: Suk, Szeryng, Chung, Perlman, Zukermann, Menuhin, the incomparable Stern and Leonidas Kavakos, who was her closest friend. Jessica particularly adored the Suk recordings of the Brahms sonatas with Julius Katchen – and George agreed: probably the most sublime renderings of Brahms's tortured genius.

In fact George was not unfamiliar with music people, since he had habitually made it his business to queue up, just like any other Joe Soap, for autographs from the Barenboim–du Pré duo, the Menuhin duo – Yehudi and his sister Hephzibah, whose playing of the "Spring" sonata he would never forget. The 'greats' whom he would love to have heard in live concert, but didn't, were David Oistrakh, Heifetz and Josef Szigeti. Jessica had heard – and met – them all, so they were able to listen occasionally to their recordings, provided that didn't interfere with her current work. The 'anxiety of influence' is professed by so many of today's great players, but secretly indulged.

But Menuhin and Szeryng were now past their "sell-by" date. Nigel Kennedy ("Nige") was, as Jessica said, "Good, but not that good." As were Jan Pascal Tortelier (not a patch on his father, whom George had heard so many years ago in the Beethoven sonatas) and Gidon Kremer, whose playing George had always detested and was delighted to discover from Jessica that he was personally one of the most disliked members of the profession.

But with Jessica there were many after-concert

receptions, dinners and cocktail parties, as well as private occasions in the houses of her colleagues. So much so, in fact, that he wondered how she could cope with such a series of debits from the time she needed for her own music.

George preferred the company of people of his own level – not exactly mediocrities, although sometimes in the mornings, looking in the bathroom mirror, he wondered whether his work was of any merit at all. Compared to Jessica's standing in the music world, his own in the academic milieu was far down the rankings, and, he often mused, there were very few requests for interviews, even when his books appeared, other than the general run of thesis-hunters that any academic with any reputation at all for original research has to put up with. But no requests to put his picture on the cover of *Hello!* or *Uomo Vogue* and certainly no celebrity interviews like Jessica gave to *BBC Music Magazine* or *Classical Music*. He didn't even merit an article about Woodlawn in *Country Life* or the *Shooting Times,* because the estate had passed to Uncle David and, after him, to Alex who certainly was keen on publicity for new developments such as the riding centre that he was setting up. (How Uncle D would have pulled everyone's leg about a 'riding centre'!)

But the bathroom mirror was so vehement in its questioning – would his work be read by anyone in twenty years' time other than meticulous scholars headed in their own way down the tunnel of oblivion, making footnotes on his interpretation of Pater or Fowles – or, worst of all, would it have been better if he had never written them at all? That when he designed his bathroom in Karponisi, he deliberately omitted a mirror, much to the chagrin of Al, who was keenly advising him on the fittings and overall décor.

She had thought of several more-than-eligible

partners: Alexis Weissenberg, Alexander Melnikov, and even Vladimir Ashkenazy seemed obvious choices and, she knew, all were willing to play with her. But she settled on a young but already established pianist who was also an up-and-coming composer, Angél Davidoff.

The new partnership worked well at first, but as the rehearsals progressed, the demands of the music seemed to become the demands of the pianist: although infinitely junior to Jessica in status and musicianship, Davidoff was taking control of her attention, as if these were sonatas for the piano with a violin thrown in. Nothing was said openly, but Jessica, and George too, felt the tension rising – tension which, they all hoped and believed, would result in magnificent performances – as they did.

After two hours of working intensely, Angél seemed quite calm and undisturbed, while she was drenched in sweat both physical and emotional; her face was drawn with fear and anguish. George wondered how could anyone put themselves through such turmoil in order to become a great artist? The fact is that Angél was driving Jessica, but he wasn't driving himself. He was using her to achieve an effect, as if he were a film director provoking and punishing an actress in order to win a great performance. George had heard from James Esposito that this had happened in the case of Nicole Zoffany in *Love, Fear, Hate*, driven by director Joanna Hampton beyond the limits of tolerance. This, he now saw, was what Angél Davidoff was doing to Jessica, and he couldn't do anything to halt or prevent it.

Brahms was a total bastard, and Angél was his instrument of torture, Jessica his victim. But what a willing victim and, ultimately, a triumphant victim. It turned the whole idea of a 'contradiction in terms' on its head: this was a contradiction that succeeded through its audacity, in being more than two opposites, its capacity to defy fate, reason and love itself, to sacrifice the self in the ritual of transcendence, and thus to emerge whole and clean at the other side.

George knew this just by sitting in the rehearsal room. Imagine what it did to audiences in London, Paris, New York, Moscow ...

It may have been living with Jessica that started his serious interest in Brahms, although the fascination had always been there. The fact that she was working so manically on his concerto, and performing it for the first time at the London Proms, where Ida Haendel had pulled off the same miracle several times already. A challenge, only suited to a woman with balls. Hearing her in the next room, he came to feel the deep soul of Brahms, or at least as much of it as a non-musician could appreciate. And talking each evening with Jessica helped him to understand why it had been dubbed a 'concerto against the violin.'

How could it be that George's ideas about Brahms were cerebral in theory but so sensual in practice, as he listened to Jessica in rehearsal and performance? Watched her every move, the lithe, slim swaying figure, the utter commitment, the intensity of every bow-stroke, the attention to her partner; he bathed in the sound that they produced, this perfect duo, even though in both his head and his heart he feared the worst from Brahms.

Jessica's extensive traveling schedule obviously presented her with many opportunities and temptations for a casual sex life, but when their relationship had started in earnest George completely believed her – except on two occasions – when she promised him that, sexually, she was his and his alone. The two 'mistakes' had been about a year apart, and had definitely hastened the end of their relationship, which was on its final stretch in any case. George had never suspected that there might be any involvement on Jessica's part with Angél, a man he had always liked – perhaps too much so.

They both knew it wouldn't – couldn't – last, and were both surprised that it lasted as long as it did. The intensity of their togetherness was more than the relationship could bear. It had come to an end due to her desire for affairs when she was away from the apartment in London, and also in no small part (no pun intended) to his increasing ED, which, he learned, affected men over the age of fifty, with a risk over sixty of a very high dropout (or should that be "droopout"?) rate. In George's case, almost complete termination of erectional possibilities had manifested itself from his late fifties, and even though there were other ways in which he and Jessica might satisfy each other, the lack of penetration was a severe obstacle to a sexual union. 'Dysfunction' the doctors had called it. If only they had known how dysfunctional his whole bloody life had been, that this was only one aspect of a life that was on the verge of meaninglessness ever since he could remember.

Yet, from that meeting in Prague and the quick onset of their passion for each other, he and Jessica had enjoyed well over ten years of intimacy, trust and thrust. Early on, he had told her about his idea for the Brahms book, even though it was only a vague one at that stage, without any structural form. She had shown very little interest in the intellectual side of it, saying that it was too academic and textbookish for a mere musician. How right she was about the complete lack of brain in so many of her colleagues! As far as the Brahms concerto was concerned, she just played the thing, she didn't want to know that it prefigured the Schoenberg concerto (which she also played and, indeed, recorded) or that, in George's view, Brahms prefigured Mahler who prefigured Schoenberg who prefigured.... George was not a 'mere musician' and he had hoped that the sexual chemistry between them would gain by talking about the philosophy of music. But that wasn't in Jessica's music bag at all.

The erection problem began while he was still with Jessica, but became increasingly apparent and troublesome after their separation. Erection superintendents assured him that it was perfectly normal, however distressing it might be, and that they saw little hope of his regaining his former functions to any useful extent. Once ED had, so to speak, lowered its head, George had a sense of relief that he would no longer be "responsible for his own orgasm," or anyone else's. But it did aggravate his drinking. Without sex, without Jessica, without sex *and* Jessica, he felt not merely empty but helpless and hopeless. Apparently this wasn't the case with Uncle D who, despite old age and (although he did not know it) oncoming death, was still indulging in extra-curricular rumpy-pumpy. Well, if you were married to someone called Elvira Tollemache who was as strait-laced as she was hatchet-faced, you too would go for a plain bit of skirt, something called Mary Brown or Jane Smith, who said "Oh reely?" or, at the right moment, just "Ooooh!"

Drink was both a necessary companion and a betrayal. Like his book on Pater, it "filled a much-needed gap." In this case, the gap was that empty centre in his life about which he blamed everyone except himself: his father, Rugby, TCD, M, even Nanny Conneely, *even his mother*. But never Uncle D. Once he was sober – and drying out took a *very* long time, since it wasn't only a matter of eliminating the alcohol that had soaked into his every bodily fibre, but also the way it had soaked into his DNA and his imagination – he would realise with whatever clarity he could muster that he had 'only himself to blame' as everyone put it. Even James tried to convince him that he, George, was at the centre of this empty space, and that if he could only work outwards from the nightmare he might meet himself somewhere in the vicinity of his no longer addled brain.

His doubts about his status as a literary authority continued. Usually, when he had been drinking, George reassured himself after a large glass of Pinot Noir or a snipe of champagne, telling himself that he had *some* merit as a writer, if not in the first rank. And now that he was not drinking, those kinds of doubts took second place to others. As someone had said about recovering alcoholics, it was not so much abstinence from alcohol that was the real problem, as the discovery of the self, the person who emerged from those shadows and presented himself to the startled ego as a monster biding its time, someone they had never met, or even imagined, before sobriety brought them face-to-face with an 'other' who was, and always had been, the 'self.' All spies are fascinated by 'the other'; alcoholic spies even more so.

And yet he did not allow his disappointment to lessen his passion for Jessica. He simply buried his feelings. It was perhaps the day on which Jessica said: "I never liked you. I loved you. That's a completely different matter," that almost killed him and sent him helter-skelter to take up residence inside the wine bottle.

Looking back, he realized that she had been the centre of his life and that he had found himself in her. The selfish creature in him did not, however, realise that for her, *he* had been the centre of *her* life, and that she was now adrift, vulnerable to whatever chance might introduce into a life that was, as far as musical passion and excitement were concerned, empty.

After their separation, Jessica went off with her new lover, Angél Davidoff, but, as far as her public were aware, there was no change in her schedule or her availability for all the interviews and TV shows that go with celebrity life.

Until, that is, she started to cancel engagements and, eventually, went off the concert radar completely. Absolutely no one, not even her agent with whom she was so closely connected, knew anything of her whereabouts, and it was clear that she and Davidoff had parted company abruptly after only three years together. Jessica dumped Davidoff for musical reasons – what he was like as a lover, George of course had no idea, but as an accompanist he just wasn't in Jessica's league. Her recordings of the Brahms sonatas had shown her that she needed greater musical understanding. No doubt, George surmized, why so many film stars split when they realise their partner is going nowhere fast. Davidoff had been a good, even a brilliant, répétiteur, no more than that, despite the demonic way he coaxed her to glory.

George ruefully surveyed the eleven years of their own relationship, and wondered how Jessica felt about it now. He had even planned a practice room for her in Karponisi and had budgeted for a piano, but in the outcome that room was never built. It simply became yet another forty-square-metres of library space.

And then she wrote, asking him if there was any possibility of their getting back together. He was friendly, but made it clear that, if at all possible, it would amount merely to a few visits by her to Karponisi. George seemed to be oblivious to the fact that Jessica had hit a dead end and that this might have something – everything – to do with *him*, and that she was clearly uttering a cry for help, for understanding. But it was equally clear from the tone of his letter that he was not too keen on this idea. With her help, he had shut that door, and shut it should remain. There the matter rested.

However, he was very glad to hear that her musicality sustained her and prevailed, and she returned to the concert platform radiantly and decisively after an absence of two years that couldn't be accounted for. And she did it, spectacularly, in New York, with, of all works, the Brahms.

George had experienced the *real* Brahms – that is, Jessica's sensuous reproduction of Brahms's emotional sterility. She had given sex to Brahms. Now, trying to write about Brahms's music, from a pseudo-critical standpoint, George failed to translate that experience of Jessica's playing into terms the reader might understand. It was an emotional quagmire, this struggling to import into a mere book the passion, the excitement and the tragedy of Jessica's "Brahms," which was also the passion, excitement and tragedy of Jessica's "George."

Writing the book had been a struggle. If his "dispatches" seemed at times like an incoherent five-year-old describing how to do a lobotomy, Brahms underlined his ignorance of music; made it so obvious that he was amazed by his audacity. But since he couldn't give a flying ferret any more, his critical reputation couldn't suffer, could it? Until that is, he realized that Brahms wasn't the exclusive domain of scholars or even of performers like Jessica, but a public property, open for discussion.

Even the title of the book had given him trouble – especially the title. *Brahms Our Contemporary*, unpunctuated, seemed to read like a newspaper placard: "Read all abaht it! Brahms outed!" Brahms wasn't a nineteenth-century composer, he was here with us, *now*. That's what "contemporary" means. *Brahms, Our Contemporary*, with a comma, now *that* was more an indication of how the author felt: making a case for Brahms as a composer with modern, late-twentieth-century, relevance. But there were several other possibilities, interrogating *Brahms Our Contemporary? Where* that case for relevance was investigated and, perhaps, found to be baseless.

But then he thought: this will be a book that explores regions unknown to musicologists, a book that puts music and Brahms into a completely new context. Just like his "dispatches," really. Think "Gallipoli," describe "Vietnam" and write "Palestine." (He recalled how his mandarin bosses must have puzzled, or perhaps not, at George's references to the "Left Bank," when *they* assumed he meant the Jordan and *he* meant the Seine.) Just a maelstrom in a postbag, somehow the letters must have got mixed up. As they did on Brahms's alphabet which, musically speaking, only got as far as G, but included the minefields of sharps, flats and the in-between bits of the quartertones that fascinated him but would never be reduced to any sound acceptable on a concert platform.

This book would show how Brahms's mind – a mind inhibited by self-doubts, wracked by worldly worries, closeted by sexuality (Pater again!) – succeeded, after massive intellectual and emotional effort, in freeing his music in symphonies, concertos and sonatas that would engender music of the New Age. And *that*, George reasoned, is why Brahms is still our contemporary. But you couldn't put "still" into the title, that would be worse than the question mark, because it would sound as if you didn't really believe your own argument.

And remember, George addressed his yet-to-be reader, Brahms was one of the first "German" composers to be actually writing in Germany. Most of the others – Beethoven, Schubert, Schumann, Mendelssohn – had written "German" music in Austria, before "Germany" had been invented by that cunt Bismark. Only Brahms and Wagner, the two "Poles" (ha ha) of the new German music, carried the burden of creating a national medium, leading, in Wagner's case, to that awful Ring Cycle (a velodrome, Brahms would have called it had he known the term) and thence to Richard Strauss and Hitler and ...

His famous remark to the young Ravel, ready to worship at the Master's feet - "There *are* no French composers" – was worth a thought. And he didn't even say it himself, he sent a servant to the front door where Ravel stood waiting. "Mr Brahms says there are no French composers." Not quite the same thing, semantically. If Brahms hadn't said it himself, it wasn't an *obiter dictum* was it? It was reported speech. And like all reported speech, likely to be misreported. Just like dispatches, George thought. But he thoroughly agreed with Brahms. And anyway, even if Brahms *had* said it and even if he *had* thought it (two different things again, semantically speaking) he would be proved wrong in time: unless, of course, you dismissed Debussy and Ravel himself as *poseurs*, which wasn't a bad ploy, musicologically speaking. And Erik Satie, what about *him*? And that old pouf Reynaldo Hahn? But speaking from a nineteenth-century context (which, of course, Brahms wasn't if you accepted George's own argument) he was right: there was only one really good French composer, Augusta Holmès, and she was Irish, George was happy to reflect. And as a *composer* she was pretty (was she pretty?) marginal (even though another musical non-entity, Saint-Saëns admired her), but as a *woman* you could hardly call her negligible, with her long affair with Catulle Mendès, with whom she had five children. So she must have been pretty.

Then there was the unwritten Brahms, who came home at four in the morning totally polluted, smelling as if his mother had been a distillery and his father a brewery. Or so George liked to think. It would humanise the man. And it could just be true – after all, the Cockneys didn't think up 'Brahms and Liszt' all by themselves, did they?

Could it have been true, that Benjamin Britten said that he regularly played Brahms just to remind himself of how bad it was? George believed he had the explanation:

Britten was openly gay, whereas Brahms stayed safely in his closet. So Britten had to deride and bewail the fact that Brahms hadn't written *Peter Grimes*. It was as simple as that. One brave twentieth-century homosexual demonstrating in his life and work the pursuit of men and boys, while demanding that Brahms should have done the same. Asking that the clock on homophobia be turned back to embrace the closeteers, a retrospective pardon for sins that were no longer sins, offences against a society that had ceased to exist.

"I wished that you were once again in my bed and I could tickle your forehead, I think of you with tender love," Brahms wrote to a young friend. Well, come on. If he felt like that about another man, would he stop at tickling? Yes, he probably would. Lacerating himself into ecstasy. Tenderness spit-roasted and served with mocking laughter. He was said to have resorted to prostitutes, but that seemed impossible, given his timidity in all matters. Women were always the parish church of their four-square sanctity, never the cathedral that was their delta of Venus.

As a critic rather than a musicologist George found that the four symphonies and the two piano concertos posed not only the musical problems that performers always acknowledged and tried to accommodate, but huge intellectual challenges which, he was certain, had been central to Brahms's writing of those works.

There was the weight of tradition and example: after Schubert, how could anyone hope to write songs? And (more pertinently) after Beethoven, how could anyone think of writing symphonies? For a very long time, Brahms didn't dare. He wrote the two piano concertos instead. And what about opera? Opera takes us into an "other" world, a world of make-believe and fantasy, the willing suspension of disbelief – *credo quia absurdum*. Why didn't Brahms write an opera? Well, in the *German Requiem* he did, sort of. But it was more sinister than that – if "sinister" is read as the antonym of "dextrous," as "left" rather than "right," then Brahms's closet held more than just a would-be queen. It was a powder-house of pretence, a hiding place that was also a generator of antonyms which would assume musical form in the vivid contradictions and cruel reversals of his symphonies.

And, George reflected, that's what he himself did in "dispatches" if, again, we allow "dexter" and "sinister" their twin roles in the spy world, the world where nothing is what it seems, where nothing says anything that is either true or false but lodges in-between, in the hints and crevices of language, of music, of love.

Brahms's symphonies are ambivalent. Publicly, they are celebratory, but privately they are apprehensive, haunted. It's summed up in the juxtaposition of the 'Academic Festival Overture' and the 'Tragic Overture' – one joyful and humorous, the other atoning for its companion's overstepping the mark of permissible levity. Brahms was, at every moment, expansively lyrical and yet fearful of the consequences. His music is a metaphor for our own time, an age of anxiety, which continues to be disturbed by the angst of the nineteenth century. An age of neurosis, remorse and fear, still dominated by the legacies of Freud and Einstein, an inherently unstable world deeply affected by doubt and anxiety. An age in which tenderness can never divest itself of cruelty, nor hope rid itself of despair.

Brahms was born naked into this age of certainty flawed by doubt, unable to shave until he was twenty-four, determined thereafter to be identified by a massive beard which proclaimed his seniority and cloaked his face with wisdom. It was inevitable that he should seek sounds that would satisfy, yet his symphonies asked questions they could not answer, as if they were the response of the disappointed child to the unanswered questions of the nursery: Why? What for? Who? When? *Music that alienates the listener because the child was alienated in the cradle.*

The opening of his first cello sonata is a massive interrogation, asking over and over again the same appalling questions. That sonata had a lot to answer for, George thought. It was so deep, in the notes played and in its spiritual sonority, that when it was first played the cellist complained that he couldn't hear himself, and Brahms replied "Aren't you lucky?"

The first violin sonata was (with apologies to Beethoven) a "Spring Sonata" but one that longed for something rather than celebrating it. The birds were singing but they hadn't long to live. Jessica made one of her very rare statements about Brahms when she said "He's always setting out on a journey, but with something dreadful at his back." She had also told George: "Loving you comes naturally, but it brings with it much pain and it demands explanation at every step; even, or especially, when it is at its most joyous." This, he now realized, was her way of warning him of the dangers of love, but it was also a metaphor for Brahms: don't go there only for love, because love's tenderness is also a trap with monsters.

Despite his ability to write beautiful expansive cantabile*, Brahms is trapped inside the music and cannot find the exit, the way to bring the story to a satisfying conclusion – and they all lived happily ever after. Because Brahms knew that they* didn't. Couldn't. *Doubt and fear are part-and-parcel of the musical fabric.*

Like the 'stream of consciousness' literature of the same period, the music is a place of difficulty where the reader/listener is implicated in the text/music. Brahms anticipated the age of anxiety, and predicted it: more, he gave it its vehicles. The first piano concerto begins where Beethoven's Choral Symphony *left off: with cacophony, musical chaos; but in Brahms's case no-one interrupts with the admonition* "Oh friends, not these sounds" *and ushers in the* Ode to Joy. *Oh no. Brahms would be forever searching for his ode to joy.*

There would be no story well told, with a beginning in mystery and ending in positive, major key resolution. Instead, an ever-deepening descent into a vortex that would result in a world undone by the absence of love, of cherishing, of meaning.

In the symphonies, there are soaring melodies that can be sung, *but they soar* downwards *and plunge* upwards. *Arguing over the nature and purpose of sound; what was required of sound in a world grown cruel, bestial, uncaring and unfeeling. The concert hall becomes a place of struggle, of intellectual and emotional turmoil.*

An Irish poet had said that the trouble with the common reader is that he knows that the twentieth century is a battlefield, but he does not know what the battle is about. Brahms did *know. But he couldn't articulate it sufficiently to make clear his legacy of forewarning; hence the bewilderment of so many of his critics, starting with Hans von Bülow who had called the violin concerto "a concerto* against *the violin." The symphonies were symphonies against the orchestra and against the listener. You could not, it seems, have* cantabile *without also embracing* horribile.

Brahms clung to structure, but he fucked it as he used it. He refused to obey the rules he admired. They had entered his student soul and, as a middle-aged man, he could not rid himself of the demon of discipline in order to embrace the angel of artifice. He could not come. He was wilfully difficult, as if, hearing always the ghost of Beethoven mocking him, he wanted to erase the past while worshipping it, to predict a future that would be riddled with a cancerous tradition. He wrote sonatas and concertos against the piano, symphonies against the orchestra – symphonies that were unplayable and unhearable.

There were huge gaps in the music, where the listener had to catch up. It was the music of cruelty, punishing the composer, the players and the audience. This wasn't merely the fashionable Sturm und Drang. This was out-and-out warfare against an unseen and unknown enemy. But then suddenly wistful. Brahms was at his most humane when he was teasing, at his most punishing when he was damning to hell. The German Requiem wasn't for the dead, it was for the living.

Yet Schoenberg, among many, recognized the novelty in Brahms. His own Verklärte Nacht, written only just after Brahms's death, was the medium through which Brahms's angst found its transitus into that of the twentieth century. Like Brahms, Schoenberg (along with Webern and Berg) distilled their musical feelings into a condensed musical language. The intensity of a Brahms symphony or sonata becomes, in the Second Viennese School, the microcosms of their string quartets.

Brahms was, in one critic's words, "groping around for a home key." Yes, the long stretch for home, the unknown place of an empty childhood.

Nietzsche called Brahms's music "the melancholy of incapacity." So what was the final verdict? Cause of Death, unhappiness.

259

VIII

Karponisi and Aleksandra

It was after he and Jessica separated that George realized he no longer had any reason to remain domiciled in England. He would have left Lincoln, and everything else, at the age of fifty, and moved lock-stock-and-barrel to Karponisi, if the phenomenon of Jessica had not changed his horizons so completely, for a magical eleven years. After his eventual withdrawal from uni – a move greeted with sighs of relief on both his own part and that of the uni – he had plenty of time to reflect on his history as a teacher and writer. Where others staggered on beyond even seventy in secure and pointless lectureships, George had realized that, approaching sixty, he had nothing further to add to a reputation in academe that was reasonably, if not illustriously, distinguished. That is, as far as the reading public and the uni-watchers were concerned. Within uni, matters were very different.

He could have justified remaining in his post, like so many of his colleagues, churning out his annual lecture notes as Owen O'Brien had predicted but, having known the Greek islands for so long, perhaps encouraged by Fowles's not terribly inspiring experience in Spetses, he had decided, maybe as a spur-of-the-moment thing, to up sticks for good and make the final move to Karponisi. And final it now seemed to him – irrevocably so. With this tiredness which was partly *ennui*, world-weariness, partly intellectual death, or its obvious approach, there was no going back.

There was one other compelling reason for George to leave England and resettle in Karponisi: he had loved

261

'Europe' as an idea, until the domination of the European Union by Germany, and by international organisations such as the International Monetary Fund which, he suspected, was in its turn controlled by extraterritorial financial interests. It was two world wars all over again; if, as some general had said, war was diplomacy conducted by other means (or maybe it was 'war is what you do when peace stops working'), this was the *vice versa* – a pernicious extension of Teutonic influence under the guise of peace and democracy. Some years previously, he'd found the texts of a lecture series given in Berlin in 1942 by high-ranking Nazis including several university professors and the President of the Reichsbank. The lectures outlined the programme for economic renewal of Europe (and Russia) that would take place once the war was won. Comparing it to what the Germans were now proposing, there was hardly any difference between 1942 and today!

Britain was either too timid, or too careless, to comment on these troubling intentions. George had become interested in the European idea during a couple of visits to the Council of Europe in Strasbourg (some tedious committee to which he had been sentenced by his head of department, in addition to the *Via Crucis* of Scunthorpe). He had been obliged to join a working group on "The Status of the Writer in the Modern Europe," which was only one degree better than a Lincoln committee meeting to decide next year's visiting lectureship. When he had stupidly let it be known that he was an expert on Fowles, he was then drawn into another group on "Writing in the Peripheral Islands of Europe," a subject on which he knew absolutely nothing, but was assumed to be an authority merely because Fowles himself – long before he ever published a word – had once spent time on a Greek island.

At that time, membership of the Council of Europe

was confined to the so-called "democratic" states of western Europe; these included, rather improbably, the Vatican State. It was quite a chummy club, if you liked that sort of thing, but it lacked a vital dimension: socialism, or any expression of leftist views, was almost tacitly suppressed. Even the querying of the *bona fides* of the nation-state was disallowed by committee chairmen. After the collapse of the "Iron Curtain" and the break-up of the Soviet Union and its satellite states, and their conversion to some other mutant form of democracy, the Council's membership changed dramatically. Several of George's friends from the 'other side' of that Curtain were now eligible to take part in these meetings. In particular, he rejoiced that the Albanian writer Ismail Kadare, and the Czech Milan Kundera, both living in Parisian exile, could now represent their countries.

But on the wider map, Germany (and France too) had had to accommodate this radical change in the political orientation of the continent, and they did so using the same strategy that the British had employed in rebutting demands for Irish independence: they killed it with kindness, stifled it with a series of diktats, disguised as impenetrably long-winded memoranda, ententes and concordances which tied up all initiative in a Gordian knot which no-one had the balls to cut through.

But now George couldn't give a toss for Europe, which in his opinion had prostituted itself to the slogan of "unity in diversity" without ever questioning what lay behind this panacea that was in fact nothing more than a placebo. As an Englishman (and maybe this was yet another factor in the way he was so easily persuaded to start writing "dispatches") he deplored this gutlessness on the part of politicians of all persuasions, whose sole ambitions were the immediate possession (or so they thought) of power, and, after their inevitable defeat, the enjoyment of massive pensions, consultancy fees and villas on private beaches, mostly outside the European Union of which they had declared themselves to be such dedicated servants.

Britain, if it were to be a key player in post-war Europe (which everyone, from Charles de Gaulle onwards had ensured *wouldn't* happen), should have entered the Eurozone. It should have abandoned all those facets that made Britain British – the mile, the pint, the ounces, pounds, and stones, the rods, roods and perches, the belovèd acres, the Cornish pasty and the pork pie. But it had stayed aloof, probably because it knew that to seek integration would be to court rejection once again, and that was something unthinkable. "Can't afford to lose face, old boy." All that sort of thing.

And now, when all of Europe was getting to look like more of the same, Britain was going in the opposite direction, splitting up into its smaller parts – Scottish independence would be followed by Wales and, god knows, his distant relatives might even declare autonomy for Rutland. They could afford it. After all, it was only a few years since Berwick-on-Tweed – he thought it was – had made its separate peace with Germany, having been technically at war, all on its own, since 1945.

No, Europe as an idea meant nothing to him now; he was as disillusioned with it as he was with his own depressing life story, the attempt to progress towards a sort of integration of his own, to become himself, and to find home.

Karponisi – it meant 'the island (*nisi*) of fruit' – became George's new home. But, the origins of Greek naming being what they were – truly, as the cliché has it, "lost in the mists of time" – it was argued that the name harked back to Karpos, a beautiful youth, the son of Zephiros (the west wind) and Chloris (springtime), giving rise to the image in the minds of those islanders who believed it, that their island represented the wind that brings with it the springtime of sowing and, later, reaping – which was where *karpos*, the word for fruit, held its own. *Karpos* was also the word for the wrist, and if the island had had a natural isthmus between north and south it might have sustained that as an alternative meaning too, but the island was olive- or grape-shaped, with no "wrist" in evidence, so the local inclination stayed with the fruity metaphors. Lawrence Durrell had called it "an alabaster cliff overhanging one of the smallest and loveliest harbors in Greece, more a cove than a harbor." There may be nothing original to be said about islands, but there will almost certainly be something original in the way one says it.

The island's name certainly had nothing whatever to do with a town in central Greece, Karpenissi, which wasn't an island at all, and whose prominence was due to the fact that it had been the headquarters of the communist guerrilla forces during the Second World War and the ensuing civil war. His colleagues who knew of his frequent visits to Karponisi would tease him about taking up a position in what had been a hotbed of revolution, so inured to conflict and ideology, and it had taken quite a lot of persuasion to make it clear, with the use of maps, that there were two places with very similar names, and that, no, he was on an island, not a hotbed. There had been no hotbed in his life since the split with Jessica. How much the idea of two places that were the same, or almost the same, would perplex him in later years did not occur to him until much later. The fact of it being an island did not make it immune to conflict or ideology, but it bred conflicts of its own, and while it had no ideology (in the polemical sense), it certainly manifested, in its often unspoken spirit, a sense of what it was, of what perdures.

George's initial curiosity had arisen partly because the

island was so close to Spetses, in the same archipelago that clustered around the eastern arm of the Peloponnese, in the bay of Nafplion. That choice had been confirmed not only by the lack of any cosmopolitan trappings in the island itself, but also because it was *not* Spetses, which Fowles had celebrated in *The Magus*. He did not want, as a "Fowlesian," to be imitating Fowles in his choice of residence, and it was a residence, rather than a holiday home, for which he had been looking, as carefully as if he had been his faraway ancestor searching Norfolk for a place to make a home after being thrown out of Belvoir.

Another reason for Karponisi was that it isn't inundated by Brits. Standard joke: how do you know a planeload of Brits has just landed? Answer: when the engines are turned off, the plane goes on whining. George was very fond indeed of Corfu, but there was a sizeable population – many thousands – of Brits living there and complaining about everything. It was suburbia-on-sea, and this made him reluctantly cross Corfu off his list of places to settle, to make his home. His experience of Brits abroad had been exponentially worse than living among them. Lawrence Durrell left England partly because he didn't want to live among the English with their middle-class hang-ups. George couldn't tolerate their whingeing when they continually complained about 'them' – by which they meant the locals, the people among whom they lived, the host country.

As for trying to live among the Greeks and, largely, despising them, it's a colonial attitude: natives are "unfit for self-government," which was of course the policy and strategy of the British administration in the nineteenth century. Perhaps it is due to some deep discomfort within the British psyche, that it continues to send out colonial types to fill what used to be the administrator's bungalow in the tropics. As colonists during the British protectorate of Corfu, the English were able to regard the "natives" with disdain, as inferior creatures. The Corfiots were even referred to as "the Irish of the Mediterranean." That hadn't pleased semi-Irish George at all.

George's own language skills had always been basic – the limitation of someone who spends his life immersed in Eng. Lit. – so his Greek, even after forty years, was primitive. His laziness meant that his grammar was almost non-existent, so that conversation, especially the animated, not to say passionate, talk in the taverna, was beyond him. He could talk hesitantly with the shopkeeper using nouns and adjectives, with the occasional verb thrown in if he felt sufficiently daring, but it distressed – and embarrassed – him that he could go little further. One or two of the islanders had a good command of English, due to their years abroad, or the pervasiveness of the American language that was ever-present on their television screens. It enabled them to talk a sort of island Greeklish which was intelligible to them but not with any clarity to either mainland Greeks or English speakers.

He and Margaret had been fortunate in being able to find an old house with sufficient ground to enable George to build a large library room in local stone, to house not only his own huge collection but also the overspill from Woodlawn after cousin Alex had had his way. Lincoln (and also a couple of American desert-based libraries) had made him a generous offer for his archival material (mostly on Fowles), and for a large portion of the library itself, which would have increased his pension fund significantly, but he preferred to take with him the accumulation of a lifetime. Without it he would have no roots, no point of reference, no record of how he had spent the previous forty years. With it, he had something to examine during the winter nights, surveying his work and trying to reach a conclusion, as do so many authors anxious for a verdict on their life's achievement, as to whether those forty years had been spent in vain or whether he had actually succeeded in doing something worthwhile which might benefit a few avid readers. And to discover whether he had enjoyed doing it.

He had overseen the huge job of installing his books and archive in the carefully designed library – in fact two rooms which were to house 5000 books of his own plus the spillover from Woodlawn. This had been the main element in the relocation to Karponisi and had required meticulous attention – after all, it was in these rooms that he would spend the rest of his life. Bestowal of his personal effects, including some good pieces of furniture, hardly occupied him. He had been to Karponisi sufficiently frequently over the past twenty years, and of course in regular contact with architect and builder, that he was already well known by all. 'The Professor.' Never 'The Spy.'

With the exception of the "dispatches," which George now enjoyed so much that he would be sorry if the day ever came when they were no longer wanted, he led a very quiet life. As a northerner, he still surprised himself at the sight of his own lemon and orange trees, his vines, and he revelled in the ároma (the accent falls on the first syllable) of wild rígani and mint crushed underfoot as he walked on their carpet to his gate.

Even though Fowles, and his other research interests, were now behind him, and the Brahms project had required little material other than his comprehensive collection of recordings on both vinyl and CDs, George needed to nestle within his library: it was not only a resource (whether or not he needed it any longer) but also a comfort zone. Here, as a bookman, he felt secure. Wanted. But by whom?

There were two villages on the island, the main one, Agios Paraskevi, to which the harbor and its accoutrements belonged, being at the island's southern tip. This was where George had chosen to live, since the main facilities, few as they were, were to be found here. From the harbor a steep road led to the *plateia* or village square, which featured the church (with a genuine miracle-working icon, still in good order and much demand, miracles being more than ever necessary), the school and Alexis' part-time police-station-cum-lobster-depot. The other village, Agios Panteleimon, lay in the north of the island, and was connected to the harbor by a metalled road, along which traveled the island bus, an ancient creature held together by the wiles of its driver, a good deal of rope and glue, and the best intentions of saints Paraskevi and Panteleimon. Spiros the driver was also the ambulance driver (the bus also serving this purpose) and the taxi service (the bus, as the only four-wheeled vehicle on the island, undertaking this role too). Spiros was in fact the provider of all temporal transport needs. The parish priest, who ministered to both villages, had a motor-bike – a Vespa, unseen in civilized society since the sixties – which some said had been left behind in 1943 by the retreating Italian army which had stationed a token force of occupation. Of the bus itself, the prevailing legend was that it had been floated ashore on a raft...

As real estate people say, 'the property is adjacent.' It certainly was. Except to the supermarket and the DIY store, so beloved of the bourgeoisie, which were two ferry crossings away. But above all, Karponisi was adjacent to nothing but itself.

Karponisi was home to approximately 600 people, of whom 400 lived in the main village, clustered around the harbor and on the hill above, and 150 in the north, with another fifty in scattered cottages, mostly along the spinal column of the road. There was a school with fifty students, some of whom George gladly tutored in English, beyond what the local schoolmistress – a toothsome wench if ever there was one – could teach. A thankless task, as these local heroes, unlike their predecessors in Scunthorpe, were already in control of their destiny: some to stay on the island and continue their family crafts, others to go to university and emigrate to the States, Canada or Australia, where they already had many cousins.

As for shops, there was a bakery which, like the bus, served many purposes: bar, grocery, and post office and the communal oven, since hardly any house had a modern oven and few had one of the traditional indoor variety, other than the top surface of the ubiquitous *sompa*, the wood-burning stove. As George's old friend, Zissimos Lorenzatos, had written in his "Aegean Notebooks," a meal consisted of "home-baked bread, local wine, goat roasted over charcoal, garlic, a salad of tomatoes with onion, goat's-milk cheese, eggs fried in olive oil" of which, he said, it represented "our culture in its most enduring aspects." Lorenzatos may have been old-fashioned, and, in his notebooks, like so many before him, he decried much of the 'progress' that inevitable westernisation had imposed on an essentially peasant, pagan, way of life.

Karponisi also had a quayside taverna-cum-kafeneion which boasted wifi for the one or two tourists who availed of it in the season. It stayed open all year, for the islanders, some of whom still pursued the ancient work of fishing, and for the few remaining foreigners such as George himself; locals played interminable games of backgammon, which seemed to be the national pastime, and a card game of impenetrable complexity. There was very little hard drinking unless an anniversary such as a name-day were being celebrated, which it usually was, or the *panegiri* marking the feast of Saint Paraskevi. The mail boat came once a week, doubling duty as the ferry and carrier of groceries, paraffin, and anything else that supported island life, which could be ordered from the stores on the mainland. There was a Flying Ferret from Spetses to Piraeus, but George preferred, on his extremely rare visits to Athens, to take the ferry to Nafplion and the Athens bus from there.

He – or rather, Karponisi – had been spared so many of the accoutrements of modern tourism: fish baths where tiny fish nibbled the dead skin on your feet; made-in-Taiwan souvenirs including miniature pianos that played "Für Elise" *ad nauseam*; allegedly local handcrafts actually machine-made in Turkey. Thankfully there was no airport, since the traffic could not have justified one, nor was there one anywhere nearby on the mainland. But in 2005 a helicopter pad had been built, at the behest of a local vote-catcher, to allow emergency services in the event of serious illness, especially when the island was cut off by heavy storms, which was a frequent occurrence in winter. There were very few tourists, other than backpackers, for whom the enterprising postmaster had opened a camping site, and there were also a few houses which, in traditional Greek style, welcomed guests. There was an archaeological site, which was home to a small group of diggers in the summer months, and one day a report might, or might not, announce that Karponisi was, or was not, of some significance in this respect.

Once a low-flying jet, which was clearly in difficulties, came screaming overhead as if it were going to crash into the island. Old ladies fell on their faces, screaming as if supplicating or challenging the plane. One even said that she thought the sky was falling in. It took a long time to persuade her otherwise.

There were other foreign residents on Karponisi, in addition to the English psychiatrist, who seemed to have systematically divested himself of all the friends who, until recently, had been regular summer visitors: a famous novelist, a not-so-famous novelist, a world-renowned London chef and a model from the 1960s who still managed to look glamorous – without surgical assistance, it seemed. Uncle D's heartfelt advocacy of Botox wasn't needed – or was it there but not in evidence? George and the psychiatrist met once a week for dinner at the taverna, since neither could cook, and in fact George took all his meals there, except for a weekly standing invitation to one of the other blow-ins, a Norwegian woman of uncertain age and origin, and another with the schoolmistress who, despite her limited command of English, was an attractive but unattainable companion.

George was always amused when he saw a trailer for a film announcing "At a cinema near you." He thought about the travel arrangements he would have to make if he wanted to see a film at the cinema near him – in Nafplion. Very occasionally, a screen was put up in the village school and a DVD player would materialise .... *Not* a sheet stretched across the village street, or a rickety projector that broke down near the dénouement on the second reel, just like the tourist brochures for a Greece that had vanished.

Why had George ended up here? He wasn't running away from anything – well, in a sense he *was* running away from *every*thing – and he wasn't running towards anything. Not now, not at his time of life and not with his total lack of automotion. If anything, life was a palindrome – he was running back to where he began, in order to begin running forward again towards the point where he already was. Nor was he 'lured' by the magic of islands. But he was obeying that unwritten law that predicts the destiny of the uncertain types who mistook isolation for freedom. Had Karponisi given him a new lease of life, a new trajectory, a new sense of horizons, the last lap before the unanswered question? Or was it the kiss of death? He waited to find out.

On the first page of one of his "island" books Lawrence Durrell defined a condition which he called *"islomania"*: "a rare but by no means unknown affliction of spirit," experienced by "people who find islands somehow irresistible." Durrell tells us that "the mere knowledge that they are on an island, a little world surrounded by the sea, fills them with an indescribable intoxication." They "yearn" subconsciously for "the lost Atlantis."

Reflecting in his diary on his reasons for coming to Karponisi, George had no difficulty in coming to terms with himself, perhaps for the first time in his life, or for the first time in his diary, anyway: *Islands, by virtue of whatever it is that makes them attractive to islomanes, encourage selfishness, the tendency to regard oneself as the centre of the world, even if we know that essentially we are standing only at the threshold, or the outskirts, the littoral, of the island itself. Even though we islomanes have rejected the society from which we derive, we nevertheless seek – long for – a place in an "other" society where assurance can be found – a "neverland" where we can recreate ourselves. And the idea of the subconscious searching for a buried city that might very well be within oneself, buried in one's own psyche, is irresistible. The "lost Atlantis" is not elsewhere, it is within.*

Perhaps life itself is a group of uninhabited islands which we must populate with our longings, our fears, our failures. For such exiles as the islomanes, who actually live their exile, the life and the philosophy are one. Coming to an island, where one can be at peace, at rest, but never in a state of grace, you have abandoned your context and can never achieve another, because context is hinterland, it is your own background, what stands behind you. It stands behind the islander, but it can never provide you with a background. Mine is Woodlawn. Or is it?

You live without origins, and you survive without a future. In that sense, you are one-dimensional man, like the cardboard characters who populate so many novels, characters who in fact are not characters at all, but ideas posing as people, as bundles of thought rather than emotion, of propositions rather than pronouns. Some of us run away to islands because we despair of, or are exhausted or bewildered by, so-called civilisation, with its credit-card mentality, its Wikipedia, its Ferrero Rocher, its Ryanair – all the panaceas and placebos of workers' playtime that city life imposes on our already tired minds. This is what we escape from. But for others, it is not a concept of escape or rejection but of embrace, of longing. We run away because we seek the simplicity of island life, the basic living of villages and villagers.

The world does not understand us, we are not like other people, and so on. That is, we have the capacity to shut out the world and to say "No!" to find its languages incomprehensible, its grammars impenetrable, the corridors of its mind distressing to say the least. And then we jump, in order to give our own language, grammar and mind the space in which to live: the island. For those who find the challenge – another cliché would be 'the lure' – of difference and otherness irresistible, for those who surrender to the inevitable, their travel into foreignness is not a matter of prurience but of going to meet some as yet undefined part of oneself.

Some never find it – they spend all their lives, and all their imaginations, in the quest for the missing part of "life," of themselves, of identity.

Some find it immediately. An encounter which is satisfying, which finds the "missing part" and installs it appropriately in the psyche, can be immediate and revelatory. One can become earthèd in a new soil, terroir, with ease.

For most, the decision to put down those roots, to say "I am here, here I will stay, here I am 'at home'," comes after long searching of both the self and the place where it is suspected that this "home" might be. And that decision should always be accompanied by the recognition that the "place" will never in fact be the "home," but may offer the comforts and satisfactions and continuities that the first home did not offer. A sense of time which is not aggressive or, indeed, temporal; a sense of creativity; a sense of knowing that harbors gnosis for its own sake.

"Home" is where you start from. "Home," once you have left it, either by choice or force majeure, can never be recovered. "Home" as a destination is impossible. You may return to the place that was home, but both you and it will have changed, and sometimes will not even recognise one another.

If one lives a life that began in a dysfunctional childhood, the quest for 'home' is a quest for an "other" place, an imagined place, where one instinctively or intellectually believes, or fervently hopes, to become "at home." I can feel "at home" in my village house, within my own self-imposed circumstances, but as soon as I step on the threshold of the village kafeneion or sit at a pavement café in Nafplion, I am the stranger, the visitor, xenos, always arriving, threshold-wise (or threshold-unwise, perhaps), at an approximate compromise with the idea of 'home.'

To lose one's childhood is an experience for which the child seeks compensation. When a child is deprived of love, it takes whatever it can find, or invent, by way of compensation. Probably the vigour with which he pursues the prize of compensation will have a direct relationship to the degree to which he feels himself to have been betrayed in the rupture of childhood. The frustrations I have discovered in dealing with figures and statutes of authority at Lincoln have perhaps made me rebellious, cynical and, potentially, duplicitous – especially when I find that so much of my career found me engaged in so much work for the government. At least, I think it did.

As an 'intelligence' agent, with associations, if not direct contact, with the espionage industry, George saw himself as an outsider in the 'real' world, just as he had been an outsider – or certainly never a committed insider – in the university. If for one moment he could regard himself in the third person as a potential spy, the move to the island seemed to him to be a natural and, indeed, pre-ordained development. Spies hid. George was in hiding, from his family, from the academic world, from Britishness, from Jessica, and from himself. Each of these, with the likely exception of his children, or two of them at least, the two acknowledged ones, were acts of rejection, the fear of the traitor that if he did not reject the system that had rejected him, he would be the victim, rather than the master, of the situation.

It was with a great sense of arrival that he settled down. And yet, his peace was due to be disturbed. No sooner than he shut the front door, lit the fire, made himself a cup of cocoa and sat down in his favorite armchair to watch *The X-Files* than the doorbell rang. All of that is of course metaphorical, since George never drank cocoa, had no television receiver and had not installed a doorbell. Moreover, in late autumn it was still not yet time for fires to be lit. But ring the doorbell did, not immediately but about a month after he had taken up residence, in the form of a knock on the door from Spiros. George had not yet developed the island custom of watching for the mail boat and sauntering, apparently nonchalantly, down to the post office "just in the off-chance" that there might be letters for him – letters which were, in a sense, a lifeline. So Spiros had come up to the house with a few letters, one of which had a Russian stamp and a Moscow postmark.

This he opened, only to find that he had also opened a door that he had never seen before and did not want to open. "Dear Distinguished Professor Manners" the letter began (flattering enough, he thought), "Please to forgive my inclusion into your life." Holy God, he exclaimed aloud, she means "intrusion," but little did he yet know how near to "inclusion" the writer would get. "I am keen student of the work of Mr Fowles, I am a Masters degree from Moscow University and I know that you are a good friend of him and the expert on his work because I have read all your books and even the book about Mr Walter Pater." She must be very determined, he thought. "I am most glad if I can come to your beautiful island to meet you in the month of May. I will come to Greece and can I please visit you in one of the guesthouses of the island?"

This is getting complicated, he reckoned. The last thing he wanted was to encourage students to Karponisi, however much they might contribute to the local economy, and I'm finished with that part of my life. It's true that quite a number had written asking for an interview, all of which he had politely declined. Others – mercifully a very few – had actually arrived unannounced on his doorstep. He had shown sufficient good manners (ha ha, he could hear Uncle David at this joke on the family name) to give them a cup of tea before firmly showing them the door. Some, he felt embarrassed to admit, had been so assertive at the door that the family name deserted him and he resolutely closed it in their faces. "The last thing I want is a disciple." And yet. And yet.

The flattery was compelling, as of course it was intended to be. "I wait with all my breath to have your reply in letter and I hope you will say yes at my visit. Yours gratefully Aleksandra Demidenko."

What was he to do? Say yes and open the floodgates to a flight of Muscovy duck-researchers? Say no and appear churlish? Well, churlish is as churlish does, and if he had been churlish in turning his back yet again on Vicky and Al and James, then he could continue to act as a churl when confronted by blatant opportunism from a woman he did not know and did not want to meet.

The sheer brazenness of her approach! And what, he wondered, could he possibly tell her that she did not already know? She certainly wouldn't get access to the archive. If he had wanted anyone to have access, he would have sold it to Lincoln or further afield.

Yet he had a nagging feeling that maybe it was *he* who could learn from such a meeting. This worried him and he delayed any response until he had had time to think it over, and over, and over. Several weeks passed while he tried to add up all the pros and cons of the request. If the girl had sent him any kind of follow-up ("did you receive my letter?") he would immediately have said no. But it was the fact that she seemed patient enough to wait that tempted him to say yes.

It was a dreadful mistake. A beautiful mistake. He knew it when he posted the letter saying yes, and he certainly knew it after Aleksandra's visit. The time when she was there, in Karponisi, it seemed to be not a mistake but a godsend – a terrible godsend that only a cruel and malicious god could have transmitted.

Into his life came the slender, challenging beauty of Aleksandra. An epiphany without precedent in his experience. Restricted his sex life may have been, in terms of the number of women with whom he had slept, but his appreciation of women who combined beauty, sexual allure and high intelligence was infinite. This Aleksandra was the daughter of Afrodite. In Latin-speaking countries she would have been called Amanda, she who must be loved. She was one of the most beautiful women he had ever seen. No. *The* most beautiful. Here. In his house. In Karponisi. He wanted her, and he couldn't have her. There was no choice to be made: her summons to utter, impotent devotion was immediate and irresistible.

Yet there was, beside her magnetism, a *noli me tangere*, a forbidding aspect which, of course, only enhanced the allure. Who did she think she was? Nicole Kidman?

It was only after her all-too-short visit, and the beginning of the exchange of letters which at first gradually, and then rapidly, led to revelations of her – as it seemed to him – true character, that that immediate monolithic impression began to trouble him. In her company, while he was not exactly a mindless slave, there could be no such doubts, no premonition of his later disillusion. She simply *was* beauty and intelligence personified. In her superb body and her brilliant mind, she defied analysis. George was in a presence such as he had never previously encountered.

Her job, as a computer programmer in Moscow's education ministry, was hardly a fit function for someone who was so clearly bulging with brains. As the world became progressively smaller (he baulked at the term 'progress' implied there), and along with it the technological means of communication, it was perhaps apposite that this woman of the future should combine in such a slim figure a stunning beauty and a mental computer of such power. A microchip off a micro-block.

If they had not shared this compulsive interest in John Fowles – he from a position of seniority and extensive knowledge, she from her passion for Fowles's work and her inquisitive habit of mind, still at its embryonic stage –

he might, in his dirty-old-man mode, have simply thought of her as an exceptionally beautiful young woman. And, had he still had his manhood intact, have considered her as the ultimate lay. He was nevertheless fascinated by the sheer enormity of the horizon that seemed to have opened up. The idea of unperformable sex was no obstacle to his fantasies, yet they were not in fact fantasies but scenarios which, ten years earlier, could have been realized in glorious Technicolor. Now it wasn't even monochrome.

But, not least because she had come to the island with his agreement and because of this shared literary interest, it was so much more profound and pervasive than any thought of bedding her might have provided – even if it had been possible. And she, for her part, quite rightly and understandably, saw nothing sexy or beddable in a man more than twice her age who was clearly lacking (she could not have known the full details, of course) in some venereal department. She also, presumably, thought that despite what he might provide as an "academic sugar daddy," it was not worth the fuck. He, for more reasons than the purely – or impurely – physical, because he had no expectation of any response from her were he to attempt a move, and because it would, in his gut feeling, be entirely inappropriate and lead to professional suicide. He had known several colleagues in years past who had, it seemed, been honey-pots to any female wasp that came buzzing around them, looking for a quick one and, hopefully, better exam grades. One of them had indeed been sacked, due partly to jealousy on the part of the aptly named Vice-Rector. But apart from his own hushed-up incident, George had never fallen at that fence, but he had paid the price: Scunthorpe. Now it seemed that there was to be another *faux pas*, a wrong step that might land him in a place far more delicious than Scunthorpe but irredeemably and eternally punishing nonetheless. So it was that during her two-week stay on the island, despite what island gossip had decided – no doubt the marriage and the nursery were already conceived in the villagers' minds – neither had shown the slightest sexual interest in the other.

There was one residual problem for George in all this: this undeniable and reproving fact, that she was extremely beautiful. It was the first time, since he had become impotent, that there was any sense of frustration. Had he been in possession of his sexual faculties, there would have been a personal and professional choice between suppressing his lust or pursuing it, with a girl less than half his age and, seemingly, indifferent to his non-existent charm. Of course, she had no idea of his physical condition, but she cannot have been unaware of his natural attraction to her. Half of Russia was probably in the same boat. If he wasn't careful, George could be a victim of a hoax like the one Nicole Kidman (as a Russian prostitute) pulled off in *Birthday Girl*.

He had told her very little about the Brahms book, since he was quite sure from her initial reaction that she was uninterested and, in fact, did not seem to understand what it was about (would anyone?). Her interest was entirely in his personal knowledge of Fowles and his professional work in that area. She had even proposed a visit by ferry to Spetses, but he felt this was too much like work. Sitting in his library, talking to an eager student, was one thing; upping and offing to Spetses, even though it was nearby, was quite another, especially if there were any risk of a sexual advance from either side while they were, so to speak, both playing an away game.

Their conversations, in which he learned very soon to call her Sasha, the diminutive, affectionate form of her name, or, even more intimately, Sashenka, began with some fairly obvious questions, which she had very carefully thought out in advance. She had to use a notebook because he refused from the outset to allow her to tape-record the meetings. I wonder why?

As the meetings progressed over the course of the fortnight – stilted at first but better as they warmed to each other – the talking became more open and relaxed, and her questions became more profound. She very skilfully opened up the subject of the writer – both writers, in fact: Fowles as the subject and George as the critic. Although in his books George had given some indication of "the man behind the books," there was so much more to be told, and Sasha succeeded in drawing out of him some, but not all, of his insight into 'Fowles the man.'

But it was also 'George the man' in whom she was interested, and he found himself opening up to her questions in a way that surprised him and – he had to admit – pleased him. After all, if life was a book, and his life in particular, it was no great shakes to let her read him. Or so he thought, as his trust in her developed. He had always known that, whatever one writes, whether novel, drama, poetry or even the work of criticism, one is writing about oneself: the act of confession. And Sasha got him to talk about himself as a writer in a way he had never spoken before. And he was pleased that she had done so.

To say that there was nothing sexual in all of this would be untrue. Of course it was sexual. The fact that it was entirely without physical contact was irrelevant. It was profound, what he felt for this young woman, and it was only in retrospect that he accused himself of being the silly old man he had always feared to become. If she had not been so ravishably beautiful, and if she had not appeared to be ravishably intelligent as well as beautiful, it would never have excited him in the way that it did. If she had been a boring, fat old frump... But she wasn't. She was heaven on two incredible legs that started near the ground and traveled up to her shoulders, and ... beyond. They had carried her into his world, like totems, and however taboo they may have been to George, they etched themselves into his lust-diary.

Her manner, if her thirst and eagerness for information could be curbed for a moment, was very 'sweet.' Over their dinners, when he had insisted that the interrogation into Fowles and Fowlism must be suspended, she spoke of her life in Moscow, of the poor quality of life, the long winters, the darkness, the punishment for being Russian implicit in her civil service work and the Stalinist concrete block with her tiny apartment, and the unspeakable contrast between all of that and the light, air, freedom, clarity of the south.

There seemed to be no lover on the premises. If she had not been a Russian with a dose of the "gimmes," her eagerness would have been innocent and alluring. But it was ineradicable, and imbued everything she did and said and asked with the feeling that she had just joined the end of a queue simply to find out what was available at the other end. Even if there was nothing at the end of the queue, it was worth having if you didn't already have nothing. It made a something out of nothing, and any kind of something was worth having. And even if there was nothing-nothing, you got to meet a few more like-minded people.

He had learned a bit of Russian at school, and the few words he retained made a small bond between them, one over which they could laugh a lot. But he couldn't speak her language any more than he could speak fluently in Greek, since he was destitute of grammar. Grammar meant detailed hard work, and being the laziest of men he refused to even contemplate irregular verbs, declensions and conjugations, other than sexual ones.

After she left, they had had a brief correspondence

which he would have to admit was flirtatious. He enjoyed it, even if only in his subconscious. She had a good spoken command of English, but her written grammar was all over the place, and much of their subsequent correspondence would consist of his correcting her mistakes. One of his favorites was her "Can it was?," by which she meant "Could it have been ...?" That was endearing. Mistakes that he had overlooked when she spoke them, because their novelty superseded their inaccuracy. It was a sort of seduction. But even when he was correcting her written "Russglish," it was not a matter of "Dear friend, I appreciate so much what you are doing to help me" but "Thank you. Here is another query." Always the taker, never the giver. In fact, he wondered what sex with her would have been like, or even whether or not she was still a virgin.

The strain of giving so much, so often, was wearing him out. It was like donating to a charity which then proceeded to blood-suck every drop of his energy and intelligence. Finally, the camel's back was broken by a letter from her so demanding, and at the same time so accusing of his meanness, that he resolved to tell her some unpleasant home truths.

When he wrote, making it clear that there was absolutely no possibility of any future contact, let alone co-operation, he laid out the whole matter of their "relationship," both the plus and the minus sides. Due to his infatuation, he had for a long time resisted the conclusion that the relationship was a false one, and even longer before he could find the right words to write to her, but eventually it had to be done, and the harshest way was the fairest.

Aleksandra he wrote, dropping the "Sasha" into the emotional waste bin, *You are asking too much of me, and asking it for far too long. I ignored it at first as merely the eagerness of a young student who suddenly finds a unique door open to her. You were typical of the anxious, curious student persistently pursuing her subject, and you did it very well. I have to admire you for that. I myself in my younger days in pursuit of Fowles would clamber over other people (or at best, find a way round them) in order to get at the material I needed, the thirst for information being the irresistible driving force. And your beauty – I mean your beauty in body and, as I thought, spirit – was such that, for longer than a moment, I had the hope that you might be the last great love of my life. That we would share a wonderful life together. But that long moment came to its realistic end.*

I have to admit that in you I thought that the cliché of the Russian who will take anything and everything that she can get hold of, fitted you well. As an academic pursuit, that was fine. But when you left and wrote complaining that I had given you so little of my time, after all the expense you had had in getting here and staying in Spiro's house, which by the way was a minimal cost, and that I never really appreciated your enthusiasm for the subject, I realized that the character I thought I had found in you, the beautiful, elegant, appreciative woman – yes, you, Aleksandra! – was driven by a more acquisitive person whose principal motivation was to take, take, take, because that is what you Russians seem born to do: it's in your DNA, the servile experience of deprivation, of being nobody, subject to the tsar, then the commissar, and now the new tsar, Putin. In English, we have a word for it. "A touch of the gimmes." Well, this wasn't a mere touch, it was a full-blown attack of the gimmes. Looking back, I see that every day during our meetings was nothing more than "gimme! gimme! gimme!" and that it was much more serious than your enthusiasm could support, and my growing feelings for you could hide. Your last letter really told me that you simply hadn't received enough – you had been sold short on the gimmes.

Maybe I am standing on my dignity as a senior figure, but do you know of any other writer who would give that much time to a researcher – with the possible exception of a university don supervising a PhD. student, whom he is monitoring and mentoring – and all this in my still busy schedule?

He paused. This fault of which he was accusing her – the gimmes – wasn't that what he had been doing all his life? Craving affection, craving understanding, craving a place in the world, as a child, as a critic, as a lover, as an "intelligence agent"? Wasn't he constantly, in the way he unspokenly addressed life, saying "gimme love, gimme meaning, gimme myself"? Make nuffink into sumfink. So how could he reject Aleksandra with accusations of being just like him? Or was he a Russian, too? Was the whole human race crying out for attention? And if so, from whom?

Even now, I think that you might have been the last great love of my life. But your constant preoccupation with knowledge which, I assure you, is practically worthless, has been shown to be devoid of human feeling, bereft of any consideration for the giver. The idea that there could ever have been love between us dissolved immediately I realized this massive character defect in you (and I'm not saying that there aren't character defects in myself, which you so skilfully half-manoeuvred me into revealing), it was an insuperable problem. In fact, had we been in university, me as the supervisor, you as the candidate, I would have asked my head of department to assign you to another colleague, rather than have you as an unsupportable drain on my mind and my time.

James Esposito

Was there a Greek god up there, saying the same thing to *his* department head: 'take away this cup from my lips'? Oh, hadn't he stood on his dignity! Pompous prat.

With my previous partner, the 'give and take' was so precious that it brought both of us to a deeper and higher level of love than either of us separately could imagine. I was foolish enough to think that you, too, could meet me in the same way. If you had only known how to give, as well as to take... But I don't think that you have the gift of giving. A wise man once said to me that it is easy to give – and difficult to receive. How easily, how joyfully, I would have received your gift, if you had been able to offer it. Even if we had been sexually attracted, I sadly believe that you would not yet have known that to give is as important as it is to receive.

I received you as a student, and, like any teacher, I knew that my primary function – indeed, responsibility – was to give. To share with you my knowledge of the subject which occupies us both. But to share also means to be able to give as well as take. In this case, you did not recognise that I was a teacher who, even after all these years, was still in need of the student's gift, the insights – even the guesswork – of the young. And I suspect that in bed it would have been no different. If this letter helps you in any way, I hope it will teach you – yes, teach you – the importance of knowing how to give as graciously as one must receive.

And even then, she wouldn't, at first, take "No" for an answer, plaintively writing "Why? What have I done bad? Why do you have so ideas on me? I thought you really was a care at me. When I wrote to you to say my disappointment I was a silly girl, but when I came to Karponisi I was so much hope and maybe I have hope too much." You bet, he thought. So he took the drastic and, for him, uncharacteristic decision to refuse all further contact – not to respond to this 'silly girl' who wasn't a silly girl at all, but a stupid woman. Stupid to reveal the gimmes, stupid to harry him with her imprecations.

IX

George's Worlds

He looked at what he had written: "He was tired. Very, very tired." Well, it was true, but perhaps not as "true" as he might have explained it. It was the complete lack of purpose, the uselessness of what he was doing, or not doing, that bewildered him. And when bewildered, he would sit down and say "I'm tired" – tired almost to the point of living death. And at his age, bewilderment was a feeling he could not afford to entertain.

He thought about Fowles's advice to would-be writers: "Kill your parents! Kill your wife!" Well, he had done that. Or they had done that to him. He wasn't a great critic and his only attempt at a novel had been jettisoned over thirty years ago. But simply in order to be a writer he had gone down the Fowles route – one Fowles himself had not taken – and excluded from his life everything and everybody that threatened the privacy he needed to single-mindedly pursue the work in hand.

He had left home at eighteen, never to return except in memory. He had shown so little commitment to M and his children that separation was an easy and inevitable outcome from marriage and parenthood. He hadn't had to exclude Jessica because their separate lives were mutually exclusive. Even though he now knew that, had he tried harder to be less selfish and more caring, he could have held onto Jessica and prevented her leaving with Angél Davidoff. And he had shut the door on Aleksandra before it had hardly opened. They say that one door shuts and another one opens, but in his case George was happy in his room without doors.

Only his later conversion to love for the twins had kept him in any measure part of the human race, rather than merely a book-producing subsection of it. He had always loved his children, but he only realized it late in life. As a scholar, he had been, as far as he could be, blessed with M and the twins, but it was a blessing in disguise, since the constant demands of three- or four-year-olds – "Daddy, I'm hungry," "Daddy, tell me a story," "Daddy, can we go to the park?" – threatened to intrude on his scholarly existence, his scholarly identity, a threat which he successfully rebuffed. "Not now, I'm working. Ask your mother." "We did, and she's working too. She said to ask you." "Not now, I'm working" – the same gesture that his father had offered him so many years ago, but on that occasion mercilessly, wordlessly. If only his father had been as eloquent as his son in shutting the door! "May I please come in? We have much to talk about, Father." Was it a genetic defect, this single-minded exclusion of all that should have been nearest and dearest? He couldn't answer for his father, but George would have said that, of course, M and the twins *were* his nearest and dearest – far nearer and dearer than Walter Pater or John Fowles (were they nearer and dearer than Brahms?) – but he hadn't realized at the time how essential it was to recognise that and act upon it. Was it the fate of the Manners, or the manners of fate? Yuk, George, yuk.

Had he, all these years, been doing what Owen O'Brien had mistaken for the work on Pater? Was his whole life's work a "Letter to My Father"?, an *apologia* that did, indeed, say "Sorry, Father, sorry"?

Maybe the *apologia* he had never expected, and certainly never received from his father was in fact owed by him *to* his father. He had turned his back on Woodlawn, left that world, which at least offered the security of dullness and repetition, in order to enter an "other," that offered nothing except uncertainty, instability, fear.

On one memorable occasion, when he did agree to tell a bedtime story, but was in a hurry to return to his desk, he began: "Once upon a time there was a handsome prince and a beautiful princess... And they lived happily ever after. Good night children." He was on the top step of the stairs, when shrieks came from the nursery. Four-year-old Vicky had realized that they had been short-changed, and she and Al were now conducting nursery rampage. It took M several minutes to calm them down. It took *him* several years to live it down, and he wasn't sure that he was yet forgiven.

He couldn't call it a marriage, a partnership, if he left it all to M, especially as her career was in full flight, while his was plodding along. He had never paused to reflect on whether his distance – nothing compared to his own father's almost total absence, of course – had in any way harmed either Vicky or Al. And later, he thought, they had turned out ok, mostly due to M's benign influence. They were healthy, happy, moderately successful, and even spoke of each other with affection. Vicky must have picked up some of his scholastic instincts; he supposed that could be an explanation he would cherish if it were true, even if he disapproved of how she had turned her skills to the teaching of the great unwashed. Where Al got his aesthetic interests from was anyone's guess. Not from either side of the family, as far as George could see, but he, too, was happy and, in his case, settled. They both liked Tony, and were glad that Al had someone who seemed to be life-partner material. More staying power, perhaps, than many a heterosexual marriage.

Was it all real, or imaginary? He actually had no idea. Most of his life had been a fiction. The 'dispatches' were a fiction, or so he thought of them; he'd concocted them, submitted them, been rewarded for them. That's what all good storytellers do. Whether the mandarins in MI6 had actually believed any of it, didn't really matter. They had liked the stories. He thought now that his whole life was like that: invented partly by himself but mostly by others.

He likened himself to Sir James Frazer, the greatest authority in the history of anthropology, who had penned fourteen volumes on the customs and beliefs of primitive tribes without leaving the security of his study in Cambridge.

It had all been a charade, playing characters, a wonderful make-believe. If he'd had a different career – as a film-writer, for example, like James's other friend, Andrew Dalton – he couldn't have lived a more fantastic life. Everything was make-believe. His thesis outing Pater, his lies about Fowles, followed by the *truth* about Fowles, his dispatches, his just-finished book on Brahms – all of it was based on fictions, versions of untruth, the *stories* that he hadn't had time to tell to his own children, but instead had spun for academe. All of it pretending to be solid, objective scholarship, wrapped up in a bit of mystery and delivered *via* his unwitting publishers to an unsuspecting public. The fact that most of his books (except *Pater's Closet*) had sold less than a thousand copies, and most of them to university libraries, was a redeeming feature, he thought: at least he hadn't contaminated too many minds with his mendacity. And that was what they all did – all writers, especially all academics. They just thought up a reasonably plausible story and peddled it in the right emperor's clothes. "Once upon a time ..."

Pater was the thief of sex; Fowles was the thief of love; Brahms was the thief of passion. But they were all thieves of reason and he, George, was their high priest: The Thief of Reason. Reason had nothing to do with sex, love or passion; reason was sterile, cerebral, didn't even know where to find the naughty bits. But if you rob life of sex, love and passion, if you sterilise the cocks and cunts, you also rob it of reason, of any possible route to meaning, identity, self, because reason is the only way we can remember it all, and memory is the life-support of both passion and meaning. And George had stolen meaning, and taken it into himself, and had made it, and himself, an empty thing.

And he had stolen Jessica. *She* had meaning, and selfhood, and passion; *she* was the incarnation of 'aspiring to the condition of music'; she *was* music, and he had stolen it and almost cast it away.

It was just the same in all his personal lives, which now seemed more *im*personal than his scholarship. His father, Uncle David, Janet, Margaret, Jessica, Vicky, Albert, Aleksandra – they were all real. Or at least he thought they were. Of his mother he was less sure, because he had no personal evidence of her existence, other than her place in the family vault, which he had first seen as a child of six when his father had solemnly brought him there and said, tersely, "This is where your mother lies." So she *had* existed, *had* given birth to him, and *had* died. That much he could understand, even at that age, but he was more certain of Nanny Conneely than he was of either his mother or certainly of his father. Of Pirkko-Liisa he could have little direct proof and of her vanished, anonymous mother none at all.

Of the 'real' women with whom he had been involved, he did want to see each of them again, but each for a quite different reason. M, in order to find out the 'truth' about her job and his; Jessica, because he could not quell the passion that was not so much physical as spiritual; and Aleksandra because it was unrequited stupidity on his part, about which he often speculated.

He knew that, in recounting his misspent youth,

misspent early manhood, misspent marriage, misspent affair with Jessica, he had been short on dialogue, in reporting what had actually been said. But that was because, in all this misspending, he had hardly ever had what one could call a "real" conversation with anyone. All the people he had written about, himself included, showed no "development of character" – no *Bildungsroman* – that is so prized by the reviewers in the Sunday newspapers. They were all born fully rounded. Uncle D, M, Jessica, Aleksandra, were types, not real people; they were just the same at the end as they had been when they first walked onto his stage. George decided "I was born a cardboard cut-out. A cipher. If I *am* a book, then at least it's a first edition, no changes allowed, no call for a reprint or a revision." Nietzsche had got it the wrong way round: it was the incapacity of melancholy.

George came to the conclusion that the medieval cliché was true: that man, by the exercise of his free will, fulfils the pattern of his destiny. So, *orobouros*, in my end is my beginning, meeting oneself on the way back from the shop that sold lies like faulty condoms. But the puzzle remained the same: was he a man who mistook himself for a book, or a book that mistook itself for a man? He would never know, because his reading over the text was interrupted unexpectedly that day.

He sees a figure with a backpack down at the harbor, obviously looking for directions. That meant a stranger, so it couldn't be Aleksandra – or could it? As the figure approached, he has a sinking feeling that it really is her – her lithe, slender body and swinging gait, so clearly full of self-possession. He sees Markos walking with her, guiding her, without doubt towards this house. He waits on the terrace for this unexpected visitor, unable to determine, by guesswork, if it is a pushy student whom he will have to repel as politely as possible. As she comes nearer to the house he realises with relief that this is a woman older than Aleksandra. For a moment he still thinks it might be just another Fowles-hunter, there had been few of them this summer. Then another premonition takes hold of him.

As they approached, Markos fell back, leaving the girl to make her own way up the steps to the terrace where he waits. She is very, very beautiful. He says nothing, allowing her to announce herself. Which she does. In language which he hardly recognizes, words he had never expected to hear in such a way.

"I am Pirkko-Liisa Vuonen, senior officer in the Finnish intelligence service, based in the London cell. I am your 'control.' For the past twenty years, you have been working for us – and, more recently, for me." A pause, as George thought 'this cannot be happening.' Then "I am also your daughter. May I please come in? We have much to talk about, Father."

THE END

ACKNOWLEDGEMENTS

This book could not have been put together from the papers of Andrew Dalton and George Manners without the continual support of my wife, Aleksandra Demidenko and our twin daughters Coral and Bognuda Esposito, who were willing guinea pigs when I needed to know if the "Uncle Andrew" and "Uncle George" (whom they had known in childhood) emerged from my editing of their memoirs with honor and credibility.

I also owe many thanks to my secretary, Edith Oldham, for her work on my unwieldy manuscripts, to my agent Sebastian Garrett for assuring me that Andrew's and George's memoirs would find a readership. My lawyers, Thompson D'Olier & Co, have searched the text for any possible slights on figures living or dead, and have given it a clean bill of health.

To Victoria and Albert Manners, to Jessica Mausch, to Alex Manners, Oscar and Lucinda Zoffany-Dalton, Olli, Katya and Pirkko-Liisa Vuonen I owe more than I can possibly express, for their confidence and trust in my ability to edit the texts of the two friends who were so much a part of them, their honesty and their obvious love of Andrew and George.

I have tried to retain all Andrew's characteristics: his humour, his innocence, his sense of wonder, beside his obvious infatuation with "N," to allow his "authentic" voice to come through.

In George's case, I reproduce his story as he himself wrote it, only pausing occasionally to introduce explanatory sentences where George's meaning might otherwise have been unclear.

Both Andrew's and George's manuscripts and associated papers have been deposited by me in the Special Collections of the Standish Library at the University of Chicago, with an embargo that they may not be made available to the public until after the deaths of all the persons named in their two narratives.

- James Esposito

About the Author

James Esposito was born in Castellammare, near Naples, in 1950, and educated at the universities of Dublin and Oxford. He spent his professional life as a lecturer in film and drama at Leeds University before retiring to Greece. He is the author of *Book Into Film* and *George Eliot on Screen*. This is his first novel. He is married to the critic Aleksandra Demidenko. They have twin children.

The New Atlantian Library

NewAtlantianLibrary.com or
AbsolutelyAmazingEbooks.com or
AA-eBooks.com

www.ingramcontent.com/pod-product-compliance
Lightning Source LLC
Chambersburg PA
CBHW060948030726
47503CB00003B/772